Miss Seeton
by Moonlight

Heron Carvic's Miss Seeton

Miss Seeton by Moonlight

Heron Carvic's Miss Seeton

HAMILTON CRANE

Thorndike Press • **Chivers Press**
Thorndike, Maine USA   Bath, England

This Large Print edition is published by Thorndike Press, USA and by Chivers Press, England.

Published in 2000 in the U.S. by arrangement with Curtis Brown Ltd.

Published in 2000 in the U.K. by arrangement with the author and the estate of Heron Carvic.

U.S. Hardcover 0-7862-2481-9 (Mystery Series Edition)
U.K. Hardcover 0-7540-4140-9 (Chivers Large Print)
U.K. Softcover 0-7540-4141-7 (Camden Large Print)

The text of this Large Print edition is unabridged. Other aspects of the book may vary from the original edition.

Set in 16 pt. Plantin by Al Chase.

Printed in the United States on permanent paper.

British Library Cataloguing-in-Publication Data available

Library of Congress Cataloging-in-Publication Data
Crane, Hamilton.
    Miss Seeton by moonlight / Hamilton Crane.
        p. cm.
    Originally published: New York : Berkley Books, 1992.
(Heron Carvic's Miss Seeton)
    ISBN 0-7862-2481-9 (lg. print : hc : alk. paper)
    1. Seeton, Miss (Fictitious character) — Fiction.
2. Women detectives — England — Fiction. 3. England —
Fiction. I. Title. II. Heron Carvic's Miss Seeton.
PR6063.A7648 M54 2000
823'.914—dc21

                                                                99-462229

Miss Seeton
by Moonlight

chapter
1

It takes, as everyone knows, two to make a quarrel. And it takes a village like Plummergen, in Kent, to show the world how a quarrel should best be enjoyed. When Mrs. Welsted, who with her husband and daughter runs the draper's, was laid low by influenza and refused to let Miss Pydell have the key of the church for daily organ practice, words were exchanged which resulted in Miss Pydell's attending Rye, over the border in Sussex, ever after. When Mrs. Skinner and Mrs. Henderson found themselves in dispute over whose turn it would be (in three weeks' time) to arrange the altar flowers, not even the talking-to given them by Miss Molly Treeves, the vicar's sister, could do more than bandage wounds doomed in perpetuity to erupt at the slightest provocation.

And provocation, in Plummergen, is seldom slow to manifest itself. The village delights in controversy. If there is nothing controversial to be found, then it must be invented, for the benefit of all who wish to take sides — indeed, who thrive on so doing. Almost everyone in this little community can contrive controversy when required, to a degree; but the principal contrivers, virtual professors in the art, are Miss Erica Nuttel and Mrs. Norah Blaine, otherwise known as The Nuts.

The Nuts have embraced a lifestyle dedicated in almost equal parts to vegetarianism and gossip. They eat more bean salad, and monger more scandal, than anyone else in Kent. They have lived in Plummergen for upwards of a dozen years, and flatter themselves that they have been accepted by the inhabitants: but they are wrong. They are tolerated, they are humoured — and, behind their backs, they are mocked by people who were born in cottages where their grandsires were born, and where they confidently expect their grandchildren to live: cottages which still boast their original windows, whether sash, dormer, or casement, and not the net-curtained, plate-glass discordance of Lilikot, where The Nuts reside.

Lilikot, in Plummergen's main (indeed only) street — The Street, as it is formally known — is located conveniently (for The Nuts) opposite two centres of village communication, the post office and Crabbe's Garage, which runs a bus service to nearby

Brettenden twice a week. This means that The Nuts need never miss a single coming or going about the village, whether of importance or not — and, if not (and if nothing else seems promising), they will strive to make it so. On a scale of one to ten for inventiveness, Miss Nuttel and Mrs. Blaine score eleven, every time; and the results of their speculative labours are always given their first airing over the road, in Mr. Stillman's post-office-cum-general-stores.

But this morning was different. This morning, instead of being the instigators of Plummergen's usual diet of wild surmise, The Nuts were rather its victims, and everybody was enjoying themselves a great deal.

Mrs. Flax had opened the bowling. "Four pounds of granulated, Mr. Stillman, thanks. Mrs. Blaine's not the only one wishful to brew a last batch of strawberry jam." The word *brew* reminded her audience, if any reminder were needed, of her position as Plummergen's wise woman, which ensured that her views on any subject would be treated with respect: or with courteous and silent interest while she expounded them, at any rate.

Mr. Stillman quietly set two packets of sugar in front of Mrs. Flax as she continued, "Not that the poor soul's fit to be brewing jam, to my mind. Proper peaky she's bin looking, this last week or more. Two lemons, Mr. Stillman, thanks."

"Not herself at all," agreed Mrs. Skinner, and a general murmur echoed her. Even Mrs. Henderson, reluctantly, could hardly bring herself to deny what everyone knew was true.

"There's an *atmosphere* about that house," she said, with a darkling glance through the post office windows in the direction of Lilikot. "Different, somehow."

"And maybe we can guess why," said Mrs. Spice. "Not that ever in all my born days did I think I'd live to see it, the pair of 'em always having bin so thick right from when they first come here, and now . . ."

"When friends fall out," remarked Mrs. Skinner, her gaze pointedly directed away from Mrs. Henderson into a far corner of the shop, "there's always one to blame far above t'other, we all know that. Only, with her being too pigheaded to apologise, nobody but herself can do anything about it."

Mrs. Scillicough cleared her throat, and others smirked, as Mrs. Henderson sniffed. "What some folk call pigheaded," she informed the little group of shoppers, "there's others consider no more than sticking to principles. Say what you like, them Nuts stick to their principles, the pair of 'em, agree with 'em or no as you choose."

"I've never agreed with 'em," said Mrs. Flax. "It's not right, turning up their noses at honest meat like they do, let alone *inventing* the stuff, lentils and split peas and goodness knows what — flying in the face of Nature, that's what they've bin doing, if you ask me." The one person in Plummergen entitled to indulge in any inventing, concocting, or exploiting of Nature, in the opinion of Mrs. Flax, was Mrs. Flax. "Why else," she continued virtuously, "should we've bin given a good set of teeth, and stomachs, if not to enjoy a chop or a rasher of bacon once in a while? Which," she added, turning back to Mr. Stillman, who stood and waited while the conversation surged about him, "I'll take two pounds of, thanking you, and set the dial to seven. Not too much rind on, neither. No," she went on, as the huge steel disc of the bacon-slicer began to whirr in its dark red cage, "what *I* think is, Mrs. Blaine's not just peaky — not by herself, she isn't, in a manner of speaking. There's more to it than that. Some," she added, "might say as she's plain ailing, but . . ."

"She's not consulted Dr. Knight," said

young Mrs. Newport, who lived in the council houses at the end of the village, past which Mrs. Blaine would have to go to reach the nursing home owned by the doctor and his wife and run by them under the stern eye of Major Matilda Howett (Ret'd).

"She never does," retorted Mrs. Skinner, "not needing to, with all them herbs they grow." She cast a wary look in the direction of The Wise Woman. "So what's your view of the matter, Mrs. Flax? It's more than peaky from their quarrel, you reckon?"

Mrs. Flax drew herself up to her full height. "Peaky?" she repeated, raking her audience with a look which promised revelations to come. "There's a sight more than peaking about Mrs. Blaine, believe me — herbs, you say. And just who is it as looks after that garden of theirs across the road? Not Mrs. Blaine . . ."

"Miss Nuttel," breathed someone on cue, and everybody uttered little gasps of thrilled delight. "But — Mrs. Flax, you surely never —"

"Oh yes I do! If there's anyone in this village knows more about herbs than me, I'd like to meet 'em. And when being peaky comes on so sudden as it did with Mrs. Blaine — for there's no denying last week she was as bright as a button — well," concluded Mrs. Flax, pursing her lips and looking portentous, "I'm not *saying* a word, you understand. But there's no law can stop me from *thinking*," with a nod, and a frown. "To them with the eyes of knowledge, the signs is clear enough . . ."

"There's no signs of nothing," said Mrs. Scillicough in a flat voice, "save that they've not bin able to agree over that daft bit of sculpture in Brettenden. Dear knows, I'll never understand why folk should fall out over such a great mess of scrap metal, but that's what The Nuts have done — and nothing more." Mrs. Scillicough had but scant respect for the authority of Mrs. Flax since the Wise Woman let her down so badly over the soothing herbs intended to give the young mother a respite from the demands of her notorious triplets. Mrs. Scillicough in desperation doubled, then trebled the dose — which stubbornly continued to act more like a stimulant than a suppressant, resulting in permanently sleepless nights. "They've had a tiff, that's all," and she smothered a defiant yawn.

Before the startled Mrs. Flax could find words to quell this small insurrection, Emmeline Putts rushed into speech from behind the grocery counter. Emmy had a strongly proprietorial feeling for the contentious sculpture, since it had been commissioned by, and stood outside, the Brettenden biscuit factory where her mother worked. "You didn't ought to call it scrap metal, Mrs. Scillicough, indeed you didn't. Why, it's one of Humphrey Marsh's finest pieces. The managing director said so himself."

"*And* it was in the paper," chimed in Mrs. Skinner. "A masterpiece, they called it, with a photograph and everything," as if that must be the final word. But Mrs. Scillicough failed to see why *The Brettenden Telegraph and Beacon* (est. 1847, incorporating [1893] *The Iverhurst Chronicle and Argus*) should be accepted as the arbiter of Plummergen taste; and Mrs. Henderson automatically lent support to this dissent. She tossed her head.

"Scrap metal's what Mrs. Scillicough said, and I must say I agree. Looks a regular eyesore, cluttering up the front like that and nobody able to miss seeing it whenever they go past — how anyone could pay good money for a thing like that beats me."

"But it's by *Humphrey Marsh*," breathed Emmy, who'd never heard of the renowned modern sculptor until recently, but who was a splendid example of suggestibility and the

14

power of the press. When her mother had come home and told her the *Beacon* was going to print an article, with photograph, next week, and Mrs. Putts might've got herself in a corner of the picture when they snapped the leader of Brettenden Town Council unveiling *Food Chain* — and she had — Emmy became an authority on Humphrey Marsh almost overnight. She cut out the article for her scrapbook, and ordered an eight-by-ten print of the photograph which showed what her mother swore was the top of her head. Not since Emmy herself (wearing a long blond wig) had been crowned Miss Plummergen at the summer fete had the Putts family enjoyed such renown. "He's ever so famous, Mrs. Henderson. Someone's wrote a book about him, and there was a bit in my magazine, too — ever so handsome, he is. Real rippling muscles," said Emmy, sighing. "He was on the telly last night, what's more."

"Moore? Why, I saw that too," broke in Mrs. Skinner, her memory jogged by Emmy's final words. *"Another Henry Moore in the making,"* she quoted, "that's him, and never mind your rippling muscles, Emmeline Putts. Carrying all them heavy lumps of metal around, hammering and such, I've no doubt." She frowned at Mrs. Henderson. "Very modern, he is. There's people so ignorant they still think sculpture's all marble statues and carving. Very old-fashioned, they say that's become. Welding, and blowtorches, they do it like that now — the telly man interviewed this Humphrey Marsh, and that's what he told him. A-a vision for the future — or something like that . . ." She stumbled into silence as memory failed her, and Mrs. Henderson smirked.

"Vision," said Mrs. Henderson, "may be what *some* folk choose to call it — but a nightmare's more what it looks like, to my way of thinking — and not just me," she added, before the admirers of Humphrey Marsh's distinctive iconoclasm could argue back. "Nobody's noticed Croesus wanting anything of the sort, have they? It was in the paper this very week — *Anyone's* — not one word to say it's *visions* he's having stole from all over the place. *He* wants things as look like what they're supposed to, and more's the pity, is what *I* think. Because if he didn't," concluded Mrs. Henderson in triumph, "he might get his gang to come and clear that mess away from outside the biscuit factory, then we wouldn't have to look at it no more. And I'll take three packets of digestive, please, Mr. Stillman, if Mrs. Flax will excuse me. I've got better things to do with my time than talk about rubbish all day long."

This blatant disrespect had everyone gasping, but Mrs. Henderson was too carried away by her own eloquence to care. She had recognised, in the eyes of most of her audience, a flicker of agreement once she'd raised the topic of Croesus: she knew she'd scored a point, and wanted to leave the shop (and the discussion) on a winning note, which would annoy Mrs. Skinner all the more.

And Mrs. Skinner was duly annoyed. As Mr. Stillman, with an inquiring look at Mrs. Flax, produced the biscuits requested by the queue-jumping Mrs. Henderson, her rival said in an irritable tone, "*Modern* art, that's what it is. Bound to be difficult for some people to understand, Modern Art is," and pronounced the capitals in a meaningful way.

But Mrs. Henderson, heading for the door with the digestive biscuits in her shopping bag, looked over her shoulder and remarked, to nobody in particular: "And if *some people* ever stopped to consider some of the strange folk as are supposed to know all about Art, they'd not be so quick to make fools of theirselves by talking about it and giving other people the wrong idea!"

She was gone, leaving everyone looking at everyone else, trying to pretend they had no idea what she had meant: trying, but with little success. They all understood perfectly well who she'd been referring to in that oblique way, and with whose strangeness the name of Mrs. Skinner had been very cleverly coupled. Though whether anyone would come right out and say so was another matter . . .

Then Emmy Putts, who felt in some obscure way that the reputation of her hero was at stake, remarked thoughtfully: "Yes, well — she never *says* much, does she, but stands to reason she *thinks* a lot, what with teaching the kiddies and all. Ooh, yes, I wonder what Miss Seeton thinks about it, I really do . . ."

And a collective sigh of speculation filled the entire post office, before the tongues began to wag once more.

chapter

2

The subject of all this speculation was, as ever, completely oblivious to any idea that she or her affairs could be of interest to others. Miss Emily Dorothea Seeton, who gladly took early retirement from her teaching of art in a Hampstead school, has lived in Plummergen for seven years now: a septennium which, to Miss Seeton's eyes, has been as happy — and uneventful — as seven years could possibly be. There are many who would take issue with her on this latter point, among whom must be included Chief Superintendent Delphick of Scotland Yard; Superintendent Chris Brinton of Ashford, in Kent; Inspector Harry Furneux of Hastings, in Sussex; and Assistant Commissioner Sir Hubert Everleigh, of the Metropolitan Police; not to mention assorted crooks and villains whose careers, once their paths crossed that of Miss Seeton, turned out considerably shorter than anticipated.

But Miss Seeton sees nothing of this. Her eyes, for all their training in the appreciation and understanding of Art, do not so much ignore or look past the unusual as look right through it. She is unable to conceive of the adventures in which she so frequently becomes embroiled as being in any real way anything to do with her: adventures simply do not happen to a gentlewoman — Miss Seeton, therefore, does not have them. Whatever occurs that is out of the ordinary must be happening to somebody else; her eyes might for a moment wander in search of that somebody, but when she recollects herself and subdues her regrettable curiosity, she is able to dismiss the untoward completely from her mind.

At present, she had managed to dismiss completely from her mind the tremendous bustle of broom, duster, and vacuum cleaner amid which she sat quietly rereading a letter from one who had, over the past few years, become a dear friend. While Martha Bloomer threw herself with enthusiasm into the scouring of Sweetbriars, the cottage which Miss Seeton inherited from her late godmother and cousin Mrs. Gannet, the owner of Sweetbriars smiled to herself, and turned another page, and paid no heed to the flourish of feathers above her head as an unwary cobweb was swirled into oblivion.

"Hi there, Miss S.," the letter had begun

in confident black ink. "I'm writing from my sickbed, would you believe — a broken ankle, of all things!"

"Oh, dear," said Miss Seeton, and clicked her tongue, turning to the end of the letter to see which of her large acquaintance had been so unfortunate, although from the mode of address she had a fair idea.

Her idea was correct. "Yours, as ever, from my bed of pain, *Mel,*" proclaimed the signature, underlined twice and flamboyantly scrawled. Newspaper reporters, Miss Seeton remembered, needed to make notes of what they were reporting as quickly as possible — shorthand, so useful, although not something she herself had ever needed to learn. But all the girls in the Commercial Stream had been taught it before leaving school, and some of their friends would borrow their books to teach themselves the rudiments, ordinary lessons requiring one to make notes — except Art, of course, where it was surely more important to See for oneself rather than to scribble down the mere words of another's way of Seeing. She supposed. It was certainly the way she had tried to teach her classes: to think, to see for themselves, and then to draw what they had seen so that others could share it . . .

"A broken ankle, of all things!" Miss

21

Seeton read on, expecting to learn what manner of accident had befallen poor Amelita Forby, demon reporter of *The Daily Negative*, but Mel had too much consideration for her maidenly correspondent's blushes. Miss Forby's relationship with Thrudd Banner, the freelance star of World Wide Press, wasn't exactly a secret from their friends, but she saw no need to dwell on the more private moments in detail: neither she nor Thrudd were movie actors, tycoons, or minor royalty. Besides, Miss Seeton had been a skilled practitioner of yoga for several years now, and would therefore be unimpressed by the physical activities being enjoyed moments before the brittle crack of a broken bone put an end to all the fun.

The next few paragraphs contained an amusing wordsketch of Mel, her crutches, her experiences as an emergency Out Patient ("Guess what my next exposure's going to be, Miss S.? Got it in one — the National Health Service!"), and Thrudd's limitations as a nurse. "But never say die, Miss S., you know me. I've been sending the boy out to work to stop him driving me crazy fussing around — we women can look after ourselves a darn sight better when the men aren't cluttering the place up!!" And

Miss Seeton, pausing for a brief spell of judicious thought, had to admit that dear Mel — *poor* Mel, she supposed, although it hardly sounded as if the young reporter was suffering too much — was probably correct.

"Anyway, he's been working hard as well as (trying to!) look after me, and this week's *Anyone's* is running a Thrudd Banner exclusive we both thought you'd be interested to see, hence the enclosed. I know you don't spend a lot of time reading the newspapers — and who's to say you're not right? Not Mel Forby! — so you'd more than likely miss this. Don't you think the lad shows promise? But just wait till I'm out and about again — *scoop* won't be the word, believe me!"

Miss Seeton looked again at "the enclosed," which was an article bearing Thrudd Banner's byline beneath the heading THE CROESUS COLLECTION! *Crooks Suspected of Stealing Works of Art to Order.* She sighed, shook her head for the sorrier aspects of human nature, and began to read once more.

The headlines really told the whole story, but no reporter worth the name will miss any chance to display his (or her) investigative skills in attention-grabbing paragraphs. Miss Seeton read Thrudd's description of how he had come to recognise, then to pursue, a hitherto unsuspected connection between various art thefts which had recently occurred in Europe: thefts masterminded, or at the least instigated, by one man, to whom he gave the nickname "Croesus"; thefts of pieces so rare, indeed unique, that they could never be put on the open market. "Only someone as rich as that proverbial king could afford to keep these treasures in the conditions they need, special conditions which museums and art galleries can supply. They control the humidity, temperature, and cleanliness of the surrounding air . . ."

"Mind your feet, dear," said Martha Bloomer, paragon of cleanliness, as she pushed the carpet-sweeper towards a few crumbs it wasn't really worth fetching the Hoover out for. "Why don't you go into the sitting room to finish reading that? I've done in there already."

Miss Seeton obediently pushed back her chair, though she had just reached the last line of Thrudd's article and would be unlikely to read it again — or not for a while, anyway. "But there is still my reply to be written, of course," she murmured, stepping nimbly out of Martha's way. "I must convey my thanks for letting me see this most interesting article, as well as my sympathy — for the broken ankle, that is." She frowned. "I suppose it is in order to combine the two — or maybe I should send a get well card, and enclose my reply in the same envelope — or maybe," and a sudden smile danced in Miss Seeton's eyes, "I could draw a little sketch based on the descriptions in her own letter. So very vivid — which I suppose is only to be expected, though one might *not* have expected her to be so cheerful, making light of her misfortune in such a clever way — but it is her job, though with a broken ankle one must suppose she will be unable to work for a while, which must be most distressing — and then I should be sure of catching the post. Not having to go out twice, you see," she explained, as Martha (who had been listening with half her attention while she hunted out crumbs with the rest) turned a puzzled face towards her. "Because I don't believe," Miss Seeton went on, "that I have one in the house — a get well card, I mean. Which is what I think I will do," and she gathered up the sheets of Mel's letter and Thrudd's article, preparing to leave Martha in peace.

"Some poor soul broke their ankle, have they?" remarked Martha, who was used to her employer's occasionally erratic trains of thought. "Anyone special? I didn't recognise the handwriting when I picked it off the mat."

Miss Seeton flourished the letter vaguely in Martha's direction. "Poor Miss Forby, though I must say she sounds remarkably bright about it, and such an interesting copy of an article by Mr. Banner, too. So very kind of them both to think of me."

"Oh, your reporter friends." Mrs. Bloomer's attitude towards the Press was ambivalent. She enjoyed a good story as well as anyone, and would devour page after potentially libellous page with relish — unless her dear Miss Emily was involved, when she would become a flaming sword. Martha had heard about the Feudal System during school history lessons; her attitude towards her employer was part servitor, part overseer, part protector. The latter came very much to the fore whenever Miss Seeton was off on another of her adventures: but over the years Thrudd and Mel had earned Martha's grudging respect. They never took the advantage of Miss Seeton's innocence which others less scrupulous (as Martha knew well) would have done; if anything, they strove to protect it, as Martha always did, as the police who counted her a colleague tried to do. Since Chief Superintendent Delphick no less (who first co-opted Miss Seeton into the force, and thanks to whom she could afford the washing machine and other labour-saving household appliances which made Martha's job so much easier) seemed to approve of Thrudd Banner and Mel Forby, Mrs. Bloomer felt she could do worse than follow his lead in permitting Miss Seeton to enjoy their friendship . . . and she wasn't jealous in the least, of course.

"Your reporter friends." Martha sniffed as she whisked her duster across the table on which Mel's letter had lately been lying. "Sent you something to read, have they?"

Miss Seeton nodded. "Apparently, Mr. Banner has an article in this week's *Anyone's*, which as you know I never see, and they have kindly sent me a copy, about works of art from all over Europe being stolen, and how rich he must be — the man who is paying the others to steal them. The paintings and statues, I mean."

Martha's ears had pricked up at the mention of *Anyone's*. "Oh, I saw that this morning — some funny name, he's got, this rich man." Not for worlds would she have admitted that she wasn't sure how to pronounce it. "But I never knew it was Mr. Banner wrote it. Well!" And she looked suitably impressed. The journalistic credentials of Mel and Thrudd had always seemed slightly dubious before, but when what they wrote was printed in a paper read by half the households in the country . . . "And poor Miss Forby with a broken ankle," said Martha, shaking her head. "Well, well. And you going to do her a little picture to cheer her up . . . She'll like that, I'm sure. Just you pop along now to the sitting room, out of the way of the dust — and," she added, "you might say I'm sorry, when you write *Anyone's*, indeed. And Mr. Banner writing all about paintings and sculptures and things like that . . . Wonder what he'd make of that ugly great mess outside the biscuit factory?"

Miss Seeton tried to be fair. "It is *modern* art, Martha dear, and though I confess myself to be not as sympathetic towards Mr. Marsh's ideas as perhaps I should be — teaching, after all, ought to broaden the mind of the teacher just as much as that of the pupil . . . but it does at least provoke *thought*. Modern art, I mean. Which must be considered as being the next best to sight — having sufficient knowledge, that is, to understand that it is necessary to *think* about where to start looking for what the artist intends us to see — his personal vision of the world. Though it is not always easy to communicate," said Miss Seeton with feeling, "one's ideas to others — which is why others must make the effort to see what was intended — if they can," she added, for she was an honest woman. "Sometimes, of course, they can't. Which has to be a failure on the artist's part . . ." And she sighed, thinking of her own limitations.

Martha snorted. "I'll say it's a failure! There's that clutter, for clutter's what it looks like to me, large as life and twice as expensive, from what the *Beacon* said last week — remember I brought it over to show you — and neither rhyme nor reason to it at all, say what you will. If people are paid good money to, to *vision* what looks like somebody squashed a couple of old tin cans and a sewing machine together, then I'm taking my dustbin up to Brettenden on the next bus, and ask what they'll give me for it. *Food Chain,* indeed! What's it supposed to mean?"

"Mechanisation," replied Miss Seeton after some thought. "The factory — conveyor belts, or do I mean production lines — and the biscuits, which of course are intended to be eaten and which used to be made by hand . . ." She frowned. Surely there had been a far better explanation than that in the interview which Humphrey Marsh had given to the *Beacon*? Who, for so young a man, seemed to have very decided views . . .

As Martha snorted again, and muttered of rolling pins, pastry boards, and a good dose of common sense, Miss Seeton broke into a smile. There was a twinkle in her eye as she said, her voice quivering:

"I'm sure the fault is mine, Martha dear, for being so blind to Mr. Marsh's talent, but I have to confess that I was not at all sure, when I first saw the sculpture, of what he was trying to show me. It reminded me, indeed, of nothing so much as one of dear Cousin Flora's stories — no doubt you remember? About her young days as a member of the bicycle club, and how they tumbled together into a ditch when the president's machine was frightened by a horse — or, rather, the horse was frightened, and bolted. I was riding it at the time, which made me recall — the horse, that is — or rather, my bicycle. Past the factory. Which of course is another sort of machine, or at least has machines inside — to make the biscuits." Miss Seeton looked surprised. "Why, perhaps I am not so unsympathetic to the work of Mr. Marsh as I supposed . . ."

And, much cheered by this evidence of

her ability to see at least something of what had been intended, Miss Seeton hurried off to write her letter, leaving Martha to wage war to the death on every last particle of dust.

Miss Seeton read Mel's missive through once more before composing her reply, in the final paragraph of which she reminded Miss Forby of the first time they had met, and how the young reporter had suggested that the art editor of her newspaper might be interested in a few Seeton sketches. Not that she was suggesting for one moment that the enclosed was anything other than a personal greeting, but since Mel had been kind enough to express that interest, she might find Miss Seeton's attempt at a get well card amusing, in view of her own clever words, and the crutches . . .

Miss Seeton drew her sketching block towards her, worked out in how many sections the sheet would have to be folded to fit in the envelope with her letter, and closed her eyes as she tried to rough out a little cartoon strip, perhaps, of poor Mel's adventure: something she could read in different ways, depending on how it was folded. Which would take rather a lot of thought, to make the lines of various parts of the drawings match up . . .

Good gracious. Miss Seeton blinked. Her eyes had been open for longer than she'd realised, because she'd managed to fill the entire sheet of paper — but not with a picture that would mean anything to Mel Forby, unless she'd had her accident while riding in a pony and trap. One of the people in the trap was definitely female in form — but surely Mel, no matter that one knew young people of today to be so very liberated in their views, would never go out so scantily clad? For the female figure appeared decidedly lacking in dress: a few draperies, nothing more. And the pony — or was it a horse? "Hands," murmured Miss Seeton, recalling conversations with earnest young members of the Pony Club, and the measurements which could bar one from entering certain competitions. "Four inches, I believe, or was it six . . ."

But she had other matters to puzzle over than the height of horses and ponies. There could be no possible connection between Mel Forby and this sketch and anything that made any sense — unless . . . Of course. She had been talking to dear Martha about making biscuits by hand — and Cousin Flora's story of the bicycle (the wheels of the trap were so very clearly drawn) and the horse that had startled the president of the club. Her subconscious had jumbled together the conversation just past with poor Mel's present predicament. No doubt the obviously female form was a representation of Mel in her hospital robe, being prepared for the operation when her broken ankle was to be set. And the other figures in the trap must be the nurses, or the hospital porters, escorting her to the theatre . . .

But Miss Seeton decided that it was perhaps a little too obscure for an invalid's bedside; and certainly not amusing, as she'd intended it to be. She tore the drawing from the top of her pad and pushed it to one side before settling down to start again.

And she did not stop to wonder, as she put everything back in her portfolio and fastened it neatly, whether there might be another meaning in that pony-and-trap picture which would be of interest to others of her acquaintance besides Mel Forby . . .

Such as, for instance, the police.

chapter
3

It should be explained that around half the population of Plummergen are avid readers of *Anyone's*; the other half will learn of anything of particular interest contained in that popular periodical by hearing everyone else talking about whatever-it-is — usually in the post office. But, as it was still too early this morning for Lady Colveden to have gone out shopping, at Rytham Hall the conversation was of a more general nature.

"More coffee, anyone?" Lady Colveden gauged the weight of the silver pot. "Yes, Nigel, I know about you, but would you mind just taking a quick look behind the paper first, to see if your father's finished his?"

Nigel pulled a face at his mother. "I know you can't help subscribing to the view that your spouse comes before your offspring — it's the way your generation was brought up — but may I just point out that I work twice as hard as Dad thinks he does, if not harder." The newspaper concealing Major-General Sir George Colveden, Bart, KCB,

DSO, JP rustled in a pointed manner. Nigel grinned. "And when the weather's as hot as this, a working farmer really needs to replenish his fluid intake before he dehydrates . . ."

He withdrew from behind *The Times* an empty cup, and held it, with his own, across for his mother to fill. "Perhaps I ought to add a pinch of salt," he suggested. His mother shook her head at him.

"You shouldn't make fun of your father," she reproached him. "Though I must admit, it would sometimes be nice to have him properly with us — yet it does seem rather a mean trick to play, just to wake him up . . ."

The Times rustled even more, and Sir George cleared his throat as Nigel was about to speak. "Boy's talking sense, Meg. Saw it in the desert, many a time — pinch of salt for heat stroke. Two spoons, please."

Lady Colveden opened wide eyes in silent apology to her grinning son, who reached for the salt cellar and plunged in his spoon. She shuddered, and pulled a face, turning to the window so that she wouldn't have to watch. There were times when her menfolk teased her beyond belief, and she was never entirely sure how far they meant what they said. It made for an exasperating, if interesting, life on occasion.

"Oh look, here comes Bert. He's late today," she said, above the brisk rattle of Nigel's spoon.

"You mean *oh listen*," he corrected her with a chuckle, then a choke as he sipped his coffee. Maybe he'd risk heat stroke after all. "I do think the Post Office ought to buy him a van with a more reliable engine. I wonder if he'd like me to take a quick look at it for him?" After years spent with a spanner either under the bonnet of his little MG or inside the farm tractor, Nigel thought himself (with some justification) reasonably expert on most matters of internal combustion.

There came a series of cheerful pips on the van's horn as the village's favourite redhead, the young postman who had the Plummergen round one week in three and was trying to make it a full-time appointment, rattled his way up the rest of the drive and juddered to a halt by the main door.

"Might be something exciting in his little brown sack," said Nigel, "and not just bills. Shall I go?"

As he pushed back his chair, his mother looked anxious. "It's sure to be against the union rules, or something — for you to start tinkering with the motor, I mean. And suppose you make it worse?"

"Can't have you blamed for bringing the entire GPO out on strike," agreed his father, above Nigel's protest that he could hardly make it worse than it already was, and in any case he knew perfectly well what he was doing. "Remember what they say in the Army," he added. "Never volunteer." Nigel stopped in his tracks.

"Perhaps I'd better not," he said, sounding regretful but resigned. There came a clatter from the hall, followed by a dull thump. Nigel chuckled. "I could always fix that wire basket back on the letter box," he remarked, with one eye on *The Times* and the other on his mother.

Lady Colveden flashed him a warning glance as the newspaper trembled in his father's hands. Sir George's balding pate had, on a recent occasion when he stooped to tie a shoelace and stood upright without thinking, borne the brunt of a sneak attack from one of said wire basket's well-meshed and uncomfortable corners. The baronet, after cursing with some of his fine old Forces epithets, had wrenched the offending basket from its hooks and hurled it down the hall. Martha Bloomer's comments upon seeing the scratches she'd have to spend hours polishing away had been almost as pithy as those of Sir George . . .

Nigel caught his mother's eye, spluttered, then headed out to the hall to collect the little bundle of letters. He was vaguely disappointed to see that there was nothing for him, but he hadn't really expected any envelopes addressed in a feminine hand. He was between girlfriends at the mo— No, here was an envelope addressed in a feminine hand, all right — but it wasn't addressed to him.

"One for you, Mother, and the rest for Dad — circulars, bills, that sort of thing." Nigel returned to the dining room to hand out his booty. "The postmark's all smudged on yours, so if the phantom blackmailer's trying to cover his tracks he's done a good job."

He passed Lady Colveden her mystery envelope, then went round to the other side of the table and deposited the rest of the letters neatly under his father's nose. Sir George grunted his thanks, and carried on reading the newspaper. Nigel returned to his seat, pausing to collect a clean cup from the sideboard, and favouring his mother with a pleading look. As she was too busy opening her letter to pay attention, he helped himself to the remains of the coffee and pointedly stirred in a generous dollop of sugar.

"Good gracious!" exclaimed Lady

Colveden, beginning to read. Nigel looked up. "The poor thing!" His mother came to the bottom of the first page, sighed, and continued reading. "How dreadful . . ."

Sir George lowered *The Times* and gazed sideways at his son. Nigel shrugged, and shook his head. Sir George went back to his newspaper.

"Oh, dear," said Lady Colveden. "How exciting, though."

"Mother!" Nigel could bear the suspense no longer. "If it's so dreadfully exciting that you're giving us a running commentary on it, do at least give us a *detailed* commentary, please. What on earth are you babbling about?"

Lady Colveden lowered her letter and regarded him with a sorrowful expression in her eyes. "Nigel," she said, sadly. "As if I ever babble —"

"You know you do, darling, when you're all excited about something." Nigel waved a coffee spoon at her. "And don't try to pretend there isn't a gleam in your eye, because it's perfectly obvious from where I'm sitting." *The Times* danced in Sir George's hands. "See? Even Dad's noticed — through twelve thicknesses of newspaper, what's more. If you don't put us out of our misery, he might even be reduced to asking you himself — and just think what a shock to your system *that* would be."

Lady Colveden stifled a quick giggle, and strove to look serious. "It's nothing to laugh at, Nigel. This letter is from Alicia Eykyn, and you'll never guess what she says!"

"Fire? Flood? Earthquake?" hazarded Nigel. "She's won a place on the Olympic show-jumping team? No, that wouldn't merit all the exclamations of horror. She's burgled Battersea Dogs' Home!" The young countess was a well-known lover of all that was canine or equine. "Come on, Mother, spill the beans. What's up?"

"*Raffles,*" breathed Lady Colveden, in a thrilling voice.

Nigel looked at his mother. He looked at *The Times.* It was lowered enough to permit Sir George to look back at him. Father and son rolled baffled eyes at each other.

Nigel let out a sudden groan. "*Not* another attempt to raise funds for something-or-other by offering the hapless peasantry a chance to unlock a time vault if they buy the winning ticket? Look what happened here!"

"That was hardly Miss Seeton's fault," his mother said quickly; and there was a thoughtful silence. Nigel sighed.

"Then what are we talking about?" he en-

40

quired, gently. Lady Colveden took a deep breath.

"Raffles the Ransomeer," she announced. "Of course. As you probably knew all along, and I do think it's —"

"Mother! Not the Eykyn Emeralds?" And, as Nigel spoke, there came a horrified trembling from *The Times*. Sir George cleared his throat.

"The lot?" he enquired. "Bad show. How much?" he added as an afterthought.

"George, really! That lovely parure — it's priceless. All the historical associations — worn by every Eykyn bride since goodness-knows-when —"

"Which is why he'll have gone for it," said Nigel. "You have to hand it to the chap, whoever he is — he does know his stuff. But they'll have got it back by now, won't they? Alicia wouldn't risk telling people about it while it was still missing, in case he found out and thought they'd told the police, and they never saw it again."

His mother nodded. "Sent by registered post, the way he always does. And not a sign anything had been wrong — no false stones, no broken clasps, and Alicia thinks he's even had it cleaned, because she swears it never shone like that before. Which is why the first thing Bill did was have a man down to check the stones, in case he'd exchanged them." The second thing the earl had done was double the insurance carried by the heirloom parure, a set of flawless emeralds mounted as matching bracelets, earrings, brooch, necklace, and a tiara which the countess seldom wore because she said it made her head ache. "And everything was just as it ought to be — so I suppose it looked brighter because, well, they were so pleased to have it all safely back."

"You're being sentimental, Mother. Mind you, I can sympathise," said Nigel, on whom the sight of Lady Eykyn in her full be-jewelled glory at a hunt ball last year had worked as dramatically as had Romeo's first glimpse of young Miss Capulet at her engagement party. "Gosh, yes," said Nigel, remembering with awe, and the old flutter awoke in his susceptible Galahad heart. "Pretty grim, if they'd never got it all back!"

"Bill insists on being first in line with the horsewhip, if they ever find out who took it," said Lady Colveden, referring back to the countess's elegant scrawl. Lord Eykyn was noted for standing no nonsense from anyone. "Only they won't catch him, of course. He's too clever. In fact, now it's safely over, I think it's almost romantic, in a way. And so does Alicia — she says it's rather a compliment that he thought they had something worth going to all that effort to steal."

"Pah!" came a furious snort from behind *The Times*, which was crushed to the table as Sir George harrumphed. "Women's fuss — bad for business." As a magistrate, he knew his duty not to let anyone in the Colveden family make a bally hero out of the rascal. "Help old Bill out with the horsewhip," he added, as his wife looked startled. "Anytime. Chap's a crook — no two ways about it."

"Well, yes, George, but he's a *harmless* crook," his wife hastened to remind him. "I mean, he might steal things, but he never hits people over the head, or vandalises the place, or breaks his word — when he says he'll send something back, he always does."

"Honour among thieves," murmured Nigel, as the tips of his father's moustache twitched irritably. "And, talking of effort, Mother — how did he do it this time?"

"It seems he climbed up to the roof and fastened a rope to one of the chimneys, and — what's the word — abseiled," she consulted Lady Eykyn's letter again, "down to the nearest windowsill, and then he must have *walked along all the sills* until he came to the morning-room window." She gave an expressive shudder. "You know how unnervingly high the rooms are — it makes me giddy just looking out, never mind sitting on the sill with a bucket of soapy water, the way the window cleaner does. But he left broken glass all over the carpet, so they know that's how he got in — Raffles, I mean. And then he fastened another rope to the leg of that Chinese cabinet Bill's mother used for her Crown Derby dinner service, you remember how very solid it is, and, well, abseiled down to the ground. He left the ropes behind," she said, as Nigel mouthed an "O" of astonishment. "Panache — isn't that the word?"

"It's a start," said Nigel, above Sir George's ever more furious harrumphing. "*Incredible* is another good one — think how super fit he must be, whoever he is, not to let go or lose his nerve at the vital moment. Though I could probably give him a run for his money pitching bales," he added, with haymaking in mind. "But — gosh, yes, there really is something about him, isn't there? I wonder how much longer he's going to get away with it. You can't help having a sneaky sort of, well, admiration for the chap . . ."

Nigel's opinion of the daring cat burglar dubbed by the press "Raffles the Ransomeer" was shared by most of those

44

who had read of his exploits. While the more sensational publications, such as *Anyone's*, featured every detail of his recent reign of crime (five ransoms generally known, and an unspecified number darkly hinted at), even the more sober pages of such papers as *The Times* and *The Daily Telegraph* were now prepared to mention him in the occasional discreet paragraph. Raffles, whoever he was, was News. People spoke of him in shop queues, and exchanged speculation as to his identity, and the likelihood of his capture. The well-known British penchant for the underdog meant that a sizeable proportion of the populace secretly hoped he would never be caught at all.

"The police seem to be no nearer catching him now than they were when he started," said Lady Colveden, "at least, from what Alicia says. Bill informed them straightaway, of course, and they advised him to play along while they made enquiries, but he worked out such a clever way of tricking them. He kept them hanging on for ages — you know how he does, building up the suspense and making them all the more worried, poor things — and when he eventually got round to asking for the money, he said it must be taken to a building site on one particular Sunday afternoon, and put under an overturned packing case he'd marked with red paint." She turned back hurriedly to Lady Eykyn's letter. "Or was it blue? Oh dear, I'm not really —"

"I shouldn't think it matters," broke in Nigel, as she began to scan the bold black writing in search of accuracy. "We get the general idea. What happened then?"

"I said it was clever," his mother reminded him, "and if your father twirls fifty moustaches at me I shall still say so. Because it was. The police set a watch on the place, of course, and Bill handed over the money — well, popped it in a plastic bag under the packing case, then went off and joined the watchers, and waited for Raffles —"

"With his horsewhip?" asked Nigel, grinning. There was a muffled snort from behind Sir George's moustache, which quivered. Lady Colveden said quickly:

"Alicia didn't say. But it wouldn't have made any difference if he had brought it, because Raffles never showed up — at least, they never caught sight of him."

"The Invisible Man," said Nigel, who enjoyed the cinema when work permitted an outing. "So did they track his footprints in the snow?"

"Don't be silly, Nigel, it's the middle of July," said his mother at once, before recollecting herself. "I thought you wanted to know what happened? If you keep interrupting me, you'll never find out."

"Sorry," he murmured, catching his father's eye. Even Sir George looked interested now. *The Times* was lying forgotten, one corner in the marmalade. "Go on," said Nigel, "we're all agog."

"And so you should be," his mother said sternly. "This is the nearest you're ever likely to come to a really daring crime . . ." She tailed off at the expression on the faces of her menfolk. She thought of Miss Seeton, and turned pink. "Well, you know what I mean. This is a firsthand account — and before it's been in the papers, too. He hasn't used the trick before, as far as I —"

"Mother!" Nigel waved the coffee spoon again. "Do stop fluffing and come to the point. There's a farm out there in need of due care and attention, remember."

"*Sewers,*" breathed Lady Colveden, producing the punch line with a thrill in her voice.

"Sewers?" echoed Nigel. "You mean — the Third Man, not his invisible brother?" And Sir George coughed mightily.

"No I don't," said Nigel's mother crossly,

beginning to pile crockery on a tray. "I mean that Raffles had put the packing case right on top of a manhole cover, and he crept along underground, where of course nobody could see him, and collected poor Bill's money — they used real notes, just in case it all went wrong, because they did want the emeralds back — and then he crept away again. Unnoticed. And . . ." Lady Colveden's voice shook. ". . . and . . . leaving a receipt behind."

"Gosh," said Nigel, duly impressed.

And Sir George, scraping marmalade from his newspaper with a spoon, remarked: "Feller has style, give him his due. Better him than the Croesus crowd, anyhow . . ."

chapter

4

Several days later, the Croesus Gang came up in a far less rarefied atmosphere than that of Rytham Hall: Scotland Yard. Thrudd Banner's *Anyone's* article had sounded warning bells, and ever since that journal's appearance telephone calls had been received at police stations throughout the country from anxious museum curators, owners of art galleries, and others with reason to dread a megalomaniac millionaire's acquisitive machinations.

"He must be crazy, if everything Interpol says is missing has really been pinched on his behalf," said Chief Superintendent Delphick to Detective Sergeant Bob Ranger, throwing aside one of his Art Squad colleague's anguished reports. "That is, if the chap exists at all, and he's not merely the figment of a journalist's fevered imagination."

"Thrudd generally gets his facts right," pointed out Bob in a thoughtful tone. "Granted he'll have livened it up for the sake of a good story, but I bet there's an honest-to-goodness Croesus around somewhere, collecting like mad."

"And, as I said, judging by this, the man must be mad." Delphick indicated the Art Squad report with the end of his ballpoint pen. "Nobody in their right mind could possibly bear to live with such a motley mix of artifacts: it isn't so much the variety of items as the violently differing styles. He's snatched everything from Renaissance to Rococo, and if it's all intended for the same room he must be singularly lacking in taste."

Bob, who wasn't even sure whether there were three esses in *Renaissance* or only two, tried to look knowing. "Perhaps he has a very large house, sir, with enormous rooms." There was a hint of envy in his voice: he hadn't been married very long, and the home he shared with Anne suited her tiny frame far better than his six foot seven. Maybe one day . . .

"Or perhaps" — he dragged his thoughts with difficulty away from wedded bliss — "he's planning to sell the stuff to the highest bidder, sir, instead of hanging on to it — or he might even be having it stolen to order for other people. Perhaps he's more a — a criminal mastermind, sir, than a mad millionaire wanting to build himself a palace."

"At least we know one thing about him," said Delphick in a resolute tone. "He may be as mad as a whole husk of hares in March, but he's nothing to do with us, thank goodness. Terling and his Art Squad chums may chase after fifty-foot-long cast-iron spiral staircases if they like — this office deals with more serious crimes than the pilfering of architectural fittings, of historical interest or not."

"They coshed the night watchman pretty hard," said Bob, who had first drawn his superior's notice to today's story in the popular press. Senior police officers will never admit to reading *The Blare*: they rely on their subordinates to keep them informed of anything it may contain of likely interest. "And next time they might damage someone even m—"

"I repeat, Sergeant Ranger, that this Croesus Gang has nothing whatsoever to do with us," Delphick broke in, fixing Bob with a bleak and minatory eye. "Inspector Terling was no doubt suffering from a moment's mental aberration when he sent his report along to me . . ."

There was a long, thoughtful silence. Bob retrieved his newspaper from Delphick's out tray, and went back to his own desk. Absently, he opened the paper and gazed at the headline which had caught his attention.

"Spiral Stair-Case Stolen: Croesus Sus-

pected," he read, emphasising the alliteration as he did so. "You know, sir, there's something about all these esses. I can't help thinking of —"

"No, Bob," Delphick said, dangerously quiet. "There's no need for you to think, believe me — or at least not about what my instincts warn me you're hinting at."

"Don't you mean about *whom*, sir?" burst from Bob before he could stop himself, and Delphick's eyes narrowed. Ranger suppressed an instinctive grin, shot his superior an apologetic look, and folded away his copy of *The Blare.* He found his shorthand notebook, opened it, and with a sigh settled to transcribing the concluding pages of an interview held on the previous day with a lady of dubious reputation who might just be the key witness in a nightclub protection racket.

Delphick regarded the exaggeratedly bowed shoulders of his mischievous sergeant with an amusement he struggled to suppress. He picked up his ballpoint pen and, before pulling the next pile of reports across his desk, doodled for a moment on the blotter . . .

And uttered a groan, when he realised what he'd drawn.

An umbrella.

MissEss.

"Bob, you are a confounded nuisance," Delphick informed his startled sergeant, as he ripped the sheet of blotting paper from its four leather corners and proceeded to tear it into strips. "Some malign influence," continued the chief superintendent, still tearing, setting strip upon strip with a determined hand as he did so, "has encouraged you to taunt me with thoughts of a certain inhabitant of a certain village in a certain county to the south-east of London . . ."

"Sorry, sir." Bob blinked as Delphick began to tear the strips at right angles, dropping the resulting shreds of confetti with a muffled groan into the wastepaper basket he hooked towards himself with an anguished foot. As the last pink particles spiralled into the bin, Delphick dusted his hands together, and smiled a thin smile.

"Back to work, Sergeant Ranger! And not another hint, reminder, or direct mention of Miss Seeton is to be heard in this room until the Croesus Gang has been caught — through the exclusive efforts of Inspector Terling and his men, do you understand?"

"Perfectly, sir," said Bob; and his shoulders shook.

Delphick pushed the wastepaper basket back where it had come from. It fell over. He cursed.

"You can't blame her for *that,* sir," said irrepressible Bob, as the metal bin rolled across the floor scattering a rosy trail in its wake. Delphick glared at him.

"Blame whom, Sergeant Ranger?"

"My Aunt Em, sir," replied Bob, who had adopted MissEss as an honorary relation some years past, and rarely seen any reason to regret it. "I know things tend to go a bit, well, peculiar sometimes, when she's around — but she's not around here now, is she, sir?"

"Thankfully, she is not," Delphick replied, breathing hard. Bob joined him on the carpet, collecting confetti. Between them, the detectives hunted down every last scrap.

When things were back to normal, Bob said: "D'you know, sir, I've been thinking. About how things go wobbly when she gets involved — involved with us, sir. The police. Yet the rest of the time, she seems to live a perfectly normal sort of life down in Plummergen — Anne's parents would tell us if anything funny happened, and they never do — and when Anne and I go to see her, sir, as ourselves — I mean, me as me and not as a copper — well, she seems almost like any other maiden aunt, sir. Anybody's aunt, she could be."

"Almost like," Delphick echoed him. "There you have it, Bob: she can never be exactly like anyone's aunt because, there's no denying the fact, Miss Seeton is unique. I don't see how her position as an artistic consultant to Scotland Yard, being paid a retainer fee for a small number of drawings each year . . ."

He tailed off, and fell silent, looking back on the remarkable association of Miss Emily Seeton with the Metropolitan (and, as her fame spread, other) Police: which first came about when, leaving Covent Garden after enjoying a performance of *Carmen*, Miss Seeton had interrupted a young and vicious dope peddler while he was knifing his girlfriend — had prodded him in the back with her umbrella, disapproving his ungentlemanly attitude towards the weaker sex.

"Weaker sex!" muttered Delphick in an ironic tone, recalling Miss Seeton's subsequent survival of gassing, coshing, abduction, attempted human sacrifice, bombing . . .

"But only because we asked her to, I suppose," he said to himself. "All in the line of duty, she'd say — and," he regarded Bob with a pensive look, "we're the people who pay her for doing her duty, as you've pointed out. She knocks things completely off-balance as she goes along, of course, because that's the sort of person she is — but she wouldn't necessarily be going along in that particular direction if we hadn't first asked her to . . ."

"That's what I meant, sir, yes. We sort of — set her up to go off, sir. Like a rocket. The gunpowder's always capable of exploding, but unless someone puts a match to it, it can't. And, well, we might be Miss Seeton's matches, sir."

"*I* might, you mean. As you have so shrewdly brought to my attention, Miss Seeton appears to indulge in few of her gyrations when left to her own devices. How peaceful," said Delphick, with a sigh, "life in Plummergen must be when she hasn't received any call to arms from the police . . ."

He shook his head, brooding, while Bob went back to his paperwork after having made a silent bet with himself. Give it twenty-four hours — forty-eight at most — and MissEss and the police'd be up to their ears in it again. Even after all these years, he didn't know how she did it — she didn't mean to, anyone could see that — but she only had to appear over the horizon, waving that brolly of hers, and the whole world wobbled on its axis.

In fact, she didn't even have to put in a personal appearance — someone else could set the ball rolling on her behalf. Someone like Inspector Terling of the Art Squad . . .

"Twenty-four hours," he murmured, glancing at the clock.

"Sorry, Bob, what was that?"

"Nothing important, sir," said Bob, with mental fingers crossed; and he glanced at the clock again.

It was not twenty-four hours but nineteen minutes later that the telephone rang on Delphick's desk.

"Sir Wormelow Tump? Asking to speak to me?" Delphick blinked. "I suppose I could see him if necessary, but — did he give you any idea . . . Oh. Very well, send him up, and my sergeant will meet him at the lift."

"Sir Wormelow Tump?" said Bob, every ounce of his seventeen stone sweet innocence. "I seem to know the name, sir. Isn't he that courtier chap who takes care of the Buck House collection of arty souvenirs the Queen doesn't have time to dust? I seem to remember something about a shrunken head, and a girl modelling jewellery — somewhere in, er, Kent — a village with a fruity sounding name, sir, wasn't it? And didn't this Tump go on some Aegean cruise

57

a couple of years ago — the one MissEss was given as a sort of bonus, and then you had to be called in because —"

"Bob!" Delphick slapped the palm of his hand flat on the desk, and winced at the sting. "If you don't stop grinning like that, I won't be answerable for the consequences. Sir Wormelow may have called on an utterly unrelated matter. In fact, I hardly see how he can *not* have done so. Go along to fetch him, will you? And for heaven's sake, stop looking like the Cheshire Cat. You have no reason at all to be so horribly cheerful: moderate your mirth, if you please."

"Certainly, sir." Bob pushed back his chair and rose to his feet. "It's just that I'm five quid better off than I was half an hour ago . . ."

And he made for the door, escaping through it before his infuriated superior had time to work out what he'd meant.

Sir Wormelow Tump, custodian of the Royal Collection of Objets de Vertu, was an austerely aristocratic personage of imposing height and impeccable manners. He greeted Delphick with a grateful smile, shaking hands and seeming entirely at his ease; but the look he directed, very briefly, towards Sergeant Ranger suggested to the chief superintendent that he had come on no ordinary business.

Which probably meant Miss Seeton was involved, after all — as, if he'd been honest with himself instead of letting Bob wind him up, he might have guessed, from the start. "No ordinary business" just about summed her up. There were coincidences, and coincidences . . .

"You remember my sergeant, don't you, Sir Wormelow? You met at Rytham Hall during that little affair of the Laligue jewellery."

"Indeed I do, Chief Superintendent. Sergeant Ranger and I have already renewed our acquaintance. A pleasure to meet him again." Sir Wormelow's elegant features, however, reflected little pleasure, despite his courteous words.

"Let me assure you that Ranger is the very soul of discretion, Sir Wormelow. We have worked together for several years; whatever you have to discuss with me may be safely discussed in his presence. Won't you sit down?"

Delphick waited while Bob brought a chair across for his visitor, then raised his eyebrows and indicated that the sergeant should make himself, as far as possible for one so large, unobtrusive. Behind Tump's back, Bob motioned in the direction of his notebook, and looked a question. Delphick shook his head, very slightly.

Sir Wormelow did not appear to notice the byplay: he was reaching into his jacket pocket. As Bob seated himself at his desk, a slim-fingered hand withdrew from the pocket a pale grey envelope.

"This is — a rather delicate matter, I fear, Mr. Delphick." Sir Wormelow took a deep breath. "I've no doubt that you will reproach me — justifiably so — for not having come to you before, but . . ."

He turned the grey envelope over in his hands. "There are, if you understand me, some griefs which at first one feels should remain private . . . One does not always care to speak of, well, one's emotions . . ."

"Yes, I understand, Sir Wormelow," the chief superintendent assured the unhappy man in front of him. Tump's unorthodox sexual preference (which was what Delphick supposed he was referring to) had been generally known to the police high-ups for some years, but as the man was neither blatant nor a security risk — indeed, it had been MissEss, Delphick reflected wryly, who'd helped to clear him when the finger of suspicion had pointed his way — he had been left to pursue that unorthodox preference in peace.

Sir Wormelow took a deep breath. "It was in today's *Blare* — my cleaning lady always reads it during her all-too-lengthy coffee break, and I confess to a sneaking curiosity about the more sensational forms of journalism . . . I babble, do I not, Chief Superintendent? I make excuses, and put off telling you what must be told."

"As you say, Sir Wormelow. But as long as you tell me eventually, no real harm has been done."

Sir Wormelow's sculptured lips smiled thinly. "You have a delightful way of instructing me to stop wasting your time, Mr. Delphick. I thank you for not losing your temper with me — I find it difficult to express . . . to explain . . ."

With a sudden movement, he held out the envelope across the desk. "Please read this, Chief Superintendent. Then I believe you'll understand why I came."

"If you wish, Sir Wormelow." And, as Delphick withdrew a folded letter from inside the grey envelope, Tump lowered his head. It might have been a gesture of acquiescence; Bob Ranger could almost suppose, from the set of Sir Wormelow's shoulders, that there were tears in the man's eyes.

An uneasy silence filled the office while Delphick read the letter, which was written in a fine cursive script on embossed paper. It began "My dear Wonky," and concluded with a valediction in Greek, which Delphick (despite his surname) did not understand. But he saw no need to press for a translation: the meat of the letter was in plain English, and he turned back to the beginning to read it again.

After the second reading, he looked thoughtfully at Tump for a long moment. "Blackmail, Sir Wormelow, is a crime, as I'm sure your friend must have known. It is greatly to be regretted that he felt unable to go to the police —"

"In his position — his exact position — I wonder if *you* would have gone, Mr. Delphick? I doubt if *I* could be so sure that no . . . harm . . . to myself, or to others, would ensue from such an action. It is all very well to be willing to make a sacrifice of one's own reputation in a good cause, but . . ."

Delphick nodded, saying nothing. Tump said pleadingly: "Until now, this was simply a . . . private grief — but the newspaper said that the night watchman had been brutally attacked, and was . . . was in intensive care . . . and I knew I had been a coward . . . and I remembered your . . . kindness . . . on board the *Eurydice* . . ."

Delphick nodded again. "I understand, Sir Wormelow — in part, that is. But what exactly do you want me to do?"

Tump squared his shoulders, and raised his head. "These evil people must be stopped, Chief Superintendent. Nothing now can bring my poor friend back, but others should never have to suffer the mental agonies they forced him to undergo before he . . . took the only escape he could find. You must stop them, Mr. Delphick. And — one does not wish to speak of vengeance, but I . . . will help you, in whatever way I can."

chapter
5

Chief Superintendent Delphick hesitated. "Naturally, we in the police are always grateful for the public's cooperation, Sir Wormelow, and I'd be only too happy to introduce you to Inspector Terling, who is our Art Squad expert, but —"

"No." Tump raised a hand, very slightly, to emphasise the refusal. He shook his head. "I have no doubt that the inspector is a competent man, but I would feel . . . I would prefer to work with you, Mr. Delphick. I know you, and . . . and trust you. And you, of course, know me."

"I do indeed. But, as I was about to explain, this case is nothing to do with me. Art thefts, unless they involve a loss of life, really aren't my particular concern. There's not much I can do to help, on any official basis . . ."

Sir Wormelow, a long-serving courtier sensitive to every hint, didn't miss this one. "But are you quite so helpless unofficially? I think perhaps not, Mr. Delphick."

The chief superintendent smiled. "There

is certainly no harm, in my opinion, from talking the matter over, Sir Wormelow. Might I suggest that you have already given it some thought? I'd be interested to hear your views."

Tump, returning Delphick's smile, bowed slightly. "From the moment I read the newspaper I knew that something had to be done: and I have, indeed, thought the matter over with as much care as possible, given that my knowledge of the case is limited to . . . to my poor friend's letter, and the reports of the popular press. Which, one must assume, contain some degree, at least, of truth?"

"Thrudd Banner's generally considered a reliable man," Delphick told him. "Allowance always has to be made for the journalist's hyperbole, of course, but judging by the report from Inspector Terling which I've just read I'd say Banner has most of his facts correct. Such as they are. This is one of the most clue-less cases the Yard has dealt with for some time — the speculations of *The Blare* could end up being as close to the truth as we're ever likely to get."

Sir Wormelow considered. "This . . . this mad millionaire collector is coordinating thefts throughout Europe in order to gratify his . . . his megalomania, and nobody knows his identity. His hired thugs break in to steal, and terrorise the guardians of the artefacts he craves — but they vanish without trace. If, indeed, all the thefts ascribed to the man Croesus have been carried out at his behest. Some owners of disappearing works of art might be more than grateful for an insurance payment, not to mention the *cachet* which having one's possessions craved by a connoisseur may bring . . ."

"Except that, as I was saying to my sergeant just before you arrived, if all these Croesus thefts *are* Croesus thefts, the last thing he could be called is a connoisseur. The man merely accumulates."

"Or woman," suggested Tump, as a sudden thought struck him. "May one rely on the press assumption that Croesus is male, or have the police other information which they do not wish to share with the general public?"

"According to Inspector Terling, the — admittedly few — whispers he's picked up, shared by Interpol and police forces throughout Europe, suggest that Croesus is a man. Not," added Delphick, "that it makes much difference, really, as nobody suggests Croesus carries out the thefts him — (or her) — self, or hits night watchmen over the head — excuse me, Sir Wormelow. In this job, one becomes, unfortunately, rather hardened to the more brutal facts of life — a form of self-preservation, you understand."

"I think I do. You dwell in a less rarefied atmosphere than I, Mr. Delphick. However," and the fine-featured aristocrat squared his shoulders, "even a member of Her Majesty's court knows when facts must be faced." He favoured Delphick with a shrewd look. "You say that you have been reading the report from one of the senior officers involved in the case. Am I correct in assuming that it was sent to you, despite your . . . ah, tenuous official connection, because of the-the strong artistic influence?"

Behind him, Bob Ranger uttered a choking exclamation of suppressed mirth. Delphick glared at him, felt Tump's eyes brighten, and cleared his throat. "A colleague's courtesy, nothing more, Sir Wormelow. You no doubt know that my nickname is The Oracle. And oracles are supposed to know everything that happens. Inspector Terling was merely pandering to my conceit in wishing to justify . . ."

As Tump continued to regard him fixedly, Delphick found his own gaze faltering as he ran out of words. He glared at

Bob again, cleared his throat with incredible vigour, and took a very deep breath.

"We can hardly involve her officially, Sir Wormelow," he said at last. "You know how . . . chaotic any case in which she becomes embroiled always becomes, and, as I explained, this Croesus affair is nothing to do with me. Yet," he found himself adding, to Bob's evident glee. "That is — dammit, Sir Wormelow, whenever Miss Seeton shows up, even on the periphery of anything . . ."

"I know, I know. But she does — excuse me — achieve the required result, does she not?"

"She does," Delphick acknowledged grimly. "At considerable risk, on occasion, to herself, and to others. She sees it all as her duty, of course, and can never really believe anything's going to happen to her — which, so far, I suppose you could argue, it hasn't — but one day her luck may run out — and I feel that if we want to take advantage of her remarkable talents we ought to . . . save them for the most . . ."

Once more, he drifted into an uneasy silence, under the interested gaze of Sir Wormelow, with Bob Ranger in the background, ever watchful. There was a long pause.

"You've worked with her before, haven't you? One might almost say she's a friend of yours," Delphick said, as he'd known all along that he would. "This isn't a police state, you know. One could hardly prevent a friend from visiting another friend without an outcry from the civil liberties people — and if police officers are careless with reports," he added, stretching across the desk for his ballpoint pen, knocking to the floor a document with the Art Squad stamp on its cover, "they have only themselves to blame if members of the public pick up those reports, and read them, and maybe act upon the contents. Reprehensible, in the eyes of the law, though that would be . . ."

He stood up, stretching again. "You'll excuse me, won't you, Sir Wormelow? I'm rather busy this morning, I fear, and must leave you to the tender mercies of my sergeant, who will show you the way out. Ranger, why not take Sir Wormelow on a little tour of the place before he leaves? I feel sure he'd be interested in all our up-to-date crime-busting equipment — in particular, the photocopier . . ."

Ten minutes later, he was back in the office, brooding over Inspector Terling's report (which was back on his desk), while Bob sat and watched in a tumult of curiosity, not daring to breathe a word. First time he could remember the Oracle breaking, well, bending the rules like that, but this Tump wasn't just your ordinary member of the public. More like an honorary comrade-in-arms of the Miss Seeton Irregulars . . .

Bob chuckled, and Delphick looked up from his brooding. "You think it's funny, do you, Bob?"

"Sort of, sir. Sorry."

"What happened to Tump's friend — and, presumably, to an unspecified number of other unfortunates — wasn't funny. He killed himself rather than betray his trust. The gang put pressure on him to show them the best items to steal and the best way to go about it, or they'd publish his homosexuality abroad and ruin his career, at the very least. Caught on the horns of a very uncomfortable dilemma, Bob. If he went to the police, maybe helped set up a trap to nobble the gang and give some sort of lead back to Croesus, he'd still know that his little weakness wasn't private anymore. Tump was right. I doubt if, in the circumstances, I'd have been all that quick to ask for help."

"But to kill yourself, sir — bit drastic, surely? Much better to let them pinch the stuff, if he couldn't bring himself to cooperate with us. I assume he was an intelligent chap, friend of Tump's and a curator, warden, whatever — seems a terrible waste, to me. Almost criminal."

"But suicide's no longer a crime, Bob, even if I agree with you that it's a waste. However, if that's the only choice Sir Wormelow's friend felt he had . . . and freedom of choice is, after all, the liberty we fought two world wars to preserve . . . Still, something useful may well come out of all this. If the gang applied similar methods in their other robberies, at least we now know it's worth investigating vulnerable members of staff in each place that's been robbed, to look for possible leads — see if there were any unexpected suicides or dubiously accidental deaths around that time. This is just the sort of angle that might not have been checked as thoroughly as, with hindsight, we can see that it should. We've something to thank Sir Wormelow for, at any rate . . .

"And I only hope we'll still be feeling grateful to him once he's brought Miss Seeton into the case. Because . . ."

It was later that afternoon when Sir Wormelow, having found Miss Seeton's telephone number through Directory Enquiries, asked if he might wait upon her the following day and take her out to lunch. Miss Seeton, surprised and delighted, accepted the invitation, and recommended Plummergen's George and Dragon, conveniently situated and noted for good, wholesome meals.

Miss Seeton was in a slight flutter next morning by the time Sir Wormelow walked up the short path to her front door and rang the bell. She had tried on four of her distinctive cockscomb hats, unable to decide which, if any, she should wear; it wasn't one of Martha Bloomer's Days, and she hardly felt she could interrupt her in her work at Rytham Hall just to ask for advice. The light tweed suit and discreet blouse with its gently frilled neck were her best lunching outfit, so there had been no difficulty there: but the hat, now that she had a choice, was more of a problem. In nearby Brettenden there was a shop where Mel Forby, on a recent visit, had found the perfect headpiece. Miss Seeton, not envious but admiring, had resolved to visit "Monica Mary" in the not-too-distant future and treat herself to something a little special. Now, trying on one hat after the other in turn, she was beginning to wish she hadn't succumbed to the milliner's skill and saleswomanship with such enthusiasm: it was, she told herself, no doubt an indication of weakness of will — but it had, and she smiled at her reflection in the glass above the hall table, been rather fun.

In the end, she closed her eyes, took her hat pin, and made a jab at the hats as they sat in a row in front of her. Good. She would pack the other three away quickly, before Sir Wormelow arrived; gentlemen had little sympathy for the feminine preoccupation with clothes unless they were married — and sometimes not even then.

"Which Sir Wormelow is not. Married, I mean," she told her reflection, "and therefore he is unused to it — having to wait for people to make up their minds, that is, which of course I have now done." She swept the three remaining hats together, and turned towards the stairs. "And as to which umbrella I should take, how fortunate that in this instance there can be no possible doubt . . ."

She paused halfway up the stairs to gaze back at the row of neatly furled umbrellas clipped in their rack beside the hall table. All were serviceable, sedate in colour, sensibly crooked of handle. One, only one, had a handle that was made neither of wood, nor bamboo, nor leather-bound metal. Metal, indeed, this one in particular was: but a metal that gleamed dull and yellow in the indirect light of the hall — dull, and yellow, and golden: because it was made of gold. Hollow, not solid, as Miss Seeton was always quick to point out — the weight, and the expense — but certainly (in response to incredulous query) hallmarked gold. It had been given to her as a memento of a little adventure by the most courteous gentleman with whom she had shared it. The adventure, she meant, not the umbrella. Though there was plenty of room for two underneath, of course — the umbrella, that was to say.

"My very best umbrella," she said with pride, and took the rest of the stairs two at a time. Really, the difference her reading of *Yoga and Younger Every Day* had made to her knees — to her life — was most gratifying. Only this morning, she had achieved the pose of the Dancing Serpent for ten minutes: and when one looked back only a matter of months, there had been some doubt when she first began to contemplate stretching her spine in such a manner that she would ever achieve one step, let alone the complete dance. So very relaxing, so soothing, so calming . . .

What a pity she had lost her mental advantage by so much foolish anxiety over which hat she should wear. Miss Seeton deposited the three rejects on her bed, and again headed for the stairs. She was at the bottom, in the hall, before she began to wonder if the hat pin had made the right choice — the light in her bedroom was different from that coming into the hall, and perhaps one of the others would be a better match, with her suit — or should it be the blouse . . .

And it was at this point, much to Miss Seeton's secret relief, that the doorbell rang.

chapter

6

Sir Wormelow had remembered, from his first visit to that part of Kent, that one took the Dover train from Charing Cross and changed at Ashford for the Brettenden branch line. An asthmatic car, he recalled, lurked in the station forecourt, and if its driver could be distracted from his copy of *The Sporting Life,* and if the engine could be persuaded to turn over and keep turning, was available to transport visitors the half dozen miles to Plummergen: which were, fortunately for the car, mostly downhill.

His admirable plan to hire Mr. Baxter and his motor was thwarted, however, when on arrival at Brettenden no sight of any waiting car was to be seen. The station call box had been vandalised — nobody seemed to know when the GPO might condescend to repair it — and the station master couldn't rightly take it upon himself to allow a member of the public into his office to use the telephone. Certainly not. And it was nothing to do with whether he was willing to pay for the call: he wasn't an official, was he? Nor a member of the Union? Well then, he wasn't covered by insurance, so if he was to slip on the floor and break his leg there'd be no end of trouble, make no mistake about that.

"Then perhaps," suggested Sir Wormelow, with one hand in his trouser pocket and the discreet chink of coinage as an encouraging obbligato, "you would be so kind as to telephone a taxi for me? I wish, you see, to travel to Plummergen, which is far too far to walk, you will agree."

"Matter of six miles, that's all," retorted the station master. He was a Holdfast Brother, a member of the Brettenden extremist sect who disapprove of practically everything except mortification of the flesh. They endure teetotalism, cold baths, and a compulsory annual pilgrimage (on foot, and with dried peas in their shoes) to Canterbury, over twenty miles distant on the far side of the county; they are vegetarian, have no sense of humour, and hold fast, with great pride, to the absolute letter of the law.

"Six miles," repeated Sir Wormelow, aghast, jingling the coins more loudly. "I really don't think — it is a matter of a luncheon engagement, you see . . ."

"Rich living and sinful drinking, no doubt," the station master said, with a gleam in his eye. "Overindulgence, and wicked waste. Do your soul as much good as your body, so it would, if you was to walk all the way there — aye, and all the way back, as well."

Sir Wormelow gulped. He turned very pale, and his eyes begged for help while his tongue refused to grovel to the sanctimonious one. The station master regarded him with a disdainful eye.

"You don't much look like a man as can manage six miles, I allow, downhill or not. Not," he added quickly, fearing that any hint of weakness on his part would be exploited by the stranger, "that I hold with such decadence, mind, being strong for the Lord as I am, but there's a bus goes to Plummergen twice a week — and today's one of the days. And the stop's over there," he admitted, after a pause.

Sir Wormelow, ever the courtier, thanked him with great relief, then hurried across to the stop, dreading to learn from the timetable that he'd just missed a bus and they only ran every other hour, or something equally inconvenient. He was in luck, however. The timetable told him that a bus to Plummergen would appear in ten minutes; and, righteous as a Holdfast Brother, it did not lie. Twelve minutes later, Sir Wormelow Tump was sitting in the front seat downstairs, receiving a free massage from the springs as the bus rattled its way out of Brettenden.

At about the same time as Sir Wormelow boarded his bus, in Plummergen post office the morning's shopping routine was well under way. Little Mrs. Hosigg, wife to Sir George's farm foreman, had popped in, quiet as ever, for some tinned stuff for the baby. Not a word beyond *please* and *thank you,* and paying her money from a purse that looked awful empty — and so early in the week, too.

"No more than a couple of kids themselves, they are, and the last to be affording kiddies of their own," opined young Mrs. Newport, with a sniff. Mrs. Newport was twenty-two; Lily Hosigg's age was uncertain, though generally supposed to be in the late teens.

"He keeps her short, I reckon," said Mrs. Spice. "Everyone knows Sir George pays well — but there she was, rootling around in that purse for the last penny."

"Drinks it away, probably," suggested Mrs. Skinner. "Her all alone at home with the baby, and him off at the pub — it doesn't bear thinking about."

Everyone thought about it: with some delight. The young Hosiggs had always kept themselves very much to themselves — and were, moreover, known to be staunch supporters of Miss Seeton, which was enough to damn them in many village eyes.

"That marriage won't last," said Mrs. Newport, from her rich knowledge of the marital state. "He'll be knocking her and the babby about when the drink's in him, most like."

And, even as Lily Hosigg congratulated herself on having saved all but the last two pound fifty she needed for the smart new working jacket she'd decided Len should have for his birthday, her home life was dissected down to the ultimate detail; with the overall conclusion that any day now she'd be leaving for good, because a body could only take so much, and it was a crying shame . . .

But speculation did not sparkle as brightly as usual. Though the post office contained a crowd of its regular customers — who from time to time remembered why they were supposed to be there, popping over to the counter to purchase something and keep Mr. Stillman happy — a seasoned observer, as Mr. Stillman reluctantly acknowledged himself to be, would have sensed some sluggishness in the speed at which the busy tongues wagged. The postmaster wondered at the reason for this lack of enthusiasm; there was something —

someone — missing. He might almost say it was peaceful . . .

And, just as he was debating with himself whether such a word could ever, in all honesty, be applied to Plummergen, the bell above the shop door tinkled.

Every head turned. Every eye stared. Every tongue was stilled. A stranger stood on the threshold.

"Excuse me," murmured Sir Wormelow, hesitating for only a moment before threading his way through the assembled huddle of Plummergen ladies towards Mr. Stillman, behind his counter. With all the unease of a confirmed bachelor, Tump preferred to trust his own sex rather than the distaff side when directions were being sought. "I should be most grateful if you could remind me where, er, Sweetbriars is. It is some time since I was last here, you see."

"Sweetbriars, sir? You'll be visiting Miss Seeton," Mr. Stillman said, delighted that one of his favourite customers was to have so distinguished a caller, although puzzled — as was the rest of Sir Wormelow's audience — that anyone should need directions in a village with five hundred inhabitants and one main street. "You can't miss it, sir — if you just step over here a moment . . ."

Mr. Stillman escorted Sir Wormelow back to the door, ushered him outside, and indicated the correct way with great care. The Street runs south in a gentle curve, and ends in a sudden narrowing to form the bridge over the Royal Military Canal: Sweetbriars stands on the corner of that narrowing, its back garden bounded by a mellow brick wall, its front by a smart wrought-iron fence. "You can't miss it, sir," repeated Mr. Stillman; and, like the Holdfast Brethren, he spoke the truth. Sir Wormelow thanked him, and headed in a southerly direction at a dignified pace.

The postmaster was hardly back behind his counter before the tongues, busy as ever, began to wag once more.

"Well!" exclaimed Mrs. Skinner. "And who d'you reckon as *he* was, popping out of nowhere like that? Sounded a regular gent, for all he was dressed so scruffy."

"No more scruffier than Sir George, most times," pointed out Mrs. Henderson (automatically in dispute) with some justification: Sir Wormelow, without any conscious thought, had selected for his day in the country the traditional attire of his class — good (if elderly) tweeds, a soft shirt, a tie knobbly woven. Any farmer would have worn the same, even when planning to call upon a lady; knight, baronet, or plain esquire, it would make no difference.

"Sir George lives here," said Mrs. Skinner, indisputably. "We know him. But *him* — pretending to be a gamekeeper, most like, excepting he didn't have no gun."

"He might," suggested Mrs. Spice, "have left it outside — being as he brought it with him for disguise, only he forgot it, which is why we never seen it." She paused, on the off chance that Ms. Stillman would confirm or deny this hypothesis; but the postmaster had long ago been abandoned as a source of possible gossip by everyone who took their gossip seriously. The village knew it was up to others with more community spirit to show the way.

"So it must've bin there waiting for him," breathed Emmy Putts, with a delighted shudder and her eyes round with the horror of it all. "Waiting till he gets to Sweetbriars, and then . . ."

There was a thrilling pause, as everyone considered the likelihood of Miss Seeton's future involvement in a running gun battle up and down the Street. Such was her reputation among a certain element of Plummergen's populace that the idea seemed not the least bit incongruous. A solitary voice murmured that it might not be such a bad thing if PC Potter knew what could soon be happening, but went unheeded in the welter of wild surmise; and, after due consideration, everyone came to acknowledge the probable correctness of Emmy's suggestion — grudgingly, however, because (while hoping it was true) they wished they had thought of it for themselves.

The next matter to be considered was the stranger's mode of travel. Assassins, everyone agreed, tried to remain as anonymous as possible, so it was unlikely he'd come in anything too flash. A Land Rover, said Mrs. Spice, would have been most like a farmer (or gamekeeper); but nobody could recall having noticed any strange vehicles pull up outside at the appropriate time. A few optimists spared a moment for Mr. Stillman to say what he'd seen when he stepped out of the shop, but Mr. Stillman had had enough. With a quick word of excuse, he left the grocery counter, motioning to Emmy to take over, and went to lock himself away in peace, behind the post office grille.

It was then proposed by Mrs. Skinner that the man must've left the car — oh well, Land Rover, if Mrs. Henderson wanted to be pernickety, but *car* would do so far's *she* was concerned — somewhere out of sight, with the gun hidden in the boot. Most people were willing to accept this, except Mrs. Henderson, who gleefully recalled that the Brettenden bus had arrived just before the stranger, which meant it was far more likely that he'd used public transport. In which case, he'd hardly have been carrying a gun, would he? Somebody would've noticed, and questions been asked.

"The bus," said Mrs. Spice quickly, before Mrs. Skinner could say anything else. "I was wondering . . ." And her eye swept round the shop, which, though filled with a host of Plummergen ladies, still seemed to be lacking some vital element. Enjoyable though all the foregoing discussion had been, the basic inspiration was missing . . .

And then the bell above the shop door tinkled. Every head turned; every eye stared; every tongue was stilled, as two figures crossed the post office threshold. One was tall and equine, one dumpy and pouting; the missing element was missing no longer. Miss Nuttel and Mrs. Blaine had come: The Nuts were here at last.

Though they entered at the same time, they were not, it seemed, together; or at least not in the usual sense. Erica Nuttel tossed her head and whinnied a brief greeting to the shop at large; Norah Blaine darted button-black eyes about the assembled crowd, mumbled something, and trotted straight to the grocery counter.

"Six lemons, please, Emmy," she said. "And three large grapefruit — I'm trying a different flavour of marmalade. Bitter." Saying which, she shot a dark look at Miss Nuttel, who was hovering by the circular book stand, and now gave it a pointed twirl.

"Late today, Mrs. Blaine," remarked Emmy, as she bustled to sort out the fruit. "We was just thinking you'd gone into Brettenden on the bus, instead —"

"Missed it," Miss Nuttel snapped, while Mrs. Blaine's lip trembled. "Timetables don't wait, though."

"Usually reliable, the bus," agreed Mrs. Spice. "Comes all the way from town — and all sorts on it, too. Nothing personal, of course, Miss Nuttel."

"The bus," Mrs. Blaine announced before Miss Nuttel could open her mouth, "isn't what it was, any more than Brettenden is. Too uncomfortable, with so many strangers — one can't feel altogether safe — thank you, Emmy. On the bus, I mean, not in the town, although one does see some very *odd* people there — and some

86

very odd *things,* as well."

So the squabble about the biscuit factory sculpture was still unresolved. Everyone noted this for future discussion once The Nuts had done their shopping and departed; but, for now, there were more important matters to discuss. How to lead up to them was the question. Emmy and Mrs. Spice hadn't done too badly, but neither of The Nuts had taken the bait.

Yet. Mrs. Blaine said: "I won't bother with much sugar, Emmy, I still have some at home. This marmalade is supposed to be sour — unlike some I could mention."

She dropped the bitter citrus into her shopping bag and began fumbling for her purse. Emmy asked: "That everything, then, is it?"

"Thank you," said Mrs. Blaine, "yes."

"No," said Miss Nuttel. She abandoned the book stand and strode across to the counter. "Missed the bus — nothing in the house. Packet of plain biscuits, please."

"Talking of the bus" — Mrs. Spice, as Mrs. Blaine let out a little squeak of horror at this libel on her culinary skills, decided to try again — "and strangers . . ."

She paused invitingly. Could either of them resist?

"Tall man in tweeds," said Miss Nuttel

promptly. They'd been watching, after all. Plummergen heaved a collective sigh of relief: it wouldn't seem right if The Nuts weren't there at the windows of Lilikot, peeking out to see what was going on.

"He looked," Mrs. Blaine remarked, "as if he didn't know what he was talking about — I mean," with another scowl in Miss Nuttel's direction, "as if he didn't know where he was going. Too impulsive. Didn't he come in here?"

Which was sufficient encouragement for everyone to join in. Before long, The Nuts knew as much about the stranger as anyone in Plummergen. The comfortable casualness of his attire was analysed in depth. Miss Nuttel opined that someone so scruffy could be an artist of sorts, especially since he intended to visit Miss Seeton; Mrs. Blaine thought he had looked too peculiar, and was less likely to be an artist than a sculptor, concerning which class of person she would never be surprised.

Mrs. Spice hurriedly spoke of the gun, or rather the lack of one; Mrs. Skinner voiced her gamekeeper theory; Mrs. Henderson insisted that the man had sounded far too posh to be anything of the sort. Looks were exchanged, and theories furiously sought.

And it was Miss Nuttel who, having

thought most furiously of all, announced that the man's identity must be obvious to anyone. Whereupon it was Mrs. Blaine (for old habits die hard) who exclaimed eagerly, urging Eric to elucidate.

"Perfectly clear," said Miss Nuttel, tossing her head. "Well-spoken — says he's been here before yet asks for Miss Seeton — must be an actor, trying out a part. From the BBC, with a voice like that. Going to be," concluded Miss Nuttel enviously, "on television . . ."

chapter
7

Sir Wormelow, like most members of the establishment, had a high regard for the British Broadcasting Corporation without necessarily wishing to be thought of its number. News and views in Plummergen travel fast. Even as he lunched at the George and Dragon with Miss Seeton and her gold-handled umbrella, he was vaguely aware that the waitress was paying him far more attention than he was accustomed to. Young Maureen had heard rumours that a man from the telly was in town, and hoped that by fluttering her eyelashes, pouting her lips, and thrusting her bosom forward in provocative poses her path to instant stardom would be assured.

It was, of course, the very last way to attract Tump's interest, and it was not until she saw the size of the tip that Maureen, disappointed, realised she'd been wasting her efforts. She flounced back to the kitchen, and dreamed of meeting a millionaire. Even that Croesus she'd read about in the papers would be better than sticking in this boring dump for the rest of her life . . .

"So very kind of dear Mel to send me the article, don't you agree, Sir Wormelow?" Miss Seeton nodded and smiled at the guest on the other side of her sitting-room hearthrug: something had suggested that his purpose in calling on her was too important for the garden, although what a gentleman of Sir Wormelow's stature and position could want with her, an ordinary, retired teacher of art with limited talent, she had been unable to guess. Over lunch, however, she had listened attentively as he talked, and gleaned a few ideas.

"It has saved so much time now, however, has it not," she went on, "although of course it is a great pity, poor thing. Her broken ankle, I mean, even if without it she might not have thought of sending me dear Mr. Banner's piece, as I believe it is called, although anything less *peaceful*," Miss Seeton added, with another smile for her little joke, "than the criminal activities of these Croesus people is not easy to envisage, wouldn't you say?"

Sir Wormelow nodded; hesitated; and spilled the beans. All that he knew, all that he feared — all except the letter from his friend: he told her what had happened, but couldn't bring himself to go into details.

Miss Seeton heard him out attentively, interjecting little exclamations of dismay and shock, pitying the anguish on his face.

When he had finished, she shook her head. "It is indeed a very distressing affair, Sir Wormelow — not just the death of your poor friend, but the wicked loss of so many works of art for a mere whim, as one must suppose it to be, from what Mr. Banner has said. Although it is possible he may be mistaken," she added: with regret, for she was fond of Thrudd. "The press — sometimes, I fear, not entirely accurate . . ."

"I don't think so in this case, Miss Seeton, if you'll excuse me." Tump reached into his jacket pocket and drew out the photocopy of Inspector Terling's report. "Judging by the list at the back of this, Banner's spot-on in what he says — that most of the crimes we know about are the work of one man, or at least they are carried out at his instigation — and the chap's not bothered whether it's good art or bad. He simply *acquires* it, like a . . . a jackdaw, or a magpie."

"Such attractive birds, but sometimes so vicious," Miss Seeton murmured, as she flicked absently through the pages of the report. "I'm afraid, Sir Wormelow, I really don't know what you want me to do with this . . ."

"Just read it," he begged. "I myself have tried to make some sense of it all, but there is little I can see that may be regarded as being of any use — my views, you understand, tend to be on the orthodox side." He smiled faintly, before continuing: "The police, too, are hampered by the . . . the limitations of the official mind, if I may so express it. But you, Miss Seeton, with your knowledge of art — your keen eye and unique imagination . . ."

Miss Seeton blushed, and uttered a modest disclaimer of the importance attributed to her little efforts at sketching IdentiKit cartoons for the police. The chief superintendent and his colleagues were kind enough to say that her drawings had been of use in some of their more, well, unusual cases — indeed, as Sir Wormelow might know, she was paid an annual retainer for her services — but she felt sure this was mere coincidence. That they had been useful, she meant, because they were all so hardworking, so professional — the police, that was to say — while she was no expert and certainly (she blushed again) no professional, as anyone must know. They would no doubt have been just as successful without her, well, amateur interference . . .

Sir Wormelow, smiling, ignored all this,

and again urged her to read Inspector Terling's report. The Scotland Yard heading informed Miss Seeton that it merited due attention, whether she felt she would understand it or not; if Scotland Yard, to whose generosity she owed so much, thought it her duty to read this report, then read it she would.

As she did so, Tump leaned back in his chair, more weary than he had expected to be. Emotional exhaustion had taken its toll: he had relived the loss of his dear friend twice in twenty-four hours, and Miss Seeton was his final hope of laying the ghost of bereavement and — yes, it must be said — cowardice. He should have gone to the police just as soon as the letter came: one life would have been lost in any case, but perhaps he could have prevented the grave risk to another. The night watchman was still on the critical list. Sufficient warning might have spared him . . .

Sir Wormelow's eyes drifted about the room as he brooded on his own shortcomings, and fastened at last upon a watercolour over the mantel. It showed a stark black branch in the foreground, with a few desperate leaves still clinging, the sky behind it a looming mass of cloud, grey and stormy above the yielding heather of the moorland beneath. It was a bleak, cheerless scene. Sir Wormelow shivered.

"Oh dear," said Miss Seeton, looking up from the last page. "Such a warm day, too. I do hope you have not caught a chill, Sir Wormelow. Would you care for a cup of tea?"

"Perhaps later, Miss Seeton, thank you. At the moment, I am more interested in your views on that report."

Miss Seeton frowned. Her views? Would it not be rather an impertinence for her to voice an opinion when the experts — to judge by what the inspector had written — admitted they knew nothing? Dear Mr. Banner's article had made, or so she thought she recalled, the same point. That nobody seemed to know anything at all about what was going on, except that it was clear there was someone, somewhere, arranging to have other people steal things for him. Paying them to do so, in fact. Urging them into crime when perhaps, without his urging, they would never have been, well, corrupted . . .

"Which is hardly to be encouraged," said Miss Seeton, in her best schoolteacher's tone. "Corruption, that is to say — most reprehensible, to take advantage of the weaknesses of others. If you will excuse me for a moment, Sir Wormelow, I should like . . ."

Tump, looking flustered, nevertheless rose to his feet as Miss Seeton hurried from the room. When she returned two minutes later with Mel's letter in her hand, he sat down again with a relieved sigh. Miss Seeton handed him Thrudd's article, remarking that she supposed he, too, did not often read *Anyone's* and thus might have missed it.

"But it is interesting, as I think you will agree — that is, if I have remembered correctly, which I feel sure I have — the coincidence. One could not help noticing, having read what Mr. Terling has to say . . . or rather the lack of it, at first sight — between the two lists, I mean. Mr. Banner's, and that of the police. They do seem, from what I recall, rather inconsistent as to the identities of all the various pieces stolen on behalf of this man Croesus — understandably so, for one can hardly suppose that his, er, *gang* leave any calling card behind so that one may be sure. Which makes it impossible for there to be absolute agreement over whether they *have* been. Stolen, that is. Because," explained Miss Seeton earnestly, "while the lists clearly *overlap*, and some items appear on both, there is considerable discrepancy as well. From what I have been given to understand, a journalist is always eager to report what he sees as a good story without always, I fear, making sure of his facts — and one must make allowance also, of course, for the natural human wish to make oneself and one's property, well, more interesting than they otherwise might be. So much more romantic, is it not," she twinkled at him, "to be able to say that an international gang removed one's ancestral portrait, rather than an ordinary thief — if one could, that is. Because it seems to me they haven't. Taken ancestral portraits — or at least, not many. Very few, indeed. And the ones they have taken — not just portraits, but landscapes as well, and even the statue — the ones on the two lists, I mean — there did seem to me," Miss Seeton concluded in an apologetic tone, "to be an obvious connection — though of course I may be mistaken, and especially if you have noticed nothing. Which I gather must be the case, or you would not have brought it to me, would you? The report . . ."

And she fluttered the pages under Sir Wormelow's bemused nose, while he tried desperately to work out what on earth she had been trying to tell him.

Courtiers and diplomats, trained almost from the cradle to rise to any occasion, can think fast. Sir Wormelow was no exception.

If he could understand what a Japanese, or a Greek, or a Russian was trying to tell him, he ought to be able to make sense of Miss Seeton.

Barely missing a beat, he said: "I would be most interested to hear your opinion of the matter, Miss Seeton: and in detail, if you would be so kind. If you have discovered some link which has escaped the notice of everyone else . . ."

"So very *cold*," Miss Seeton said. His eyes wandered at once back to the painting over the fireplace. "Oh, no," she said quickly, "or rather, I suppose, yes. A grey day, you see — although, now that I know him so much better, I would hardly care to be so, well, precipitate in my judgement. Not that he has ever complained, you understand, and indeed dear Bob, I mean Sergeant Ranger, thinks that it very much resembles, or at least reminds him of, the chief superintendent. And so many of the others were as well, were they not — cold, I mean. Wouldn't you agree?"

"Your views," said Sir Wormelow smoothly, "are so much more expert than mine," and tried not to grit his teeth or to scream. Why didn't she get to the point? And, when she finally did, would it be worth all the effort?

"The others," said Miss Seeton. "The ones Croesus stole or had stolen for him, that is. So many seem to be, well, *chilly*. The Wynter family's ancestral portraits — the name, you see, so suggestive — and so many landscapes — one could hardly help noticing. *Racing Skaters on the Fens,* and *The Pleasure Dome* — as I recollect, a reference to Coleridge's 'caves of ice' in *Kubla Khan* — *Aspect of Snowdon from the South* — such a suggestive title. *Pine Trees at Christmas,*" Miss Seeton continued with her list, flicking through the pages of Terling's report and Thrudd's article, frowning as she cross-checked one against the other. "*The Retreat of Napoleon's Army from Moscow* — one remembers one's history lessons, Sir Wormelow. Being taught that the Russians had the army of winter on their side, as well as an army of men, that is. Not that I know this picture, but one can imagine the scene all too well . . ."

Sir Wormelow sat enthralled as Miss Seeton trotted out instance after instance of the Croesus Gang's apparent obsession with snow, ice, and low temperatures. *The Glacier of Mont Blanc at Sunset* — *The Iceman Cometh* (hailed as a modern masterpiece, although Miss Seeton's expression suggested the artist was still at the apprentice stage) — *Battle Between the Rime Giants and the Hosts of Valhalla . . .*

In all, she must have mentioned two dozen works of art — paintings, sculptures, even a stainless steel mobile constructed by one of the Functionist School, entitled *Electric Hailstorm* — while Sir Wormelow, his head starting to spin, fastened his eyes on the "Grey Day" picture, and felt the glimmerings of an idea beginning to stir.

". . . unfortunate catholicity of taste," Miss Seeton said sternly, "with little, one must suppose, true appreciation of art — acquiring it for the sake of having it, and not for its own sake, I fear. As you so rightly said, Sir Wormelow, rather a jackdaw than a good judge."

Sir Wormelow blinked. "Did I say that? I suppose, as it seems you support my views, Miss Seeton, that I must have done. I was in the right without realising exactly why; but now your own views and comments have illuminated matters for me to a remarkable extent. You have indeed been of help, Miss Seeton — as I always knew that you would. And as Chief Superintendent Delphick also knew . . ."

chapter

8

At Scotland Yard next morning, the telephone rang in the office of Chief Superintendent Delphick. Inspector Terling was on the line.

"Oracle? Thought you'd like to know the night watchman in that Croesus business just died, poor devil. It isn't a matter of a few daubed canvases and the odd chunk of marble any longer." The Art Squad inspector claimed that cultivating a strongly Philistine approach to all matters aesthetic worked wonders for his sense of proportion, and thus his sanity. "It's murder now, Oracle. Any, er, ideas?"

"I'll be in touch," Delphick told him, knowing perfectly well what he meant. "Someone went down to Kent yesterday to see her" — no need to mention that *someone* had been an unofficial envoy — "and he'll be letting me know shortly if she came up with anything . . ."

"So MissEss is on the case after all," said Bob, as Delphick hung up the handset, with a thoughtful frown in the direction of his blotter. The memory of that umbrella he'd doodled not so long ago was still with him.

"It would seem," he said cautiously, "that she may well, before long, receive the summons to action, heaven help us. When we've heard from Sir Wormelow we'll have a better idea of what, if anything, she can —"

The telephone rang again. Bob looked at his chief, and grinned. Talk about coincidence. Delphick shook his head at such levity, but could not suppress a sigh of amused resignation as he picked up his handset again, indicating that Bob should do likewise. He cleared his throat. "Delphick here . . . Who?"

It was one of the duty sergeants from the Back Hall, as Scotland Yard's entrance is traditionally known. Delphick was so sure that he was going to be told of the arrival of Sir Wormelow Tump that he had to ask for the message to be repeated.

"Faulkbourne? Belton Abbey? Oh, yes — stolen pictures a few years ago, smuggled to Switzerland for exhibition and sale . . ." The Duke of Belton, he reflected, hadn't been the only person to benefit from MissEss's unmasking of the over-painted pictures, thus ensuring their safe return. She herself had collected a nice little reward from the insurance people. And well deserved, too.

"To see me? Does he say why?" Delphick frowned again, his ballpoint pen in his hand. Another confounded brolly was trying to find its way out . . .

"Confidential? He's better off seeing a priest than a policeman — no, don't tell him that, for goodness' sake. My unfortunate sense of humour, nothing more . . . Insistent, is he?" Delphick glanced at Bob, shrugged, and said: "For ten minutes only, then. My sergeant will pop down for him — and let's hope," he added, as he rang off, "that it won't be too long before we hear from Sir Wormelow. One mystery connected with Miss Seeton I can just about cope with — as for two, words fail me. And stop grinning like that. Go and fetch our unexpected visitor, Sergeant Ranger . . . Faulkbourne," he murmured, as Bob, still grinning, left the room. "I thought the family name was Bremeridge, but . . ."

The man who came into the office with Bob a few minutes later looked every inch the aristocrat; and the number of inches he boasted were many. Well over six feet tall, he was not as bulky as Ranger, and beside him looked almost slim; by himself, he had an appearance of quiet strength, both of body and of mind. He radiated confidence and dignity — or (as Delphick decided after

103

a second glance) he would do in normal circumstances.

"Chief Superintendent Delphick? It is most kind of you to see me at such short notice. My name is Faulkbourne." He cleared his throat in a restrained manner. "I have the honour to serve His Grace the Duke of Belton in the capacity of steward to the household."

Delphick nodded. "Take a seat, Mr. Faulkbourne, and tell me what the problem is. Not another picture robbery, I hope — we can't guarantee the same success as last time."

Faulkbourne permitted himself a slight smile. "It is on the subject of that success that I venture to approach you now, sir. One could not help recalling . . ." The smile had faded, to be replaced with the frown which Delphick guessed had been on the steward's face for some while. "The return of the pictures was most gratifying to His Grace, sir, safe and speedy as it was. But — forgive me — am I not correct in remembering that the greater part of the achievement was due to the, ahem, efforts of a particular member of the public, and not those of the constabulary?"

Above Bob Ranger's muffled snort, Delphick said sternly: "A particular, not to say unique, member of the public, as you say. Who is attached to the police force in an advisory capacity, and to that extent may be regarded as our official representative, but —"

Faulkbourne coughed. "Excuse me, sir, but I intended to suggest no dissatisfaction concerning either the conduct of the case or its outcome. As I said, His Grace was delighted with the safe return of his stolen property — as, indeed, it must be supposed that the insurance company also was." And another fleeting smile appeared in his eyes.

"Coveral Assurance," said Delphick, having thought about it for only a moment. "But all that happened two or three years ago. I'm afraid I don't quite see why —"

A louder cough on this occasion. "We have received certain instructions, sir, to approach neither the police nor the insurance company until the items have been returned. In other words, sir, once the ransom has been paid . . ."

Delphick knew at once what Faulkbourne meant. "You've had a visit from Raffles the Ransomeer?"

"Not I myself, sir." The steward raised a discreet eyebrow. "The robbery at the Abbey took place in one of the rooms opened to the public. His Grace's collection of snuffboxes was rifled, sir, and several of the most valuable, and rare, items have been taken. With a ransom note left to the effect that they will not be returned until the sum of" — he could not suppress the quiver in his voice — "ten thousand pounds has been paid. In a manner which is to be communicated to His Grace in due course, sir."

Since Raffles had neither killed nor seriously injured anyone thus far in his raptorial career, such information as Delphick possessed on his methods had been gleaned from the press, and from the general comments of his constabulary colleagues. He knew enough, however, to understand at once that the crime now being reported followed the usual pattern, although the sum demanded was by far the highest yet. He regarded the steward with interest.

"As the note instructed you — I beg your pardon, the duke — not to communicate with the police, Mr. Faulkbourne, might I ask why, rather than approaching your local force in some cautious fashion, you have chosen to come to Scotland Yard? We are hardly an unknown body, I would have said."

"Precisely, sir. It is so bold and straightforward an approach that one must suppose Raffles would never conceive of its use: a double bluff, one might say." The flicker of self-satisfaction which crossed Faulkbourne's face as he said this could have been regarded, in one less stately, as verging on the smug.

Delphick was interested in such evidence of conceit in a man otherwise so self-effacing — no, someone who was steward in a household as large as Belton could hardly be considered that. He would need presence (as he undoubtedly possessed) and authority: but these would go with the job. A job which must involve discretion, and a strong inclination to serve, and loyalty. "How long," he enquired, "have you been at the Abbey, Mr. Faulkbourne?"

The steward looked startled at this abrupt change of subject, and bent his noble head for an instant, no doubt in order to look away from Delphick's keen eye while he consulted some mental calendar. "Eighteen years and seven months, sir. I began as His Late Grace's under-footman."

"Then it comes as no surprise that the present duke felt able to entrust to you the task of arranging this meeting. A man with so long a period of honourable service is . . ." But at Faulkbourne's hasty shake of the head, Delphick fell silent. The steward's face no longer looked anything but anxious, and his manicured fingers wreathed themselves into a knot of frustration.

"His Grace is away from home at the moment, sir, and has been for some time. He and Lord Pelsall — His Grace's heir, sir — are in South America. Mountain climbing." A shudder said more than words ever could about the steward's views of such energetic pursuits. "In the Andes, I believe, although the household has received little news of the party for some weeks now. The duchess," he added, as Delphick seemed about to speak, "is travelling by cargo boat to meet up with them in due course, sir: at Lima, possibly, or Santiago — or perhaps Antofagasta. Her Grace's plans were uncertain when she left ten days ago, I fear."

"If the whole family's gone globe-trotting," burst from Delphick before he could stop himself, "then who on earth is minding the shop? You?"

"Oh no, sir." Faulkbourne contrived to look shocked at the very idea, though the gleam in his eye suggested that he knew himself capable of minding an entire chain of supermarkets, should duty require it. "His Grace has left the Abbey in the care of his younger son, Lord Edgar Bremeridge. Lord Edgar, I must explain, is unaware that I am here." Faulkbourne frowned. "I would appreciate it if you were not to tell him of my interference in this matter. His lordship is young: this is his first, ahem, solo effort. His feelings, as you will appreciate, would be deeply hurt. Moreover," he added, as Delphick prepared to utter a few scathing words on the topic of pampered adolescents, "I fear that I might run some risk of losing my position, for having thus imposed and gone against Master Eddie's — I beg his pardon, Lord Edgar's — orders. One could not be at all certain that His Grace, upon his eventual return from the trip, would view with much sympathy so, ahem, blatant an example of disobedience. I do not wish to be branded unreliable, sir. One has one's professional pride — as you yourself understand, I feel sure."

"But, good heavens, man, in a case like this, no one in their right mind could possibly blame you for coming to us. It's what we advise all members of the public to do — never mind if this young lordship of yours thinks he knows better. At that age, they nearly always do . . ." Delphick looked at Faulkbourne with an enquiring eye. The steward dropped his gaze once more.

"Lord Edgar is just twenty-two, sir, and of what one may politely term an excitable temperament on occasion — as, it must be confessed, the whole Family might be described. His Late Grace — the present duke's father, that is — was noted for his, ahem, volatility, sir."

"Volatile is one word, I suppose, though not the first that springs to mind to describe a family whose idea of fun is mountaineering in the middle of winter — the Andes, after all, are in the opposite hemisphere to this, and it's high summer here — or a tramp steamer trip to goodness knows where, for heaven knows how long."

"His Grace, sir, has a decided aversion to warm weather, and Lord Pelsall has inherited his father's preferences. As for the duchess, though not a Bremeridge by birth she enjoys considerable . . . robustness of spirit, as one might term it. A craving for adventure, sir. Wanderlust is a noted characteristic of the Family, going back through several generations. An earlier Lord Pelsall visited Tibet in 1803, and returned with what was widely believed to be the skin of an Abominable Snowman. It is on view in the public rooms to this day, sir. His lordship studied yoga during his two-year trip, and claimed that its practice helped him considerably during his, ahem, lengthy wait to succeed to the dukedom. His father lived to be one hundred and two, sir."

A warning bell sounded faintly in Delphick's head, but he ignored it. "I believe I'm beginning to see the picture — itchy feet and uncertain tempers all round, am I right? Which means there's likely to be nobody on your side when the chips are well and truly down, Mr. Faulkbourne."

"I fear so, sir. Which is why . . ." The steward stared at his interlocked fingers, and sighed. "When the Abbey was robbed of its pictures, sir, the duke and duchess were away: in Turkey, as you may recall. But Lord Pelsall was not with them, and was able — and willing — to set investigations in motion. Lord Edgar, however . . ."

"Is young, impetuous, and a know-all." Delphick offered this ruthless précis with a smile, which Faulkbourne weakly returned. "So — as you're not here officially, so to speak — what do you want me to do? Unless Lord Edgar changes his mind and decides to ask for police help, you know, I don't really see how I can help you."

The steward's smile grew broader, and Delphick might almost have said there was a twinkle in his eye. "One must venture to take issue with you on that point, Chief Superintendent. As I implied earlier, the loss of the four paintings, and their safe return, made no small impression on the household

111

at Belton. One was particularly impressed by the actions of that member of the public whose observation and knowledge received their just reward from the Coveral Assurance Company . . ."

As Bob (who had listened to the whole exchange right the way through without uttering a sound) now couldn't prevent an exclamation of glee, Delphick smothered a groan. They'd known it all along, of course. It could hardly be anything, or anyone, else that had brought the Duke of Belton's right-hand man hotfoot from the Abbey in defiance of his nominal master's orders . . .

"Miss Seeton," sighed Chief Superintendent Delphick.

chapter
9

"He didn't seem awfully happy, sir," said Bob, after Faulkbourne had departed. "Was there really nothing we could do for the poor bloke?"

"Without having been called into the case officially, our hands are pretty well tied. Of course, we could always have a discreet word with the local boys — issue the odd warning about security with particular reference to Croesus, say. Then they might drop in on young Lord Edgar, and somehow manage to persuade him to talk to them about Raffles, without letting on they already know . . . It's always worth a try, but he sounds a stubborn young brighter. Were you as bad at twenty-two? I suppose everybody is, and we choose to forget it as we grow older and more — I hope — sensible. Just wait until you have children of your own."

Bob grinned weakly, then rallied. "I'm blowed if I'd leave 'em for an unspecified period of time while I clambered around a load of mountains in blizzards and what-have-you, anyway. This duke sounds an odd sort, all right."

"*Eccentric* is the term, when applied to the aristocracy, Sergeant Ranger. Only plebeians such as you and I are odd. Which reminds me: as we're talking of the aristocracy, isn't it about time we heard from Sir Wormelow Tump? Even if he didn't come in, I would have thought he'd telephone."

"MissEss probably tied him up in so many knots yesterday he's still recovering, sir," suggested Bob, with a chuckle. "She'll have been so confused by it all, for a start — with him being there unofficially official, as you might say, and she gets muddled enough at the best of —"

As if in response to the mention of Miss Seeton's name, Delphick's telephone rang. The chief superintendent picked it up with one hand, and found the other closing on his pen. The third brolly was on its way, it seemed . . .

And so was Sir Wormelow Tump. The duty sergeant in the Back Hall reported the courtier straining at the leash, so to speak, and would Sergeant Ranger please come and collect him as soon as possible. Delphick's expression brightened.

"Sounds as if he's come up with something — or rather he got something out of MissEss. Hurry along, Bob." And with a swift motion he sketched an umbrella on his blotting pad.

Sir Wormelow was full of apologies for not having been in touch earlier. "But I wished to be absolutely sure, in my own mind, that the scheme I am about to propose — if you will excuse the liberty, Mr. Delphick — would stand a reasonable chance of success. My first action, naturally, was to check on the information . . ." He frowned. "Well, perhaps that is not, strictly speaking, the correct word. To check on the *suggestion* given me by Miss Seeton . . ."

And he explained to his enthralled audience the "winter" theory of the little art teacher. "The correlation between the two lists — the police report, and that compiled for the *Anyone's* article — is substantially as she proposed. There are a great many missing items, Chief Superintendent, which have a distinctly chilly air about them. Croesus, while evidently a wealthy man, would appear to have a . . . a fixation with the cold — and I feel that it should be possible to exploit that fixation in some manner."

"In some manner," said Delphick with a

smile, "which my instincts tell me you have already decided, Sir Wormelow."

Tump reddened. "I would hardly be so presumptuous, Mr. Delphick, although — I admit, yes, I have certainly thought out a plan which, with a great deal of good fortune, might lead us to Croesus, or at least to his . . . henchmen. People who prey on others, Chief Superintendent, must feel no surprise at being preyed upon in turn."

"The floor is yours, Sir Wormelow," Delphick said, with an expansive gesture. "Sergeant Ranger will take notes."

"We must bait a trap," said Sir Wormelow simply. There was a brief silence. He made a deprecating face. "It seems the obvious thing to do, does it not?"

"Go on," invited Delphick.

"What could better suit the taste of Croesus than a work of art designed with his . . . his fixation in mind? He has a catholic taste, as we have noted. He acquires items from no particular period, and in no particular style: not all those items listed may in fact have been stolen on his behalf, but of those about which there is some form of consensus it was, to Miss Seeton, evident that the 'winter' correlation is far higher than might have been expected in any normal list. And I agree with her. Anything with a suggestion of the brumal is likely to attract him: my argument is, therefore, that if we could supply a painting with a winter theme, and make its possession desirable . . ."

"Trumpeted in all the newspapers as the masterpiece of the century," said Delphick, leaning forward eagerly. "Then he'd be keen as mustard to own it, if he's as much of a megalomaniac as everyone seems to think. We could stake it out — a rota system, surveillance — nobble the gang when they turned up to pinch it, follow the trail back to Croesus . . . Yes, I like it, Sir Wormelow. The only problem is that we need a painting for him to pinch. Ah." Delphick caught the gleam in Tump's eye. "Keep talking, Sir Wormelow."

"If we could enlist the cooperation of the press, there is something which I feel would do splendidly, with little alteration. A watercolour which I noticed yesterday, above Miss Seeton's sitting-room fireplace: she called it *A Grey Day*, and it is certainly . . ."

He broke off as Bob spluttered behind him, and Delphick tried to show no emotion at all. He failed. Tump regarded the chuckling chief superintendent with surprise. Delphick recovered himself, and apologised

117

for the constabulary outburst, adding:

"As my sergeant would no doubt be over-joyed to inform you, that particular water-colour appears to be Miss Seeton's personal impression of — well, of me. If memory serves me aright, the insubordinate Ranger thought it rather cold, but a nice-looking picture on the whole." Delphick glanced over at the desk where Bob sat with his shoulders shaking, and tried to scowl. He did not succeed. He sat up straight.

"I agree with you, Sir Wormelow, it's a splendid choice, and I would be delighted to think that my, er, efficiency as a deterrent of crime continued even *in absentia*, but it must rest with Miss Seeton, of course. Though she presented my sergeant's wife with her vision of him as a muscle-bound, thick-headed footballer" — Bob choked in protest — "it seems she took a more consid-ered view of her portrayal of myself, by keeping it. Perhaps she thought I might be offended, or perhaps she just took an unac-countable fancy to it. But for whatever reason, it remains her property, and she might not want to submit it to any risk. Al-though, knowing Miss Seeton, I'd take a bet on her being only too happy to help."

"And so, if I were a gambling man, would I." Tump drew vague shapes in the air with his fingers. "The addition of some snow, perhaps a sparkling of frost on the leaves in the foreground — a title such as *The Dying Year* or *Winter Desolation*" — Bob choked again — "and, as I said, the cooperation of the press in announcing the discovery of this masterpiece in, oh, somebody's attic. An elderly person has just died, maybe, and the heirs are clearing the house before selling it — a young married couple explore their new home, and —"

"Hey!" Bob didn't so much choke as erupt. Delphick and Tump stared at him with startled eyes. Bob turned as red as he'd ever done in his life, but managed to blurt out an apology of sorts before adding: "What about me and Anne, sir? We haven't been married long — and MissEss wouldn't be half as bothered about lending the thing if she knew it'd have us to look after it for her, sir. After all," he said, as Delphick seemed about to speak, "it'd be keeping it all in the family from her point of view, wouldn't it? Sir."

Delphick looked at Tump. "I should explain that my rash young sergeant and his bride have adopted Miss Seeton as an honorary aunt: a position which requires the holder to keep her nephew's body and soul together by the judicious application of vast quantities of gingerbread —"

"Oh, I say, sir!"

Delphick ignored Bob's splutterings. "Since Miss Seeton appears not to resent this, er, obligation, as evidenced by the size of Sergeant Ranger's waistband —"

"Sir!"

"— we may safely assume, Sir Wormelow, that she would indeed feel able to entrust her brainchild to the tender care of her surrogate family. And," he added with a frown, "to the tender mercies of the press, which may be rather more difficult to arrange. We require a reporter of great discretion for a trick like this to stand any chance of succeeding. An idea, however, begins to burgeon . . ."

After a search for, and, following that, through, the telephone directory (which Bob swore he'd replaced on top of the filing cabinet, but which Delphick eventually found inside it), Scotland Yard was soon talking to the editorial department of *The Blare. The Blare* was impressed by the identity of its caller, but regretted that it was unable to help: Thrudd Banner didn't work for them, not really. He was a freelance, and could be most easily contacted through the offices of World Wide Press.

World Wide Press sounded somewhat

doubtful of Delphick's *bona fides,* and insisted on calling him back before divulging the sensitive information he'd requested. There was an annoyingly long wait before they did: but at last they produced an address and telephone number, and Delphick sighed in some relief before asking whether Thrudd was likely to be at home. World Wide Press said there was only one way for him to find out, really, wasn't there? And rang off.

"Some you win," muttered the chief superintendent, as he spun the dial, "and some you lose. Let's hope — ah. Well, at least it's ringing . . ."

He heard only three rhythmic chirrups before somebody at the other end grabbed the receiver. A woman's voice said, "Banner, if that's you out there, bring another couple of tins of talcum powder home with you, okay? I'm itching fit to burst myself in here."

A sudden light danced in the eyes of Chief Superintendent Delphick. "And greetings to you, Miss Forby — er, that *is* you, Mel, isn't it?"

"I recognise those dulcet tones," replied the voice on the other end of the line, after a pause. "Now wait — don't tell me — Oracle, is that you?"

"If that's you, Mel, this is me — or possibly I. Chief Superintendent Delphick, at your service."

"Amelita Forby, at yours." Mel giggled. "Guess it was hardly my services you wanted, though, or you'd never have rung this number. Thrudd's not here just now."

"So I gathered, from your opening words. I won't ask why you feel in such urgent need of talcum powder, but —"

"If you'd got a plaster cast wrapped round *your* ankle, driving you half-crazy this hot weather, you'd need talcum powder too! Several hundredweight of the stuff, just for starters — but you don't want to hear about my problems." Mel stifled another giggle, as she recalled the circumstances in which she'd received her injury. "You wanted Banner, the Boy Wonder — and I'd like to know *why* you wanted him. My newshound's nose is twitching, Oracle. Something tells me there's a nice juicy exclusive in the offing — and that you were thinking of giving it to Thrudd, you louse. What's wrong with yours truly?"

"A broken ankle, by all accounts," returned Delphick at once. "I'm sorry to hear you've been in the wars —"

Mel giggled again. "Make love, not war," she murmured.

"— but it would be unfair to impose on you when you're unwell. I have an interesting, er, proposition to make to a — an interested reporter —"

"So go ahead and make it. I'm right here listening, as interested as they come. It's my ankle that's broken, not my wrist. I can still write every bit as well as Banner — and telephones were made for talking down. I'd be phoning in my copy before the ink was dry."

"Perhaps not as quickly as that, thanks, Mel. I'm still waiting to talk to — the other person concerned — before the plan can be finalised. The reason I rang was to find out if Thrudd — if a trustworthy reporter — would be willing to go along with me for a while in exchange for an eventual scoop, though it may mean waiting for some time."

"Banner's out fixing himself a scoop this very minute, Oracle. You'll read all about it in tomorrow's *Blare*. He needs another right now like I need to run a four-minute mile — but Amelita Forby needs a scoop, all right. Memories are short in Fleet Street. While I'm laid up on my sickbed someone else is writing my column — with me keeping a watchful eye on it, sure, but it isn't the same. There's a whole hungry generation of cub reporters howling at my door — so do the hero bit and scare them away for me, okay?"

chapter
10

It was late next morning when Bob Ranger returned to London from his Plummergen trip. Miss Seeton had been surprised when Delphick telephoned yesterday to say it would greatly oblige him if she could touch up the Grey Day picture along the lines suggested by Sir Wormelow. Not wishing to confuse her, he gave only the basic facts of the case; and Miss Seeton did not press for enlightenment. She feared she understood his motives only too well. While she had been pleased enough with the painting when she first completed it so many years ago, she had since, as she'd told Tump, come to wonder at her (and she blushed) presumption. Naturally, the chief superintendent did not care for being so, well, *emblazoned*. It was a pity that one could not easily alter watercolour, but she thought something of the required effect might be achieved with pastels. And of course she trusted the dear sergeant to take care of the picture for her — and Anne. To take care of the picture, not his wife — both of them — not that she supposed for one minute he wouldn't . . . and if Mr. Delphick wished, she could have it ready for dear Bob, she meant the sergeant, to collect next morning.

So Bob left his Bromley home after kissing Anne goodbye, promising her a treasure hunt when she came back that evening from her part-time job in the doctor's surgery.

"If we're, or rather you're, going to have to tell the world the picture was found in our attic," he pointed out, "it'll help you no end to put the story over if it actually is — found in the attic, I mean."

"You're starting to sound like Aunt Em," Anne warned him with a laugh. "Not much, but a little — perhaps it's catching. Give her my love, won't you?"

Miss Seeton sent back her own, together with the painting, which to Bob's impressionable eye looked even bleaker and more wintry than it had before. Not so much like the Oracle any longer: just as well. He wouldn't fancy working for anyone quite as cold and hard as that. But she'd done a marvellous job — if Mel Forby played her part right, Croesus would never be able to resist it.

He shivered once more, wrapped the painting carefully in brown paper, pecked

Miss Seeton fondly on the cheek, and set off for Bromley, and his house, and the attic. There was a convenient corner behind the water tank which seemed made for the purpose . . .

Everything was set fair, thought Bob, as he emerged from the lift and headed for the office he shared with the Oracle — time to ring Mel, and report all systems go. For pretty well the first time in their dealings with MissEss, they'd hit on something which didn't seem likely to involve her and her Misguided Missile personality, as somebody once called it, any farther. No brolly-waving chaos, no frantic chases in police cars, no kidnapping — she could stay nice and quiet in Plummergen, and leave it to him, and especially Anne, to do all the work.

He might have known it was too good to last.

The Oracle was on the telephone as he came in. He waved Bob to his desk, on which that day's copy of *The Blare* lay open at the boldly printed heading: *Belton Boxes Burglary — Raffles Returns!* bearing Thrudd Banner's byline, and a photograph of the Abbey with arrows superimposed to show the nerve-racking route taken by the ransomeer from the roof, to the windowsills, to the ground two floors below.

Thrudd had obviously done his homework. The rarity and great value of the snuffbox collection was discussed, with historical snippets about the Prince Regent and an oblique reference to the then Duchess of Belton. There was a brief résumé of the Raffles career to date, with emphasis laid on his daring, physical prowess, and remarkable good fortune in escaping detection yet again; there was a society photograph of the current duchess, taken by the renowned Cedric Benbow, showing Her Grace in full court dress. It was lucky, Thrudd pointed out, that the splendid jewels worn in the photograph had been sent to Garrards for cleaning while the duchess was away, their usual place of concealment being a not-very-new or well-hidden wall safe, which Raffles would easily (in the opinion of the reporter) crack.

"The ducal family has a penchant for adventure, but is unlikely to be pleased by the attentions paid it by Raffles, the adventurer thief," wrote Thrudd. "This is not the first time that Belton Abbey has been in the news . . ." And for the delight of his readership he related a scandal, comfortably distant in time, when a young woman claiming to have been seduced by the then duke stabbed herself in "Belton's famous Palladian temple to the goddess Hiberna. This temple stands in the Abbey grounds, conveniently near the main building. It was here that the duke and his maidservant used to meet: it was at the feet of the statue to Hiberna that a pool of the young woman's blood was found next day, staining the white marble red . . ."

"Rubbish," snorted Bob. "Dried blood's brown, not red — I'd have expected Thrudd to know that."

"Reporter's licence," said Delphick, who had concluded his telephone conversation while his sergeant read the newspaper. "I'm surprised he didn't describe her as weltering in gore. It's the sort of touch the normal *Blare* reader rather enjoys, I fancy."

"Too busy giving 'em a potted history lesson," muttered Bob, re-reading the part about the Prince Regent. "Some of it's interesting, I suppose, though it isn't as if anyone's likely to care much nowadays whether there's a temple to the goddess of Ireland or not. He only put it in because of the white marble and the blood, of course — but you know, sir, I think it's probably just as well Mel's going to write up the Winter Painting discovery. She'll be a bit more . . . well, a bit more tasteful about it, if that's the word."

Delphick shrugged. "Horses for courses, Bob: Mel writes for the *Daily Negative*,

Thrudd for *The Blare*, among others. It's a totally different readership. And, for all we know, Croesus reads *The Blare* avidly. We'll just have to hope he, or one of his minions, spots the story — talking of which, that was Faulkbourne on the line just now. Not, I suppose, that he'd take too kindly to being thought a minion, but he is one of the duke's employees, though I'd hesitate to call him 'mere.' And very much the loyal retainer. As soon as he learned about this *Blare* article — I wonder who in the servants' hall reads so plebeian a publication — it struck him that, with the story out in the open, the police would be duty bound to take notice. Which means he's asking again about the possibility of having Miss Seeton pop along to perform one of her little miracles . . ."

"She is," Bob reminded him, "at a bit of a loose end at the moment, sir. And she might enjoy an outing to Belton — the place'll be swarming with trippers now, mad keen to see the Temple of Hiberna and the bloodstains on the floor, and the window Raffles climbed in by. She'd be invisible among all the rubberneckers, sir."

"I thought," said Delphick, regarding him with a curious eye, "that you'd begun to wonder whether it wasn't the evil influence of the constabulary which was responsible for Miss Seeton's involvement in so much that is untoward? You tried your best to persuade me to ease up on her — and convinced me, what's more. Why have you changed your mind?"

Bob looked uneasy. He opened his mouth, hesitated, then shut it again. He took a deep breath. "Croesus, sir," said Sergeant Ranger; and for the first time sounded worried.

Fifty miles away in Kent, there was a remarkable coincidence of conversational matter: or perhaps, all things considered, not so remarkable. Plummergen's post office had been humming with hypothesis and conjecture almost since Mr. Stillman opened his doors that morning.

Mrs. Bloomer had provided the stimulus for this particular spasm of speculation, not that Plummergen tongues need any great stimulus to start wagging. Martha had popped in for a tin of scouring powder, two packets of chocolate biscuits, and a slab of gingerbread. It was one of her days for obliging Miss Seeton, so the scouring powder came as no surprise: but Plummergen can read a clue as well as any Scotland Yard detective.

"I thought," remarked Mrs. Skinner, before the bell above the door had finished tinkling behind Miss Seeton's cleaning lady, "as Martha Bloomer's gingerbread was supposed to be so good — I mean, they give her a prize for it at the last village show, didn't they?" And Martha's ribbon had rankled with Mrs. Skinner ever since, she herself having been awarded a dubious Commended. "So why d'you reckon she's buying it now, instead of baking?"

Mrs. Henderson couldn't resist a little dig. "Her fruitcake's even better, what with the judges giving her the red rosette over all." Mrs. Skinner's fruitcake had sunk disastrously in the middle, so that she hadn't even dared take it along to the marquee. "But some has a gift for cakes," said Mrs. Henderson, "and some hasn't — and you need time to bake a good cake, that's true. But if there's a guest expected at short notice, well . . ."

Only one of Miss Seeton's friends was generally known to enjoy vast quantities of gingerbread. There was a brooding silence, before Mrs. Spice said:

"It was in the paper about that Raffles this morning — how he's pinched a load of snuffboxes from the Duke of Belton. Him as had his pictures stole a few years back, when Miss Seeton went to Switzerland and found 'em . . ."

131

"Bought a new washing machine with the insurance money," said Mrs. Scillicough, with heartfelt envy. Plummergen's notorious toddling triplets lived with their parents in one of the council houses at the end of the village, and were very hard on clothes. Mrs. Scillicough's twin-tub tried its best, but was generally supposed to be fighting a losing battle. "Maybe she's after a reward for them boxes," she said, and sighed. Life could be so unfair . . .

In Plummergen, everyone knows who is meant by "She" when the word is pronounced in a particular way. Mrs. Skinner was quick to point out, however, that there was little chance of Miss Seeton's claiming any reward, as Raffles would be holding the boxes to ransom like he always did, and the police never had no clues, did they?

"That'll be why Bob Ranger's coming to see her. Stands to reason," chipped in Mrs. Henderson, with scorn.

"Could be any number of reasons," retorted Mrs. Skinner. "He's married to Anne Knight, isn't he? Suppose the two of them's coming down to see her family, and calling in just to be polite?"

"There's nothing been said at the nursing home," someone pointed out. Dr. and Mrs. Knight did their best to maintain the privacy of themselves, their staff, and their patients; it was uphill work. "So it must be really unexpected, like Mrs. Henderson said . . ."

"Personal, then," suggested somebody else, and the floor was open now to all.

Several ideas were floated almost at once. Some thought that Bob and Anne, married for two years, had found at last that the strains of a policeman's career were bringing their marriage to the brink of failure. Anne was therefore coming to confide in her parents, Bob (for some reason unspecified) in Miss Seeton. The latter view was quickly vetoed, on the grounds that, a confirmed spinster, Miss Seeton would be as much use in a marriage guidance capacity as the vicar, who was a bachelor, bullied by his sister. (A minority held Miss Seeton to be rather more effective than the Reverend Arthur Treeves because it would hardly be possible to be less; but this argument was soon abandoned.)

In which case, Anne was going to see her parents, alone, either to say she was coming home for good, or to tell them — what? Married for two years, and her dad, for all he said he'd retired from that classy London practice, a doctor — if it didn't mean a babby on the way, well, the speaker didn't know what did.

Married for more than two years, said someone else, and no sign of a babby yet. It only went to show that you could never tell from looking at a man, for all that the sergeant was such a big chap, and poor little Anne crying her heart out over the empty nursery, and wondering whether there was something her father might be able to do . . .

Miss Seeton's part in all this was still being thrashed out when the doorbell jangled, and The Nuts came in. Every eye brightened. If Miss Nuttel and Mrs. Blaine didn't know, nobody did.

"We've just seen that large young policeman who is such a crony of Miss Seeton driving down The Street towards her cottage," announced Mrs. Blaine, once the formalities of purchasing a few unimportant items had been completed. "Too suspicious, at this hour of the morning. He must have left home very early to avoid the rush hour."

"Poor little Anne'll have bin dropped off at the nursing home, I shouldn't wonder," someone said, and others prepared to impart to the newcomers the results of the speculation up until now; but were given no time. Miss Nuttel's voice rose above all the rest.

"Conspiracy, no doubt about it. The Raffles business in today's paper. Young Ranger," enlarged Miss Nuttel darkly. "Strong, physical type . . ."

Along with loyal Bunny's bleat of "Oh, Eric, of course!" (it seemed that the squabble was, for the moment at least, over) came a general acknowledgement that yes, he certainly was, and they'd all been saying so not a moment since. Miss Nuttel looked slightly resentful at thus having her thunder stolen, and was observed to be thinking fast.

Mrs. Blaine's blackcurrant eyes gleamed. The squabble, it now seemed, was only in abeyance, not abandoned for good: the chance to go one better than her friend was irresistible. "Raffles, too sinister, yes — but Raffles isn't the only case that has the police puzzled. Or so they say," she added, with a wealth of meaning in her tone. "Really, one can't help thinking — too convenient, the Croesus robberies — anyone might claim that a work of art had been stolen by the gang, and who would know any different?"

"Need to recognise a work of art, for one thing," retorted Miss Nuttel promptly, in her turn unable to resist the chance to snipe. Bunny's plump face puckered into a scowl. Everyone held their collective breath: was the Hot Cross Bun about to live up to her village nickname?

Then the door burst open, and Mrs. Putts rushed in. Emmy waved from behind her counter, but had no time to say hello before her mother, breathless, announced:

"It's gone! Somebody's took it! When we come out of the night shift, there it was — stolen away!"

Mouths dropped open and breaths were drawn in. Everyone knew at once what she meant. Mrs. Putts had worked in the Brettenden biscuit factory for so long, she had been awarded a canteen pass and a clock that struck the quarters as well as the hour.

Emmy, remembering her prized scrap-book, leaped into the startled breach with a horrified squeal. "Why, that's a wicked thing to do! Humphrey Marsh's master-piece, that was — and somebody's took it. It's . . . it's a crime!"

"It's Croesus," said Miss Nuttel firmly, throwing back her head and staring Mrs. Blaine straight in the eye. "Said it was a work of art, didn't I? No argument about it now!"

And Mrs. Blaine, her face puckering once more, uttered an angry little cry, stamped, threw her bag of shopping on the floor, and rushed out of the post office in tears.

chapter
11

Two days later, Miss Seeton's telephone rang. When she went to answer it, she was surprised and pleased to find Amelita Forby on the other end.

"You're not much of a one for the newspapers, are you, Miss S.? Make an exception today, and go splash out on a copy of the *Negative* — I'd have sent you one myself, if I'd been mobile. Still will, if they've sold out by the time you get to the shops, though I've kept your name out of it so they shouldn't have done." Mel laughed. "Banner's not the only one who knows how to write up a scoop, believe me. My editor thinks I'm just the cat's whiskers, working from my sickbed and all — but it's thanks to you and the Oracle that I've been able to — and the Rangers, of course. Bless every one of you!"

Miss Seeton, though she certainly did not object to the cost of a *Daily Negative*, recalled that it was the regular paper taken by Martha and Stan, who lived so conveniently near. She would telephone across to ask if they could spare it for a short time, while she read . . . whatever it was that dear Mel thought she should know about. Something in which it seemed her own name had not been mentioned; but then why should there be any mention of her name in the newspapers? Miss Seeton knew — which all her friends must also know — that she lived a very quiet life, retired in a pleasant village where she minded her own business, and rejoiced when others minded theirs. But Mel Forby's business, as a reporter, was (Miss Seeton sorrowfully acknowledged) to chronicle for those one must suppose were interested (though she could not imagine why they should be) some of the doings of people who might be of interest to them — people in the public eye, so to speak. Which Miss Seeton knew, emphatically, that she was not. In which case, whatever it was that Mel wished her to read about must be something of particular interest to herself, which surely meant something to do with art . . .

And Miss Seeton, pleasantly curious to know what had so excited Mel and her editor that the *Daily Negative* had run an exclusive article about it, dialled Martha's number with no thought at all of the Grey Day painting she had, just two days ago, handed to Bob Ranger as a favour (he had said) to Chief Superintendent Delphick.

Which she had been delighted to do, of course. So flattering — and such a relief that he (dear Mr. Delphick) had not thought it an impertinence on her part to have painted it in the first place . . . Mel had been bubbling with too much enthusiasm to go into details over the phone; she never supposed (despite having known Miss Seeton for several years) that the little spinster would fail to connect her work with a national newspaper scoop. She had forgotten that in Miss Seeton's opinion her working arrangements with the police were a private matter, and not newsworthy; but on this occasion it hadn't so much been work as a favour to one who had, over the years, become a friend. She had touched up the Grey Day painting because she'd been asked to, but, though Mr. Delphick had said something about baiting a trap, one must suppose it to have been his particular sense of humour, of course. One had not cared to seem too curious, or too conceited, as to the real reason behind his unusual request. One was merely thankful that he did not see it — the painting, that was to say — as presumption on her part. It had been intended as a purely personal impression — personal to herself, that was to say, though one sometimes tended to forget, in the inspiration of the moment, that one was running a risk that the other person concerned might (with some justification) object to having so personal a remark made about him. Even though the remark was, as one might say, made without words. Or her. Having so personal a remark made about her . . .

Miss Seeton, waiting for someone to answer the phone in Martha's house, daydreamed back to the first occasion when she had met Mel Forby. Such interesting bones — the eyes and colouring, so unusual — irresistible to an artist. She had sketched the young reporter's face in a manner which, she had been careful to insist, was intended as purely personal — and Mel had replied that she (Mel) had always considered her (Mel's) face personal to herself, which naturally she would. Yet — so very fortunate — she (Mel) hadn't thought her (Miss Seeton) ill-mannered after all, which had been a relief, as it might have turned out rather different. So embarrassing. She really must try to stop herself dashing off her little cartoon impressions of people. One day she would encounter someone less understanding than dear Mel, or Chief Superintendent Delphick . . .

"They must be out," she told herself, realising suddenly just how long she'd been standing with the telephone in her hand. "Now, I wonder —"

"Hello?" came a breathless voice: Martha's. "Sorry to keep you waiting, but I'd locked the door and all when I just heard the ringing. Who is it?"

Miss Seeton announced herself, and Martha laughed. "It was you I was coming to see, dear. Fancy me running back to answer the phone, when if I'd been a minute later you'd have seen me anyway! What were you wanting?"

Five minutes later, Miss Seeton was studying Mel Forby's piece in the *Daily Negative*. No wonder she had been so gratified with the results of her hard work — such large type, and so very eye-catching, which of course was what it was supposed to do. Catch the eye. Might that be why, wondered Miss Seeton, they were called *head*-lines? Because that was, after all, where one found the eyes . . .

Bromley Bride Finds Winter Wonderland, proclaimed two rows of bold black print, above a photograph of —

"Good gracious," breathed Miss Seeton. "Surely that's — no, I must be mistaken — but it does look very like . . ."

"It is," Martha told her. "That's why I was coming over to see you — know that

141

picture anywhere, I would, never mind the one they say's found it in her attic. Take a good look at the other photo . . ."

It was Anne. Anne Ranger, formerly Knight, spinster of the parish of Plummergen, friend to Miss Emily Seeton, wife to Miss Seeton's adopted nephew Bob. The Rangers. So this was what Mel had been talking about!

Miss Seeton eagerly scanned the paragraphs below Amelita Forby's byline. Really, it sounded a most remarkable story: so romantic. A dusty attic, a cobwebbed shape, a chance decision to send the painting to auction because it didn't match the young couple's colour scheme . . .

Mel had written it with great care. All the emphasis was on Anne; Bob was mentioned, but only briefly, and with no hint of what he did for a living. The photographs showed lucky young Mrs. Ranger in a fairly blurred fashion, but the reproduction of *Ilkley Moor on a December Day* was as crisp and clear as the printing department could make it — Mel had seen to that, nagging her editor down the wires until, for the sake of his ulcer, he'd promised hand on heart to stand over them while they worked on it.

As Miss Seeton read, she remembered. Good gracious. So the chief superintendent had really meant what he'd said — and how very gratifying, to have such public recognition for one's work — not that one would have chosen, perhaps, such a title for the painting. Miss Seeton knew nothing of Ilkley Moor except that it was in Yorkshire — and there was a song, of course, *On Ilkley Moor Baht 'At*. One verse after another until the worms, although why people who lived in the north of England should pronounce "without a hat" in such fashion was beyond Miss Seeton, who had taught art, not linguistics. And why, of all places, Ilkley Moor?

Mel Forby, who came from Liverpool and had a sense of humour, could have told Miss Seeton, if she'd asked; it was pandering to the good old "anything-north-of-Watford-and-it's-the-sticks" attitude of most of the *Negative*'s readership. But Mel wasn't there, and Martha Bloomer was.

"That's your picture," said Martha, as if Miss Seeton hadn't known. "You painted that, I'd swear to it. So why's that reporter woman said as it was painted by someone called Crockerton? Changed your name, have you? You've never gone and — No, course you haven't." Miss Seeton and matrimony just didn't go together. It was unthinkable.

Miss Seeton, only half-hearing Martha's complaint, took a closer look at the caption beneath the photograph of her — yes, definitely her — painting. "The newly discovered work by nineteenth-century landscape artist Sibyl Crockerton, RA, renowned for her then bold mixing of watercolour and pastel techniques, is sure to attract great interest when it comes up for auction," Mel had written. Making the masterpiece the work of a woman was partly her little joke, partly a muted compliment to Miss Seeton. She had enjoyed herself hugely inventing a history for Sibyl: a tale of jealousy, obstacles overcome, eventual recognition of genius triumphant, and (Mel revelled in this bit) early death from consumption, followed by oblivion "from which she is only now beginning to emerge. But collectors are starting to pay high prices for Crockertons when, all too rarely, they appear on the open market. Fine art auctioneers Sothenham and Sons quote prices in the region of £50,000 . . ."

"Good gracious," said Miss Seeton faintly.

Just then, the telephone rang.

Response to Mel's article had been all that Delphick wished. Anne Ranger was interviewed, herself and the little house in

Bromley photographed, and the point clearly made that, as the Rangers were uneasy about keeping this valuable item at home, it had been handed over to Sothenhams. There it would be displayed for all to admire until the auction — the date of which was given. Young Mrs. Ranger was quoted as saying she could hardly wait. "Not just the money, but the romance of it all," wrote Mel gleefully.

"I knew we could rely on Mel. She's done us proud," said Delphick, re-reading the page with relish. "If Croesus can resist all that, he's not the man I thought he was."

"I suppose so, sir." Bob looked again at the picture of his wife, and their home, and wondered what sort of monster might have been unleashed. "Anne's doing her best, sir, but she's no actress. This has all been a bit more, well, overwhelming than we expected — they've even tried to talk to her at work, and the doctors don't like it. Medical receptionists're meant to be efficient and self-effacing — which nobody can manage when there's a crowd of reporters camped on the front doorstep. And I think she's a bit worried now they might put two and two together, sir — about Plummergen, and me being a copper — and Miss Seeton, of course."

"You started to say something of the sort once before, but didn't get very far. Let's hear it all this time, Bob." Delphick regarded his subordinate with amusement. "You're afraid I've set in motion something I can no longer cope with, and that Anne and MissEss will be swept away in the flood and no one will be able to rescue them?"

"Something like that, yes, sir, I suppose." Bob looked unhappy at criticising his superior, but the set of his jaw was firm. "Things tend to, well, to happen to Miss Seeton, you see —"

"Then you," Delphick interrupted him, "see this," and produced from his breast pocket a folded white envelope. "Go on, take a good look — and then dare to hint that the Oracle is losing his grip. Rank insubordination, Sergeant Ranger, that's what I'd call it if I didn't know you better — as it is I'll settle for plain heresy." And, as Bob took the envelope and began to examine its contents, Delphick sat watching him, smiling to himself.

After a few minutes, Bob said, "Sorry, sir. For getting steamed up and, well, not thinking it right through in the first place — and for not realising you'd have been bound to even if I didn't. Think it through, I mean," and he turned red. He was starting to sound as muddled as MissEss — but what could you expect, once she was involved in a case? You just knew everything would go all wobbly — even you . . .

"Apology accepted, Sergeant Ranger. And, on your part — holiday accepted?"

"Yes, sir," said Bob, a broad grin of relief spreading across his face. "It's so obvious, now, but —"

"But that's why I'm a chief superintendent, and you have some way yet to go. You need foresight, Bob, and inspiration — and," Delphick added, "the ability to kill two birds with one stone. We'll be keeping your wife and your dear Aunt Em out of harm's way, just in case — and we'll be keeping Faulkbourne and the rest of the Belton crowd happy, at the same time. It's a comfortable pub, my spies tell me, in attractive surroundings. Just the place for a maiden aunt on holiday with her devoted family — and with a fair number of rubberneckers longing to see the crib Raffles cracked so easily and, dammit, with such panache." He shook his head. "This chap — he's different. I can see why they make a fuss of the blighter, crook though he is — a crook with class, real class, is pretty rare these days. If we ever succeed in nobbling him, his doting public might surprise us by the force of their outcry."

"He's got style, sir, no doubt about it. Everyone says so. There'll be dozens — hundreds — of people at Belton to take a good look. MissEss and Anne'll be more or less invisible, won't they? Safety in numbers. Not that I really think they're not going to be safe, sir, but when Miss Seeton's around, well, you know how it is."

"I certainly do. Which is why you'll be with them for a day or two, while they merge into the background. Something you," Delphick said with a chuckle, "will never be able to do unless you find a time machine and revert to your extreme youth. You'd have won the Bonniest Baby prize every time, I feel sure."

Bob turned scarlet. Delphick blinked. "Good lord! Bob — don't tell me —" He broke off, choking. Bob blushed all the more, and mumbled into his boots. The Oracle smothered an outright laugh, and enquired in a quivering voice:

"Might one ask, er, how many times?"

"Three in a row, sir," confessed the unhappy winner, his blushes monumental. "It was all my mother's doing. My dad didn't approve of baby shows, but she — well, she was . . . was proud of us both, sir, me and my brother, and . . ."

"And I'm sure she still is. One son a promising young detective with a delightful wife, the other, as I recall, a wine merchant. Not to mention the daughter who has made you an uncle, as well — while you, in your turn, have increased the merry throng by the addition of an unexpected maiden aunt — in short, an utterly splendid family, Bob. I won't ask why she didn't submit your sister to the same, er, exhibition" — Bob turned purple, and coughed unintelligibly — "and I won't, I promise, breathe a word to Anne about it all. I'll bet you've never told her your guilty secret, have you? I thought not," as Bob mumbled again. "Besides," the chief superintendent added, "I probably couldn't reach her by phone in any case. I confidently expect that, right now, the line is engaged while she explains to her dear Aunt Em that the car will be coming to pick her up right after lunch this afternoon . . ."

chapter
12

Their first view of the Belton Arms showed a hotel at least twice the size of Plummergen's George and Dragon. There was a sizeable car park, thickly gravelled, surrounded by flower beds which were some gardener's obvious pride and joy; there were benches set out under trees here and there about the spacious lawns; and, discreetly screened by a holly hedge, a small play area for children, comprising a sand pit, slide, and assorted sizes of motor tyres painted in bright colours, arranged in tunnels and hoops.

"Eat your heart out, Charley Mountfitchet," murmured Anne as Bob swung the car into a suitable space. "The Oracle was right: this place looks busy. We'll be swallowed up among the throng — which is probably just as well." She glanced quickly at Miss Seeton, then away. "A nice friendly crowd of tourists, with us trailing along and nobody paying us any attention — we hope," she added, in a lower tone.

"It looks," said Miss Seeton doubtfully, "although one of course feels reluctant to make comparisons, which can be so odious — but I agree with you, Anne dear, that Mr. Mountfitchet's hotel is considerably, well, smaller. And, one must suppose, cheaper. And one cannot help wondering —"

"It's a merit award," said Bob, at exactly the same time that Anne said:

"Another part of the country, Aunt Em. It's just not possible to make any comparison, because the cost of living is so very different. So don't you worry about it — we're not going to. Are we, darling?"

"Oh! No. Of course we aren't," said Bob quickly, after a brisk prod from his spouse reminded him that he was meant to be keeping Miss Seeton happy. "Shall I take the luggage in with us, or had we better check in first?"

Anne thought it better to check in; just in case, by some mischance, their booking had been lost. There was no reason why he should have to carry the bags there and back unnecessarily, although (she added with a chuckle) the exercise might not do him any harm.

"Wouldn't you agree he's putting on weight, Aunt Em? Never mind about his feelings — tell me what you really think. Remember, honesty is the best policy."

"I wish everybody thought that," muttered Detective Sergeant Bob Ranger, while Miss Seeton, smiling, maintained a tactful silence. "Although, if they did, I'd be out of a job. Which isn't likely, human nature being what it is — which is just as well for us, because the money comes in handy." He opened the door of the little car, which had been Anne's before they married, and which they still hoped to sell in part exchange for something larger — one day, when they could afford it. But setting up house seemed to cost a great deal more than they'd ever expected, so . . .

Bob bumped his knees, as he always did if he wasn't careful, on the steering column, but Anne and Miss Seeton emerged from the car unscathed. Their steps crunched comfortably across the gravel towards the main door of the hotel, and they had plenty of time to look about them.

What they saw was delightful: rural England at its best. Windows sparkled in the sunshine, sparrows danced and darted about the lawn, pigeons cooed in the trees above. A lazy labrador retriever yawned hugely in the shade of a beech, golden fur dappled on dappled green grass. Miss Seeton's fingers ached with a longing to capture the scene on paper, and she tried to remember whereabouts in her suitcase she had packed her sketching pad.

The reception area was large and luxurious. The floor was carpeted richly, the armchairs had plump cushions, and the desk itself gleamed with lavender and beeswax. Behind the desk was a young woman, so at her ease there that it was plain she never had to double, as did Plummergen's Maureen and Doris, as waitress, washer-up, or barmaid. Those nails, thought Bob as he strode across the deep pile of the carpet, had never known a sink of dirty dishes; those eyelashes had never lost their mascara by a brush from the back of a weary hand. Their owner was paid to be glamorous and efficient at one particular post, and there and thus she would remain.

Her attractions were evident to others besides Bob. The reception desk was set at a discreet angle to the door, out of the direct line of any draught, and for added protection flanked by some impressive specimens of potted plant: ferns, bromeliads, and a cheeseplant Charley Mountfitchet would have offered to buy on the spot. Amongst all the foliage, neatly arranged, were more chairs — on the most comfortable looking of which lay curled a large Ginger cat and a low table. And with one foot carelessly on the table, his elbow resting on the leather inset of the desk, stood a young man, bending close to the attractive young woman, making her giggle and blush as he talked.

The feet of the Plummergen party made little sound on the deep-piled carpet, and the pair at Reception were deep in conversation. Bob, preceding Miss Seeton and Anne, was almost at the desk when the young woman looked up, uttered a little exclamation, switched on a professional smile, and said, in a hasty aside:

"For goodness' sake, Eddie! I'm busy. I'm on till half nine tonight . . . Good afternoon," she greeted Bob, directing the rest of her smile past him to his companions.

"Oh, gosh," said the young man, straightening up and turning round in one smooth movement. His expression was rueful as he observed the three strangers. "Caught in the act, I'm afraid." He smiled, and his eyes danced: it was, Miss Seeton thought, far more real than the smile of the young woman. He had something of dear Nigel Colveden about him, she thought, always so ready to admire a pretty girl, but not always a good judge of character — those nails, such black lashes that nature had never, surely, intended . . .

The smiling young man was still speaking

as Miss Seeton tried to dismiss from her inward eye a vision of the young woman as a harpy, with rapacious claws, preying on innocent youth. "I'm so very sorry," he said, as he prepared to move away. "Your need is greater than mine, of course. I shall take myself off, and leave you in Beverley's expert hands." He bowed gracefully, smiled again, and, with a little wave for Beverley, was gone.

Beverley did her best not to show her disappointment at his going, and, professional that she was, did it well. She seemed, almost at once, utterly delighted to see the visitors, and made just the right amount of fuss over them.

"Mr. and Mrs. Ranger, you're in Room 24, overlooking the front, and we've put your aunt in 25, almost opposite — if that's all right. The one next-door was already booked, I'm afraid — we're rather busy at the moment." She regarded Miss Seeton with an expert eye, and a look of relief showed clearly as she added, "There's no lift, but if you'd like to leave your cases here we can see about someone helping you upstairs with them later . . ."

The formalities were done, the keys handed out, the car locked again after Bob's trip for the cases. Miss Seeton had unpacked a few necessities, and was gazing now out of the window at the back lawn, listening to the babble of some small children romping in the play area. Overexcited, she thought sternly. One wondered at the parents, in this hot weather — surely it would be wiser to settle them under some shady tree . . .

She drifted back to her suitcase, and retrieved her pad, pencils, and eraser. The dog, the dappled sunlight, the lazy summer cooing of the doves — how it had made an impression on her, at the time! But could she remember it now?

She thought she could — she found she could not. Somehow, the difference between vision and reality had blurred: the yawning retriever was now a snarling wolf, above whose head swooped not doves, but dark, darting, sinister winged creatures with vicious teeth: not birds, but vampire bats. And beside the wolf was a figure part bird, part woman — a woman with Beverley's face — a harpy. "Oh, dear," breathed Miss Seeton in dismay. What had happened? Where had it all gone, that sunny summer afternoon? The trees, instead of being in full leaf, were stark and grasping against a sky heavy with an approaching storm; the hotel was a crumbling ruin, its vaulted ceilings and arched windows looking more medieval — a castle, perhaps, or a church — than the elegant Georgian pile her eyes had shown her.

But what her eyes showed her now, she decided sadly, was that nothing was quite as it seemed . . .

After a stroll around the grounds and an early dinner, the three of them wandered into the Residents' lounge, where Anne and Miss Seeton settled happily to watch *Casablanca* on television, and Bob fell asleep. The spirited café rendering of "La Marseillaise" roused him from his slumbers; he stretched, yawned, and left the room.

When Rick and Louis had disappeared into the swirling Moroccan mists, Anne and Miss Seeton left everyone else sitting in front of the News, and, sniffing a little, emerged from the lounge to look for Bob. They found him at last, after a search through the crowded public rooms, in the bar, with a pint mug and a philosopher. He looked bored.

"Which," Anne teased him, once they had extricated him from the conversation of the travelling salesman, "will be a lesson to you not to neglect your wife in favour of selfish pleasure. We'll have a sherry each, please, to make up for it — and while we're drinking it," she added quietly, "you can tell us what you've found out."

Bob grinned, bought the drinks, and admitted that everything had been pretty busy — holidaymakers, businessmen, a honeymoon couple — and all he'd managed to learn from the barman was that the Abbey opened for three days every week, but that there was talk it might be increased to four, after the sudden interest shown. Which, Bob pointed out, didn't come as much of a surprise, in the circumstances. But they, or rather the Oracle, had certainly picked the right time to arrive, because tomorrow was one of the "open" days.

"Tomorrow," said Anne, "is another day. I adored *Gone With the Wind* when I saw the re-release, but I'm sure Bob would have fallen asleep if he'd been with me — I sometimes wonder if he has a soul at all! And, talking of sleep . . ."

Miss Seeton smothered a ladylike yawn and smiled: such a long journey, and so many different sights to admire. One's mind needed time to absorb it all — and then there were her exercises, too. This morning — so unexpected, such a rush — not that it did any harm to curtail the routine, but yoga was intended as a relaxation, and really . . .

Bob grinned. "I doubt if I'm going to be

particularly relaxed after tonight, sleep or no sleep. That four-poster bed is obviously an original, and those were the days when people just didn't come my size."

"There's always the floor," said Anne brutally, as Miss Seeton's eyes lit up with the romance of it all. "Gorgeous thick carpets, and you can take the bolster — we've even got a bolster, Aunt Em, just think. Real feathers, too."

Miss Seeton was thinking. "A genuine four-poster bed? I have never even seen one, except in museums, of course. And stately homes. And in the cinema . . ."

"Let's hope it isn't haunted by some genuine ghosts," said Bob, and chuckled. "And there's only one way to find out — and it's getting late. We'll see you in the morning, Aunt Em — and then we'll go and see whether Belton Abbey has a four-poster bed of its own."

The little car waited for a moment behind a coach more than half-full of trippers, the driver of which evidently hadn't been warned about the tightness of the turn into the Abbey gates. He managed it without too much difficulty, however, and the Plummergen party followed the coach in queueing to buy tickets from the man in the gatehouse booth.

Belton Abbey was a sight to make Miss Seeton catch her breath. Here before her were the very walls and windows she had found herself sketching last night: not a castle, but a church — or, rather, an abbey — and not ruined, of course. Any ghosts that walked would be those of monks, dispossessed by Henry VIII and with love of their ecclesiastical home lingering beyond the grave — a love which Miss Seeton, having seen the place, could now well understand.

"Pretty impressive," said Bob, bringing the car round to a stop. "We'll buy a guidebook. I wonder how old it is."

"It doesn't look real, does it?" said Anne. "I mean, of course it must, because it is — but it's almost *too* real, in a way. Like a movie director's idea for a film set."

"One has the feeling," said Miss Seeton slowly, "that it is, indeed familiar — which would be why, of course, as he will have allowed them to. The duke, I mean — to use it for a film, or a television play. It is certainly most beautiful — the setting, too, so peaceful — so very English. One wonders how they can ever bear to be away."

"Yes," mused Bob, remembering the words of the duke's steward on the

Bremeridges' dislike of warm temperatures. "Those high ceilings and great thick stone walls must be jolly cool, even in summer . . ." And what it would be like in winter was anyone's guess. Maybe there was something to be said for being middle class and mortgaged, after all: their house might be small, but at least they could afford central heating throughout.

Somehow, it was hardly a surprise, as the little party entered in the wake of the chattering coachload, to find Faulkbourne about his stewardly duty, hovering in the hall. On his face as he observed the throng was a practised look of lofty disdain, which impressed everyone very much. Here, they thought, was a regular aristocrat, worth every penny of the entrance fee, looking down his nose at them like that — not a bit like the young man with the charming smile who was stepping forward to greet them. But then Faulkbourne noticed Bob on the edge of the throng, and his expression of gracious distance changed at once to what might, in a being less stately, have been called a smile. Everyone looked round to see what could have caused such a metamorphosis: a metamorphosis which magnified into a broad grin, when Faulkbourne saw that accompanying the young man he'd last seen in Scotland Yard were two women. One of whom, an elderly little body in a light tweed suit and a distinctive hat, had an umbrella hooked over one arm . . .

Fortunately for the Plummergen party's cover, it seemed nobody else knew who they were. There was a suggestion (as Faulkbourne was so plainly a member of the ducal family) that Miss Seeton might be an old retainer, perhaps a nanny (though the hat was possibly on the frivolous side) or, more likely, a governess. Bob and Anne, it was clear, were her nephew and niece; they'd probably all be invited to go along after for a nice cup of tea and a chat, a chance to catch up on old times.

And then, as the smiling young man began to address the whole group, everyone forgot about the newcomers, and settled down to enjoy their guided tour of His Grace the Duke of Belton's family seat.

chapter
13

Bob and his companions had already recognised him as the same young man who'd been paying so much attention to the charming Beverley when they arrived at the Belton Arms yesterday. Away from the confines of the reception area, his voice was firm and clear, every syllable reaching the farthest members of his party.

Tours always began, he informed his audience, in the hall where they were standing, and would take in most of the ground floor, including the famous cloisters, and about half the floor above. The remainder of the Abbey was kept closed to the public, because it was the family's private home.

"But are we going to see the place the snuffboxes were stolen from? That's upstairs, isn't it?"

The young man's smile widened as he replied. From the amusement in his tone and the laughter in his eyes, this was obviously something he'd been asked before.

"I assure you, there's nothing of interest left to see. The ropes have all been removed by the police — clues, don't you know — not," he added with a chuckle, "that they seem to have any idea about catching the chap. He's as far out of reach as he ever was."

"I hope they were insured," muttered a dried-up little man with spectacles, a bald head, and the air of someone who understood these matters.

"The collection was priceless," he was told. "Insurance couldn't replace the sentimental and historical associations even if it could replace the money. Besides, the case isn't closed yet, remember. Not that I can say too much about it, of course, but you stop and think about it. There's been no mention yet of . . . the Ransom, has there?" And his audience shuddered with the thrill of it all.

He was certainly an accomplished showman. Having first whetted their appetites, then dashed their hopes, he finally admitted that, yes, the tour would include the morning room from which the snuffboxes had been removed. "And if anyone feels brave enough to try walking along the windowsills," he added, "there'll be a refund of his entrance fee!"

Making them all chuckle and shiver by turns, never once losing their attention, the smiling young man led his party from room to room, giving what was clearly a well-rehearsed commentary as he did so. They visited the kitchens, and the wine cellar. They enjoyed the cool air of the cloister, and the stuffiness of the gun room, all leather and oil and, to everyone's delight, dog. As they entered, a spaniel with beautiful eyes and a prodigious wag to her tail stirred from her basket, trotted across to greet the young man, then at a word of command went back to bed. Some members of the party asked whether flashbulbs would scare her, and, on being reminded that spaniels were gundogs, took photographs. Whoever had arranged the tour was clearly very good at it.

Upstairs, they found something which pleased them very much: a four-poster bed, of mammoth proportions, in what was described by the young man as the official main bedroom, although since the Abbey had been opened to the public the duke and his wife slept elsewhere. In this bed, generation after generation of Bremeridges had been born; one of the few exceptions to this tradition being Ivo, the current Lord Pelsall, heir to His Grace, whose birth had occurred in the local hospital three months earlier than expected, after his mother, ever adventurous, had suffered a fall while hunting.

"Pardon me," broke in a tall, earnest American woman who had taken more photographs of the spaniel than anyone else. "If he's to be Duke of Belton one day, why is his name — Pelsall, was it? And who are these Bremeridges we've heard so much about? Can they really be all the same family?"

"Oh, yes, indeed they can — though I do agree, it's sometimes rather difficult to understand," said the young man, his smile kind. "You're not the first person to ask that question, and I'm quite sure you won't be the last. It's all a matter of the difference between a name, you see, and a title. The family surname is Bremeridge, as yours may be Smith or Clutterbuck or Bloggs, and the present duke is Ivo Bremeridge, Duke of Belton. His elder son is another Ivo Bremeridge — it's a family name — but because he *is* the elder son he takes his father's second title, which is Lord Pelsall. We call that a courtesy title. Ivo was born in the degree of marquis, as the elder son of a duke. Now, if Ivo the Younger marries and has a son before the present duke dies, that son will take his grandfather's *third* title — but you all look thoroughly bewildered. I'm so sorry. Perhaps we've had enough genealogy for one day! But for anyone who may still be interested, there's a family tree in the next room, along with the portraits . . ."

The portraits were on display around the walls of a room with a high ceiling and, Miss Seeton was pleased to observe, a north light. The faces of Bremeridges from ages past hung in heavy gilded frames, neatly labelled, looking down on the faces looking up as the party studied them dutifully. The American woman posed several questions about which face went where on the family tree; but most people were more interested in the promised morning room, which they seemed to be taking a long time to reach.

Their guide, when asked, said that they would soon be there, which made everyone eager to leave the portraits and the family tree behind. Miss Seeton, with Anne and Bob, was the last to leave, looking back once more at the Bremeridge likenesses before, with a nod and a quiet smile, catching up with the others. The morning room, after all, was what they had mainly come to see . . .

"So nobody," enquired the young man with a grin, "has any desire for the entrance fee to be refunded? Well, well. Then I believe we must conclude that Raffles has won this round, too." He had shown them the cabinet (now filled with a hasty assemblage of porcelain) and occasional table where the snuffboxes had been displayed, and the window through which Raffles had made his entry. He had opened the window, and invited them to peer out along the line of sills to that one directly beneath the chimney, from which the rope had been suspended.

"The police," he said, "have reason to believe he's used the trick before: practice making perfect, as one might say. However, as it's probable nobody here has had much practice at walking along windowsills, shall we just say that, if anyone would care to make this their first time, here's your chance . . ." And when there were emphatically no volunteers, he chuckled richly before leading them out of the room.

As the guided tour came to an end back in the hall where it had begun, people thanked the young man for being such an entertaining and informative escort. One or two pressed odd coins in his hand, which he accepted with a smile and a bow; one or two asked him extra questions, but when Faulkbourne manifested himself impressively in the doorway, the young man murmured polite excuses, and ushered everyone to the door. Another party, it seemed, was about to arrive.

Once again, Miss Seeton and her friends

were last to leave. Bob caught Faulkbourne's eye, and the steward, very slightly, inclined his head. Anne glanced sideways to see what was going on, but with discretion: she wasn't the wife of a detective for nothing. She hadn't been the wife of a detective for very long, however: her glance was quick, but it made her step unsteady. She collided, though not heavily, with Miss Seeton, who dropped her handbag and umbrella on the flagstone floor.

"Oh," exclaimed Anne, "Aunt Em, how clumsy of me. I'm so sorry. Did I hurt you?"

"Not at all, my dear," Miss Seeton replied, even as Bob pointed out that she'd have been more likely to suffer hurt if it had been himself who bumped into her. All three of them bent to pick up Miss Seeton's belongings, then realised just in time that their heads were now in danger. Whereupon all three of them stood up straight — and laughed to see one another's confusion.

"Allow me," came a voice, and the smiling young man who had been their guide reached swiftly between them, picked up the handbag and the brolly, and presented them with a bow to their flustered owner. "I believe, madam, these are yours? What a very handsome umbrella, if you will allow me to say so. Pure silk, would be my guess, although — surely — the handle can hardly be of real gold?"

"Thank you so very much. Most kind," said Miss Seeton, accepting her property with a grateful smile. "And indeed it can be. That is to say it is. Real gold, I mean, though of course not solid. Or leaf," she added. "Unlike the portraits, or the snuff-boxes, as I recall. Valuable as well as beautiful, and also far easier to carry — the boxes, I mean, although naturally I find my umbrella easy to carry. It would hardly fit in one's pocket, would it? Any more than the ancestral portraits would, unless one cut the canvases out of their frames, which would be such a pity, since they appear to be such excellent likenesses and, presumably, of even greater sentimental value than the snuffboxes . . ."

Bob and Anne, who were used to Miss Seeton, said nothing as she continued to chatter in her attempt to explain, but the young man's smile looked decidedly strained by the time he had managed to usher her safely out through the main door as various groups of people were coming in. Bob and Anne joined her outside, and stood gazing about them.

"Let's see how much of the grounds we're allowed to look over," suggested Anne. She turned to fish the guidebook out of Bob's pocket, then stopped, and stifled a yawn. "Sorry — combination of sunshine and lack of sleep, I'm afraid. If we want to make a habit of sleeping in a four-poster bed, it really will have to be custom built."

Bob grinned, rubbing the base of his spine as he turned to Miss Seeton. "I gave up the unequal struggle in the end. A bolster on the floor isn't as bad as it sounds — but it won't be too much of a hardship for me to be back in my own bed tonight, believe me. If I *am* back, that is. Which all depends on you, Aunt Em. If you can come up with one of your drawings for me to take to the Oracle . . ."

Miss Seeton knew what was expected of her, and had arranged all her sketching equipment ready for the return from Belton Abbey. She would do her very best, she assured Bob, to give dear Mr. Delphick some idea of her impression of the morning room, but she could not promise how long it would take.

"And one cannot help feeling," she added, "something of a fraud, or at least false pretences — being under them, I mean. Being here, that is. Not that this unexpected little break is unenjoyable," hastily, in case they should feel she found their company irksome, "but there was, after all, very little to see — if anything, indeed. Of the boxes, I mean, and the ropes — because of course there was a great deal to see, otherwise. And they had been taken away, had they not? By the police — and by Raffles, as well. Or, rather, not as well, but . . ."

She paused, and looked uneasy. Anne smiled at her, and patted her arm. "You'll come up with something, just as you always do, so there's no need to worry — Bob's not worried, are you, darling? And, just to prove he isn't, he's going to stay down here and have a drink with me, while you're in your room in peace and quiet, sketching whatever comes into your head in your own good time. Isn't that right?"

Bob grinned as he hastened to reassure Miss Seeton. She hadn't really needed to pinch him quite so hard — Anne, that was — good lord, he was starting to *think* like MissEss now. Spend too much time in her company, and . . .

Whatever he'd said, it'd made her almost happy, from the look on her face as she prepared to trot upstairs. But even the Oracle, when she was in one of her worrying moods — that conscience, those incoherent trains of thought — could never make her absolutely happy about what she did. She was still that little bit ashamed of her remarkable talent, and —

No. Or rather, yes, to a certain extent it was still the same old worry, but wasn't there, surely, something else to make her hesitate like that?

"A matter of the light, you see," murmured Miss Seeton at last, twisting her fingers together to subdue the dance they nearly always started when one of her idiosyncratic sketches was on its way. Nearly, not always, because this dance was different . . .

"The light?" Anne was quicker than he was. "Which way do the windows in your room face? Southwards, of course, if ours is north. And I'm sure you've told me more than once that an artist prefers a north light, so — think how much better your picture might be if you drew it in our room, Aunt Em. We won't be in it with you, after all, to upset your concentration or spoil your mood." She fumbled in her handbag. "Here's the key and off you go — and take your time, darling. If the Oracle thinks one of your drawings is worth having, which of course it is, then he also knows it's worth waiting for . . ."

Her eyes, fondly following Miss Seeton

as, after further coaxing, she allowed herself to be persuaded, had a touch of moisture about them. "She's such a dear, isn't she? Simply longing to make believe it's her room, and her four-poster, just for a little while — not wanting to make a fuss by saying anything, but glad we worked out what she really meant — and so am I," she added. "Not simply because it pleases her, but because if she's pleased, she's likely to be more relaxed — which ought to mean she'll find it easier to draw exactly what the Oracle's hoping she will . . ."

"Whatever that is," said Bob.

chapter

14

It was still early evening when Miss Seeton, clutching three sketches in a cardboard portfolio, reappeared with the usual embarrassed look on her face; and she made the usual protestations as she handed over the products of her half hour's labour. She was sure the sketches could hardly be what dear Mr. Delphick had expected — they were personal impressions, personal to herself, she meant, which Bob must make sure the chief superintendent understood, because the retainer which the police paid was so very generous — of course one could not refuse — it was nothing more than her duty to let them see her work if they asked, but . . .

"I wouldn't say there's much wrong with these," said Bob, as he opened the portfolio for a quick peek. "Would you, Anne?" Leave it to the Oracle, of course, to make sense of the sketches: he seemed to talk the same language as MissEss — well, perhaps not that exactly, nobody could, but he did seem better than most at working out what she was really getting at, in the end. The end, of course, could sometimes be a long while coming . . .

"He'll be delighted to have them, honestly," he assured Miss Seeton, who looked as if she might be about to ask for them back, given sufficient encouragement. Anne hurried to admire the drawings, then changed the subject by asking how Miss Seeton had found the north light.

Miss Seeton had found it excellent. And such a charming room — the view — such elegant velvet curtains, and the lace — the beautiful brocade of the canopy, too —

"Don't remind me," groaned Bob. "My back's never going to be the same again. Thank goodness I'm heading home to London tonight — or rather, thank *you*, Aunt Em, for coming up trumps, though we knew you would, because you always do. And this time you've made my day. Not that I want to leave you and Anne, of course, but it's all in a good cause. I'll kill two birds with one stone — take your drawings to Delphick at the Yard, and make sure of a decent night's kip first — and it isn't funny," he said to Anne, who had giggled. "A bloke my size needs room to breathe when he's asleep."

"Blame it all on the government," Anne replied promptly. "Good wholesome food, decent drains, and the National Health Service — what else can you expect? Just remember that most people's ancestors were weedy little specimens who lost all their teeth by thirty, and were probably dead of bubonic plague or smallpox five minutes later. Be thankful for the twentieth century!"

As Bob grinned, Miss Seeton said: "Perhaps a great number, but surely not *most,* Anne dear, if you will excuse me — dying so young, I mean, when one considers the evidence. There were so many, remember, and of various ages, as well. Some may have been the same people, of course, throughout their lives, but certainly not all — the costumes, you see — and, although indeed some appeared rather unhealthy, no doubt that could be the fault of the varnish. Because it is most unlikely one would be prepared to sit when ailing or, indeed, dead. For one's portrait. Except in wax, that is, although I believe she had no choice, any more than the poor unfortunates who had been guillotined — Madame Tussaud, such a distressing occupation, so many of them so young. But the Bremeridges do seem to have lived to ripe old ages in many instances — just as, indeed, one may observe in others, and not necessarily aristocratic.

Tombstones," said Miss Seeton earnestly, "as well as vaults, and marble plaques — although one cannot deny, of course, that there were a great many who had nothing — but even in the humblest parish church . . ."

As one of her sketches had obviously been influenced by the Belton portrait gallery, Bob and Anne nodded as she drifted to a confused halt, and murmured (without committing themselves) that they supposed she was right. Then Anne became brisk.

"If you're going to catch that train, you'd better check you've packed everything while I fetch the car. Coming for the ride, Aunt Em? We could do a quick tour to admire the evening scenery once I've dropped Bob off, if you like."

After Bob had been duly dispatched on the London-bound train, Anne and Miss Seeton headed for the countryside and their scenic tour. There were no breathtaking views around Belton: no soaring mountains, no precipitous cliffs, no pine forests dark with whispers, no spreading oaks which had been spared the shipwright's axe. Instead, there were rolling hills, woods and spinneys and well-hedged fields, sheep and cattle grazing on pastureland, haystacks and stooks from the arable harvest. It was typically English, and Miss Seeton's fingers longed to capture it all on canvas.

Although she enjoyed the scenery, Anne was more taken with the villages through which they drove. She earmarked one or two junk shops which looked promising, and a cottage for sale which, she said, she'd buy like a shot if she and Bob had the money. "It's really rather a shame that Sibyl Crockerton never existed, isn't it? Mel Forby's done such a good job, I've almost come to believe in the auction myself — but then, if things go according to plan, we'll never know how much the painting's worth, because Croesus will have had a go at it, and been nobbled, and it'll be back over your fireplace with no harm done."

Miss Seeton smiled, but was silent. One understood, of course, that such deception was necessary — but it had all seemed so, well, so unreal at first, as if it were a joke — and now, with dear Mel's story in the news-papers, and Anne's photograph, although she did not appear to mind . . . it was hardly a speaking likeness, which was fortunate (Miss Seeton had no idea of how hard they'd tried to make lucky little Mrs. Ranger look ordinary) — but dear Anne was the wife of a policeman, and any serving offi-cer's wife must, of course, expect to be called upon to do her duty — just as she herself was proud to do, of course, even though her sketches were really not . . .

Miss Seeton sighed. Anne said at once: "Tired or hungry — or both? Both, probably, because I know I am. We'll get back to the hotel and have something to eat, and then, well, I noticed it's *Wuthering Heights* on television this evening. I don't know if you'd be interested, but . . ."

Miss Seeton was. Merle Oberon, so strikingly lovely — Laurence Olivier, so handsome and vital — dear David Niven, whom one admired for being so very English . . . Emily Brontë had written a masterpiece; she remembered going to the cinema to see the film when it first came out in London, and being so impressed by its power. She had always urged her girls, when it was their set book at school, that they could do far worse than use it — the film, that was — as the basis for their painting, although few had ever succeeded in capturing the spirit of the original — but there had been, she thought, several whose imaginations, which she had tried so hard to stimulate, had finally been released by *Wuthering Heights* . . . such a sad, romantic story . . .

She and Anne sat in the residents' lounge and watched in tearful delight as Cathy breathed her last in the huge bed, and

Heathcliff swept her up in his arms to show her the moor where they had run free as children, the curtain stirring in the wind. Miss Seeton blew her nose as the ghosts walked together before the final credits, and Anne cleared her throat with vigour. Miss Seeton, above the theme music for the Nine O'Clock News, collected herself sternly and said:

"Of course, if any of one's class had behaved in so very wayward a fashion . . . children, after all, need discipline — but . . . It is a great book," said Miss Seeton simply, "and a most enjoyable film." She brightened. "So very well made — such attention to detail. The costumes, the setting — even the furniture . . ."

"Including the four-poster bed," supplied Anne, with a smile, and in a tone low enough not to disturb the other residents. "I've been thinking about that, Aunt Em. Now that Bob's not here — and of course he didn't really use it, in the circumstances — how would you like to swap rooms? Your chance to sleep in a piece of genuine history — and," she added, as Miss Seeton's obvious pleasure at the offer was swiftly suppressed under a cloak of heroic self-denial, "it would stop me missing him so much if I was in a different room, you see. Do say you will," she begged, trying to look like a love-lorn bride. And Miss Seeton, who could only suspect that Anne was acting, gladly allowed herself to be persuaded.

". . . Brettenden, in Kent," came the newscaster's voice. The Kentish exiles at once turned their attentions back to the television screen, which showed the front aspect of the biscuit factory, with a figure wearing a beret, a beard, and a smock posing glumly beside the empty plinth. The camera closed in on the figure's face as the voice continued: "The sculptor Humphrey Marsh is angry that police seem reluctant to carry out any serious search for his stolen masterpiece, *Food Chain*." A brief still of the sculpture (which to Miss Seeton's eyes resembled, more than ever, two angry bicycles) was shown, and then Humphrey Marsh appeared.

"I think it's utterly disgraceful that so many works of art have been disappearing from sites throughout Europe for so long. Everyone, except the police, agrees the thefts are being organised on behalf of this man they call Croesus, yet nobody is *doing* anything. And I'd like to know why. Either the police are simply a bunch of Philistines who don't care about Art" — the capital was evident from the way he paused — "or, one can't help it, there has to be a suspicion of something more serious than plain inefficiency. *Food Chain* is irreplaceable — and priceless. It won three awards. The critics say it's in a direct line of spiritual descent from the genius of Marcel Duchamp" — Miss Seeton uttered a little squeak as she recognised her bicycle vision had been correct — "and certain of the Bauhaus Movement, though naturally one has developed one's own unique style." He tried not to, but he smirked as he went on, "And for a work that is generally accepted as a masterpiece to go missing like this — and for nobody with the power to do anything seeming to care — well, I'd very much like to know whether anyone might have been *persuaded* not to care, that's all." His eyes glittered out of the screen at an audience of millions, and the invisible newscaster concluded:

"Fighting talk from sculptor Humphrey Marsh. We asked Scotland Yard's Art Squad to comment on these controversial suggestions, but a spokesman declined our offer. Next, the Test Match . . ."

Anne was fuming as she and Miss Seeton left the others to watch highlights of the day's cricket. She talked of boiling oil, and the overworked police, and the ungrateful public; then she stopped as suddenly as she had started, and laughed. "This is doing my blood pressure no good at all! Mind you, I bet I'm not the only one seething. The Oracle and his chums are sure to be hopping mad as well, and you can't blame them. Fancy that ghastly Marsh creature insinuating that someone's been getting a backhander! As if anyone in their right mind could possibly want that ugly mess of scrap metal, and as for paying for it . . ." She looked at Miss Seeton, and grinned. "You're the expert, Aunt Em. Is it really great art, as he was making out, or am I right in thinking it simply escaped from a junkyard and rusted to death outside the factory when it stopped rolling? Doesn't it remind you of a fight between two bicycles?"

Miss Seeton was pondering her reply — she wished to be truthful, but one had to be fair-minded at the same time, which in the circumstances would be, well, difficult — when there came a discreet cough from a nearby throat. A tall, dark, stately stranger appeared from behind a potted palm. He looked vaguely familiar. As he drew near the two women, he inclined his head slightly.

"Excuse me, but am I correct in assuming that you are Miss Seeton — Miss Emily Seeton?"

Anne rushed in before Miss Seeton could

admit that she was. The two of them were, after all, supposed to be here more or less incognito. "I'm Anne — Knight," she amended, "and my aunt and I are here on holiday, looking for peace and quiet and privacy. If you'll excuse us . . ."

The stranger smiled, and spoke very low, although there seemed no risk of their being overheard. "I merely wished to establish my, er, cover, if such a term is not considered melodramatic. My dear Mrs. Ranger, I know very well who you are — both of you. Quite apart from the fact that there is an efficient registration system in this hotel, I observed you, and your husband, and, er, your aunt together at the Abbey only this morning" — of course, the man in the hall who'd looked so pleased to see them join the guided tour — "and, moreover, recently became acquainted with Detective Sergeant Ranger at New Scotland Yard, on the occasion of my consulting Chief Superintendent Delphick. One of them may have mentioned the matter to you. My name," with another bow, "is Faulkbourne: I am steward to His Grace the Duke of Belton. And you are, are you not, Miss Seeton?"

"I am," she confirmed, with a worried smile: should one, or should one not, shake hands? One did not, she felt sure, when introduced in the house — but they were in the Arms, not the Abbey — but that might still be regarded as Belton territory — but Faulkbourne could be here in a private capacity, which meant that one perhaps should . . .

Faulkbourne spared her any further worry by indicating a secluded group of easy chairs, and suggesting that all three of them might sit down. Miss Seeton hesitated, but Anne had no doubts. Bob, with Delphick's permission, had indeed told her something of Faulkbourne's visit to the Yard, and how he had asked for Miss Seeton's help, even if Miss Seeton herself had no real idea of the exact purpose behind her little holiday. She'd been told that a few sketches, if she could manage them, would be appreciated, but it had seemed better — as it always did — not to confuse her by explaining in too much detail.

Because, *confusion* was sometimes a definite understatement of what happened when Miss Seeton became involved in a case . . .

chapter
15

When they had all settled themselves, Faulkbourne enquired of Miss Seeton, with a degree of emphasis, whether she had found her visit to the Abbey of any interest. Miss Seeton assured him that she had. Such a beautiful setting, was it not? And so very historical — so many interesting facts, and the guide so knowledgeable and amusing — which was only to be expected, in the circumstances . . .

"Oh, yes," she said, her eyes twinkling at his start of surprise: or at what in another less stately would have been a start, but in Faulkbourne, steward to His Grace the Duke of Belton, was the raising of his eyebrows by a fraction of an inch. "Oh, yes, there could be no doubt, of course, when one had seen so many ancestral portraits. Heredity can be a remarkably persistent influence, Mr. Faulkbourne. The eye sockets, almost unique — and the structure of the nose, even if the colouring is quite different. But no doubt at all. He was obviously enjoying himself a great deal — just like

Nigel," she added, with a nod to Anne. "Don't you think they share a similar sense of fun? Playing tricks — not that I know of Nigel's ever pretending to be someone he was not, but one can easily imagine them both laughing about it afterwards — and when he was offered the tip, and accepted it, one knew for certain, of course, because that is exactly what dear Nigel would do, and tell everyone about it once the person who had given it was gone, for fear of hurting their feelings. Nigel is, you see," she explained to Faulkbourne, "a very kind and considerate young man."

"As is Master Eddie," replied Faulkbourne. "I beg his pardon, Lord Edgar. One finds it hard to reconcile oneself to the thought that he is no longer a harum-scarum youngster — an inevitable reluctance to acknowledge the passage of years, no doubt. When one remembers him and his brother as urchin schoolboys . . . But those years have indeed passed. His lordship was deemed by his parents capable of caring for the Abbey during their absence — as one feels confident that he would be, in more normal circumstances. The circumstances, however, are far from normal, are they not?"

"Are they?" Miss Seeton blinked. "Or

rather, that is to say — aren't they? My understanding of such matters is very limited, but I would have said that it was being run most efficiently, from the little I could observe as we toured it — the Abbey, I mean, or at least that is the impression with which one came away. That it was running very well. Which, after being open to the public for some years, is what one would expect — and you yourself must have learned a great deal in that time, Mr. Faulkbourne. I feel sure that in you Lord Edgar has a helpful and sympathetic friend on whom he could call, should the need arise."

Faulkbourne regarded her shrewdly. "I have done my best to advise him, but the young — I speak in confidence, Miss Seeton — can be very headstrong, I fear. His lordship is . . . not easily advised. The Bremeridges are noted for their high and haughty spirit, Miss Seeton. To employ an equine metaphor, they prefer the freedom of the range to the discipline of bit and bridle. Lord Edgar listens, but takes no notice — and says nothing in return, or certainly not to myself. But did he, perhaps, speak to you at some time while you were at the house?"

"To me? Certainly not. Why should he? I beg your pardon," said Miss Seeton, a gentle flush staining her cheeks, "but there were others present besides myself, and I cannot see why Lord Edgar should single out a complete stranger in whom to confide — and, indeed, it would be rather foolish of him to do so. As I explained, I have little knowledge of running a stately home — none at all, in fact."

Faulkbourne had looked puzzled as she began her denial, then smiled with relief. "Others present — of course, Miss Seeton, I completely understand. The need for discretion — in my natural anxiety, I have been perhaps careless." He glanced around the reception area. At one or two of the low tables, enjoying a quiet chat, a few groups of people were sitting. "Privacy, Miss Seeton, or should one say security, must be maintained."

"Oh, yes, indeed." Miss Seeton nodded. Her privacy, as that of any gentlewoman, had always been important to her — although why Mr. Faulkbourne should speak of *security*, when it was the Abbey which had suffered such a daring robbery — "Oh, yes — but mine was blown up by lightning recently, and I confess that I have been rather remiss in having it repaired. So much more peaceful, you understand. Bells and alarms whenever one forgot to turn the key — and the chief constable only intended it as a . . . a guinea-pig, I believe, or do I mean market research? For those with property of some value, such as yourself — I beg your pardon, His Grace — I would certainly recommend one, but I'm afraid I cannot even recall the name of the firm who installed it. It must have been two or three years ago, you see."

Faulkbourne wasn't entirely sure that he did, though he saw enough to realise that Miss Seeton, as he ought to have realised from everything the newspapers said about her, had her own way of doing things. He was certainly learning the truth of that . . . Obviously, she intended to keep her own counsel — or, rather, Scotland Yard's, he supposed he should consider it. His visit might have prompted them to act, but in the end they must be regarded as the ones responsible for her presence here now. It might be a breach of etiquette for her to reveal what, if anything, she had found out, even to one who, over the years, had been proud to acknowledge himself the confidant and, indeed, the friend of his ducal employer. But Lord Edgar was not His Grace — and His Grace was far from home . . .

"These are difficult times for the Bremeridges — for all of us on the Belton estate, Miss Seeton," he said, and could not suppress a sigh. Perhaps it sounded theatrical: perhaps it did not matter. He must try his best to make her understand. "The Abbey, as you have observed, is an historic and beautiful place, but such places are, regrettably, expensive to maintain. Funds, I fear, are low. Much of the capital is tied up in the property, which is entailed to the eldest son — and Lord Pelsall, whom I still think of as Master Ivo, I fear" — with a rueful smile — "is far away from home at present, mountaineering in the Andes with his father . . ."

Miss Seeton wasn't sure how she was supposed to reply to this. One's acquaintance with mountains was (apart from the films, television, and of course paintings one had seen over the years) limited to the trip she had taken when (and Miss Seeton blushed at the memory) she had flown by mistake to Genoa, in Italy, instead of Geneva, in Switzerland. She had arrived in the right place eventually, of course, and remembered that she had crossed the Alps somewhere along the way — but crossed them by air, or perhaps one should more accurately say *passed over*, except that this term could so easily be open to misinterpretation . . .

"From an aeroplane," said Miss Seeton, rather sternly, "one really cannot be expected to gain any detailed knowledge of mountains, except that they invariably seem to be covered with snow. And, in my opinion, it is far better to entrust these matters to one's bank manager — investments," she explained, as Faulkbourne's eyebrows looked startled again. "My dishwasher and automatic washing machine, for instance, so very useful. Martha was delighted. One saves so much time — but as for saving *money,* or rather making any more, I regret that I am quite unable to suggest anything — I retired from teaching, you see, some time ago. My bank manager recommended it — that is to say, when he advised me to invest, I felt it sensible to expend a certain sum on labour-saving devices before investing the remainder — one's pension, of course, as well as the retainer fee from Scotland Yard." Really, one found it awkward to discuss finance when one was hardly an expert. In happier times, money had been considered one of the topics which no gentlewoman ought to mention — but times, although still happy (indeed, one might even say they were happier since one had been living in Plummergen) were very different. If Mr. Faulkbourne had come especially to ask for advice, it might be thought rude to dismiss his anxieties out of hand, although one must certainly make it plain that one was unable to help. Which it seemed that he had understood, for there appeared to be what one might call a smile in his eyes . . .

Faulkbourne heard Miss Seeton's use of the Scotland Yard name with resignation. She was being very polite about it, as might be expected, but she was making it absolutely plain that, so far as she was concerned, she would be dealing only with the police. Which was understandable, of course, even if one had hoped to persuade her otherwise . . .

Miss Seeton, still feeling somewhat guilty at dispossessing dear Anne from her room, nevertheless felt sure she would relish every minute of her night's repose in that glorious four-poster bed. She cleaned her teeth, closed her eyes, and coiled herself down to the floor into one of her most relaxing yoga postures, revelling in the luxury of the carpet, and the lace, and the age-dark timbers. She climbed at last into bed — and one did indeed have to climb, so thickly was the mattress feathered — and cuddled down beneath the embroidered counterpane. Had it, she wondered, been made for this very bed when it was first built? And when might that have been? How many generations of Bremeridge (ought one, perhaps, to say Belton? One did one's best to observe the courtesies, but it really was a trifle confusing) dependents — or did one mean vassals, or villeins — or would *followers* do? — had been born in it; or (and Miss Seeton sighed) spent their married lives in it? Poor dear Anne. How generous of her to humour one's little fancies, though one was far from being one of the silk-clad beauties so often portrayed on the cinema screen. Rather impractical, nowadays, of course, when it seemed that laundry maids were as out of date as gentlemen who fought duels, or took snuff — and it needed so much care, or so one had been led to believe. Silk, that was to say, although one could only be glad of such modern conveniences as automatic washing machines . . . the romance, mused Miss Seeton, had somehow gone from so many aspects of life, even if it had been, from what one had read, rather a dangerous pastime, and hardly romantic, in the true sense of the word, at all. Fighting duels, not taking snuff . . .

Miss Seeton closed her eyes, and drifted off into dreams of duelling gallants with ruffles at their wrists, pistols in their hands, and snuff-stained nostrils which flared in fury at honour impugned or character maligned. She dreamed of crinolines . . . and sedan chairs . . . or was that from an earlier age? . . . and black-browed young men with rapiers, and masked highway robbers . . .

Miss Seeton slept. And woke, with a smile on her lips, and stretched luxuriously under the heavy brocade canopy of the four-poster bed. Dear Anne. How very kind. But enough was most certainly enough — she must not repay that kindness by wasting time. She hopped out of bed, resolving to banish all visions from her mind's eye by the calming influence of her yoga routine. While a reasonable amount of daydreaming did no harm, and indeed could be regarded as beneficial to one's imagination, too much (she reminded herself) was an indication of weakness of will — and, moreover, might in the circumstances be viewed as extremely selfish. Hadn't she agreed last night to go sightseeing today with dear Anne on a little tour of all those secondhand shops into which she longed to look? Married life, reflected Miss Seeton as she closed her eyes and began her rhythmic breathing, seemed to be an expensive matter. Especially when one had not been married very long, and was still settling into one's new home. She herself had been so fortunate, with her little inheritance from Cousin Flora, and in her financial affairs generally (the retainer from the police, so very useful) — even if she had been unable to advise Mr. Faulkbourne as he had appeared to wish — that it was not only her clear duty, but also a true pleasure, to help those of whom she was fond to save as much money as they could. If one could.

One could not, of course, offer detailed advice about savings accounts, as one had tried to make clear to His Grace's steward, except that it was a good idea to have one — a savings account, that was to say, not a steward. Unless of course one had a large house, which must need many servants to take care of it — which one would only have, surely, if one could afford them. Yet Mr. Faulkbourne had said that he and his family (the Bremeridges, or did she mean the Beltons?) — the duke, not Mr. Faulkbourne — were also short of money. One doubted, however, whether he would care to be considered a servant, any more than Martha would — Mr. Faulkbourne, not the duke. She had been so pleased about the washing machine, dear Martha . . . twin-tubs and washboards and old-fashioned coppers, mangles, and soap suds and aching backs . . . One wondered how many laundry maids would have been required by a household the size of the Abbey . . .

Miss Seeton had a sudden vision of the Belton portrait gallery, that long line of faces characterised by their remarkable eye sockets and the distinctive structure of their noses, all demanding clean clothes at exactly the same time; and of a laundry maid who looked very much like Martha, with a wooden stirring stick in her hand which she brandished at these thoughtless aristocrats, ordering them to wait their turn. Miss Seeton smiled. How very like dear Martha that would be, to stand no nonsense. The faces thought so, too: they flickered, and faded, and merged into one face — that of the smiling young Lord Edgar Bremeridge, who'd had such fun pretending to be an ordinary guide, enjoying his little joke at the expense of the Abbey's guests . . .

When Miss Seeton had completed her yoga practice, she glanced at her little travelling clock in sudden realisation and dismay. Had she truly spent so long in idle reverie? How late she was going to be! Dear Anne, of course, would utter not one word of blame, but this had indeed been a selfish way in which to repay her kindness. Miss Seeton jumped nimbly to her feet, completed her toilet, and hurried from the room, resolving to leave the Bremeridges behind her.

And she was so sure she had done this, their distinctive features dismissed to the limbo of her imagination, that, as she trotted across Reception towards the dining room and breakfast, she was decidedly startled to observe, talking to Anne near the doorway, an unmistakable Bremeridge.

chapter 16

"Good gracious." Miss Seeton stopped dead in her tracks, and stared. She shook her head, blinked, and then smiled. "Oh, dear, how very foolish of me — you're real, of course." The Bremeridge eyes, in those distinctive sockets, widened, looking startled in their turn. "That is," went on Miss Seeton, "I do beg your pardon, Lord Edgar, but I was only thinking just now . . . and coincidences, of course, occur in real life much more often than one would ever accept in fiction — but it was so vivid, you see. Your face . . ."

"My face," he repeated, as she drew near. "My face! So *that* was what . . ." His startled expression turned to one of sudden relief. "Yes, I suppose there would be absolutely no point in trying to deny that I was Lord Edgar Bremeridge," and he bowed, "at your service, would there?"

"None at all." Miss Seeton twinkled up at him. Such a charming smile, and so like dear Nigel. "Once we had come to the portraits, there could really be no doubt — so strong a resemblance, you see, especially the sockets and the nose — although I had begun to wonder about you earlier, if you will forgive my saying so."

Lord Edgar raised aristocratic brows. "Indeed? Didn't my little impersonation of a tour guide persuade you that I was the genuine article? You have quite cast me down, Miss Seeton. Until now, I confess, I've been taking considerable pride in my histrionic abilities."

"Oh, you were most convincing," she said at once. "Yet perhaps too much so, if you will excuse me, for an utterly credible performance. You seemed to be very much at home, you see, and somehow . . . well, you were rather more at home than one would have expected of an ordinary guide — though of course logically one should expect it, because you were. At home, I mean — unlike the rest of your family, whom one gathers are in South America. Which reminded me so vividly of a young friend of mine, Nigel Colveden — not that he has ever gone mountaineering in Brazil, you understand, or at least not as far as I know but like you he has a lively sense of fun. He would, I believe, enjoy playing a similar sort of joke, by pulling the wool over everyone's eyes — and then, of course, you accepted the tip, which I feel reasonably sure an ordinary guide would never do."

He bowed again. "Very shrewd, Miss Seeton — and allow me to point out that your *ordinary guide* would probably ask more for an afternoon's guiding than we could afford to pay. Family does it for nothing, Miss Seeton — forgive me," he added hastily, "for making so free with your name, but I couldn't help wondering yesterday when I spotted your umbrella . . . Faulkbourne has mentioned you a few times recently, you see, in connection with, well, our little difficulties, past and present. Naturally, as soon as my suspicions were aroused, I had to ask him about you to find out if my guess was correct. I'm delighted to make your acquaintance, Miss Seeton. Mrs. Ranger, of course, was with you on your tour, wasn't she? I recognised her just now as she came down the stairs — I was waiting for the receptionist to put in an appearance, but Mrs. Ranger was an even more welcome sight, I assure you. I'd intended asking Beverley to telephone your room so that I could introduce myself properly, but between you you've saved me the trouble."

Miss Seeton glanced at her wristwatch, then at Anne. "Oh dear, am I very late? Have I kept you waiting for your breakfast? I am so sorry, but —"

"You're not, and you haven't, so don't worry," Anne said quickly, "which is what I was explaining to Lord Edgar just now. I wondered whether he'd like to join us, if you didn't mind discussing — well, I suppose you'd call it *business,* while we were eating. I thought it might, well, save time," and she laughed, and turned slightly pink, as Miss Seeton's eyes twinkled at her.

But almost at once the twinkle changed to a frown. How could she have forgotten that dear Anne had wished to spend the day combing secondhand shops for bargains? Naturally, she was eager to be on her way. And by her thoughtlessness she had delayed her — although, of course, if she had *not* delayed her, they might have been gone before his lordship arrived, which would have seemed rather impolite, one supposed, as he had taken the trouble to come to the hotel to look for them — except, of course, that the attractions of Beverley would surely count for more with him than those of herself, an elderly spinster, and Anne, who was so happily married — and so, well, not poor, but certainly in need of every bargain she could find . . .

"Do please join us, Lord Edgar," invited Miss Seeton in her politest tones. "That is — unless you have breakfasted already? I believe that normally, by this hour, Nigel would be enjoying a coffee break, rather than his breakfast — but then he is a working farmer — not, of course, that I would wish to imply . . ." In a flutter of embarrassment, she broke off. One hardly cared to question the aristocracy, even obliquely, about their eating (or indeed their working) habits; but Lord Edgar did not seem to find it an impertinence. He smiled his charming smile, and bowed again.

"It will be a pleasure to escort you two ladies into the dining room, even if, as Miss Seeton suggests, I only have a cup of coffee, to be sociable. After all, my reason for coming to see you was to be sociable — or perhaps I should say welcoming. In the absence of my parents and brother, it falls to me to thank you, Miss Seeton, for your services to my family in the past, and to offer you every assistance for the future." Miss Seeton smiled politely, and favoured him with an uncertain look.

"A more detailed tour of the Abbey, perhaps," said Lord Edgar, "if you feel it would be any help — and the freedom of the grounds, of course. That goes without saying. Mind you," and he chuckled, "considering my family's parlous financial state,

I think, if you don't mind, that I won't go so far as to offer a refund of yesterday's entrance fee. And I only hope, talking of fees, Miss Seeton, that your charges aren't astronomically high. We Bremeridges are pretty broke, you know."

Fees? The retainer from the police was most generous, though one would hardly describe it as astronomically high — but really, there were limits to what ought to be discussed in public, especially with strangers, as one would have expected Lord Edgar to understand without having to be reminded. Particularly as it seemed that he had been speaking to his steward, or perhaps one should say his father's steward, and she thought she had made it very clear . . . although one could hardly appear rude, of course, in refusing . . .

"Oh dear, this is all very — That is, I have already explained to Mr. Faulkbourne that I understand almost nothing of financial matters, Lord Edgar —"

"Eddie, please." As he offered her his arm, he patted her gently on the hand. "Please don't look so worried, Miss Seeton — honestly, I'm harmless. Just behave as if I'm your young friend Nigel. He'd want you to enjoy your breakfast, I'm sure — well, so do I. If you'd rather wait — if you'd prefer not to talk this over now . . ."

Miss Seeton glanced doubtfully at Anne. "I would prefer not to waste any more time," she said, after a pause. Eddie nodded, and looked pleased. Anne, who had remained silent, gave Miss Seeton a reassuring smile.

"You don't really mind, do you, Aunt Em? I don't think Bob would mind, if that's what's worrying you. Bob's my husband," she explained. Eddie nodded again.

"The large young man escorting you both yesterday. Dear me, is he the jealous type? Tell him my intentions are entirely honourable. Which reminds me — isn't he joining you for breakfast?"

"He had to go back to London last night," said Anne, "though he hopes to be with us again soon. You know how it is — come to think of it, I suppose you don't — but there are times when you can't leave your business for too long." She was careful not to specify the nature of the "business": it never hurt to err on the side of caution. They were here incognito, after all. Lord Edgar might know who they were, or rather who Miss Seeton was — his steward knew, and others might guess — but it seemed sensible to go on trying to keep things quiet, even though (and Anne sighed with resignation) it could well be a waste of time. In a village, as any inhabitant of Plummergen (Miss Seeton excepted, of course) would testify, walls didn't so much have ears as full-blown radio-telescopic sensors. The Battling Brolly might be staying in Belton on holiday, but let one hint that the wife of a serving policeman was with her, and goodness knew what would happen. It was up to that wife to do her best to maintain at least the semblance of normality . . .

"Oh, but I do know, only too well," replied Lord Edgar, as they made their way into the dining room. "Or, rather, I know the other side of the coin. When you live right on top of the job, like us, you sometimes wish you could leave it for a while — at least, the other members of my family wish they could. Which, of course, they do. The notorious backpacking Bremeridges! I'm very much the black sheep of the family," he added, drawing out Miss Seeton's chair for her. "If not an out-and-out heretic. When I was younger — gosh, that sounds silly, doesn't it?" He caught Miss Seeton's eye, and grinned. "Actually, I'm not twenty-three yet, but when I was what I'll call a stripling I was forever being dragged up mountains and down potholes and across torrential rivers by one or other of my relatives — and I loathed every minute of it. I'm the home-loving type. I'd far rather potter around the Abbey grounds than swarm up the Matterhorn with an ice axe, a rope, and a cylinder of oxygen! Believe me, the day I came of age I made it quite clear that I never wanted to see a glacier or a cave full of stalactites or a precipice ever again — except, of course, on television."

"Such dramatic scenery," murmured Miss Seeton, as the waitress brought their menus. "And so rewarding to paint, although one would hardly suppose, Lord Edgar, that you had either the time or the inclination to carry a sketchbook with you. But I remember that when I was in Switzerland . . . although, now that I come to think of it, that was not the Matterhorn, but Mont Blanc. I found it so interesting that, from an aeroplane, the snow one sees is not snow, but clouds — while the snow is rather more like whitewash. Or cotton wool, of course — the clouds, I mean. One's eyes can play strange tricks, can they not?"

He flinched, then chuckled. "When you're camping in a blizzard halfway up a cliff, you have neither the time nor the inclination, believe me, to look for optical illusions. Sorry if that sounds rude, but . . ."

"Dear me, no, I do understand." Miss Seeton nodded, and smiled. "That there would be no time to look for them, that is — but then, would there be any need to look? Surely the point of such illusions is that they come, well, unbidden — like a mirage in the desert."

"Ah, now deserts," said Eddie, "are about the only horrible sort of place I was never forced to visit in my youth. Too hot for my family, all that sand and sun and waterless waste — and I'm unlikely to take myself off to one now, I assure you. England is good enough for me."

This was said with great firmness: a firmness which some might have called arrogant. Anne, who had fond memories of foreign parts because she'd spent her honeymoon in France, was about to say something, but refrained. Miss Seeton, however, that gently stern educationist, shook her head at him, and smiled.

"Do forgive my saying so, Lord Edgar, but you are still very young, and although I know the young are noted for the intensity of their views, one should always be alert to the risk of becoming not so much intense as *inflexible*. Surely it would be a great pity if one's earliest experiences of life were permitted to, well, to colour one's actions and attitudes in perpetuity, without any willingness to adapt — because one would miss so much, you see — or rather, one wouldn't. That is, *you* wouldn't — see, I mean. Clearly. Although sometimes, of course, one has to acknowledge the complete success of an optical illusion," she added earnestly. "Like Scarlett O'Hara's eyes, for instance, which are perhaps not the most obvious example, but are described more than once as pale green, yet she was renowned for her beautiful *blue* eyes. In the book. And so they had to be shot with a yellow spotlight in close-up — Vivien Leigh, that is, in the film. Which, naturally, coloured the whole scene, of course, although so skillfully that one hardly noticed it, as I recall — but it was, I thought, a most ingenious solution to the problem. And ingenuity, after all, is merely another way of saying *adapting to circumstances* — which is what we have been considering, is it not?"

"Is it?" murmured Lord Edgar, adding quickly, as he saw Anne's frown: "You're absolutely right, Miss Seeton, and you have a remarkable gift for explaining things." She could take that as she chose . . . "I promise I'll try to be more . . . adaptable, in future. Perhaps my view of life *is* a little narrow — but I blame my parents, of course." He smiled, and shrugged. "That's the fashionable medical view, isn't it? We're not to be held responsible, because we aren't, if I've understood it correctly."

Anne, daughter of a doctor and herself a nurse, couldn't help muttering at this, but Lord Edgar ignored her. He was gazing at Miss Seeton with great interest, his eyes bright. And Miss Seeton, who had heard his words and felt at first dismayed — trying to avoid one's responsibilities was surely neither more nor less than dereliction of duty, which was not what one expected of the aristocracy — suddenly smiled. How like dear Nigel. So very mischievous . . . She frowned again. Perhaps here there was rather more intention to shock. Indeed, when one considered the matter, there was, because Nigel's sense of fun was invariably amusing and, one could say, harmless, whereas his lordship's parents, among others, might think his attitude a trifle harsh, not to say unfair, even though of course they must know he was only joking — if, as one might say, a little thoughtlessly. Children were generally supposed to grow out of the more cruel phase of humour long before they reached Lord Edgar's age, but there were always, as one knew from one's years of teaching, exceptions to every rule . . .

As he observed Miss Seeton's concluding nod, Lord Edgar nodded back, and said cheerfully: "As I said, it's all due to my heredity. Generations of Bremeridges ducking their responsibilities by dashing off to canoe up the Amazon or hack their way through the jungle whenever things got tough at home — leaving other people to cope." He became serious. "I'm not the adventurous kind, remember. Which is why I'm . . . having this little spot of bother now." He glanced round quickly. The dining room of the Belton Arms was busy, but nobody had chosen a table too close for comfort. "The snuffboxes," he said, putting a warning finger to his lips. "I'm sure you understand me. What do you suggest I should do, Miss Seeton? Have you come up with any ideas?"

chapter
17

Anne emerged from what was now her room, and tapped lightly on what had become, over the last few days, Miss Seeton's door. Miss Seeton had been utterly captivated by the four-poster bed, and Anne certainly had no intention of spoiling her adopted aunt's fun by swapping back. With great success she applied the histrionic skills inherited from her father (who, dressed as a hippopotamus, had given a stirring rendition of "Mud" at the village concert), and managed to persuade Miss Seeton that the four-poster would remind her too much of Bob, who was still in London. Chief Superintendent Delphick had received strong indications that the nightclub protection racket was on the point of being resolved, and his sergeant's full-time presence had therefore become necessary.

"Is that you, Anne, dear? I am almost ready," came Miss Seeton's rather breathless voice from within. She had begun her relaxation from The Noose, but one should never, as the book made very plain, hurry one's movements in the advanced yoga postures. ". . . a little late today, I fear," came her muffled accents through the door. Anne called back:

"It doesn't matter — don't let me rush you, darling. If you like, I'll go on down and wait for you — Oh," as the door opened and Miss Seeton, a hurried dressing gown wrapped discreetly about her form, stood on the threshold.

"I'm so sorry —" they began together; stopped; and then laughed. Anne smiled for Miss Seeton to speak first; Miss Seeton tugged at the dressing-gown belt and looked anxious.

"It will be a matter of a few moments only before I am ready to join you, my dear. If it would not distress you too much to wait for me — that is, inside — dear Bob . . ." She motioned towards the four-poster bed. "Such a lovely room," she said, with the hint of a twinkle in her eye. She was almost, but not entirely, convinced that Anne had been acting when she claimed to be pining for her husband: she would miss him, of course, but was a kindhearted girl, and so fond of films, and realised that one was enjoying one's little taste of luxury — and as a nurse was surely much too sensible to pine. One could with confidence ask her to come inside to wait . . . she supposed. Miss Seeton

214

studied Anne's expression, and with relief observed a responding twinkle. She smiled, and opened the door wider.

Anne hesitated before entering, but took her seat in one of the deep armchairs, which seemed likely to engulf her tiny frame. "Look, Aunt Em, I don't want you to — Well, you've been coming out with me every day in the car, and I know you enjoy looking at the scenery and so on, but — Lord Edgar's offer. Are you really sure you don't want to take him up on it? The guidebook says the Abbey grounds are marvellous at this time of year, and you'd be bound to have a lovely time sketching and painting. He said you could go anywhere and do anything you liked, after all. It seems such a shame for you not to . . . well, for you to be stuck looking round secondhand shops with me, and sitting in a car half the time while we get to them. Don't think you'd hurt my feelings if you said you'd prefer to stay behind today — though I'd love you to come with me, of course," she added, in case Miss Seeton should suspect her of tactfully asking to be left alone for once. "It's always heaps more fun seeing the sights with someone else, isn't it? Someone to listen when you want to say *just look at that*, and then your artist's eye certainly comes in useful bargain hunting, too. But you mustn't miss your chance at the Belton landscape because of me."

Miss Seeton, doing up the final buttons on her blouse, shook her head. "His lordship was indeed most kind, was he not? *Noblesse oblige,* of course. But others besides the aristocracy understand such obligations," pointed out Miss Emily Dorothea Seeton, spinster gentlewoman, firmly. "It is my opinion that one should reciprocate by not taking advantage of such kindness, for it seems to me that I have really done nothing to deserve it. He did his best not to let it show — the disappointment, I mean, so thoughtful, and very much the way Nigel, I believe, would behave in similar circumstances, except that" — Miss Seeton turned slightly pink — "I think it unlikely one would be offered financial reward for merely doing one's duty. Only then, of course, he said he knew better, and wouldn't — but it was rather awkward, none the less. His mentioning a fee, even in passing. Or not, as I have done — one's duty, that is. By being unable to tell Lord Edgar anything about the snuffboxes — because it is, is it not, the constabulary who have first call on my services — so that even if I *could* tell his lordship anything, I doubt very much whether I *should.* Moreover, in this particular instance I would have supposed photographs to be of far more use than IdentiKit drawings, because they are really for faces, and though they were not mass produced in those days, as far as I know, one could never be certain that any would be sufficiently unusual to be unique, and by such means easy to identify. Especially with being so very small, for no doubt one would miss too many distinguishing details. Snuff boxes, that is. So if you would like me to accompany you again today, my dear, I assure you it will be a great pleasure."

An hour and twenty minutes later, having spent rather longer than they'd intended paying court to Orlando, the stately marmalade cat whose closer acquaintance they had been permitted to make on their second night at the hotel, Anne and Miss Seeton were bowling through the countryside in Anne's little car, with the windows down and a breeze on their faces, filling the air with the heavy scent of summer. Anne drove steadily, but not fast, around the narrow lanes, and above the engine's purr the clamour of birdsong, the lowing of cattle, and the bleating of sheep could be easily heard. Miss Seeton looked about her

217

with delight, revelling in each sight and sound and odour. So different from her dear Kentish landscape, but still so lovable, so English . . .

She sighed with happiness. Anne said at once: "Are you tired, Aunt Em, or bored? Do you want to stop at the next place we come to for a cup of tea or something?"

"Oh, please don't think that," cried Miss Seeton, afraid that she had somehow given dear Anne entirely the wrong impression. "There's no need at all to go to any such trouble on my account, truly. I am having a lovely time, and am not tired in the least. I was simply admiring the beauties of the scenery, and . . ."

Anne saw her hands dancing on her lap. She recognised the signs. "And you'd like to sketch the view? Why didn't you say so sooner? We can't stop just yet — there'd be no room for anyone to pass safely — but with luck there'll be a lay-by before too long. I'll park the car off the road, and you can set up your easel, if you like, and enjoy yourself while I stretch my legs. How would that be?"

Ignoring Miss Seeton's protests that really, she hadn't intended dear Anne to go to any bother on her account, Anne pulled into the lay-by which appeared a providential three minutes later, just past a minor crossroads, beside a giant beech. The car rolled into the welcome leafy shade, and Anne switched off the engine. "I'll get your things out of the boot," she said, and had darted round to the back of the car before Miss Seeton could say another word.

While Miss Seeton leaned her sketching block on the top of a five-barred gate and gazed at the scenery, Anne, true to her word, sauntered off to indulge in a little exploring. Miss Seeton would be perfectly happy for half an hour, at least; if she grew tired, or hungry, she could sit in the car and nibble chocolate biscuits. Anne told herself she probably would, and it was therefore up to her to replenish the stock by finding, if such a thing existed in the immediate neighbourhood, a village, with its concomitant shop — or, as it might be (a guilty giggle came bubbling up) shops. One of which might sell secondhand bargains . . .

If she hadn't lived for so long in Plummergen before her marriage, Anne might have expected a signpost at the crossroads, giving distances to the nearest signs of human habitation: but she'd grown wise in the years since her father's retirement, on health grounds, from his position as one of London's leading neurologists. The

Knights had arrived in Kent to have several cherished beliefs destroyed within a surprisingly short time. One had been that in the middle of the countryside, travellers might reasonably be supposed to want to know in what direction they were travelling. It had quickly become clear that anyone displaying such selfish needs would never be indulged by the locals. *They* knew where they were coming from, or going to, and how far that might be: why pander to the fancy notions of furriners, or encourage strangers to wander where they would? Dr. Knight diagnosed fifty percent of this reaction as due to rustic paranoia; and fifty percent to the fact that it wasn't yet thirty-five years since all the signposts had been removed for fear of invasion in 1940. It always took time to sort such matters out afterwards — and even when anyone made the effort to sort them, it was chancy to rely too much on the distances given. His prescribed formula was based on a multiplication by three and subsequent division by two, but he would add the rider that there were times when you had to apply the formula back-to-front, multiplying by two and dividing by three, because they didn't want you to feel complacent about having cracked it — and you could never tell when it might be one of those times . . .

So, even though she wouldn't have trusted one too much had she seen one, Anne saw no signpost. She saw, however, a five-barred gate, and climbed carefully up the hinged side to balance on the upper rail. She gazed in all directions: no village, or at least not for several miles. Oh, well, it was a nice day for a stroll, anyway. She went on for about a mile, and came to a stile, with a footpath sign pointing to Little Belton, supposedly three miles across the fields: too far, even if she believed it. She sat happily on the bottom step for a while, delighting in the warm summer near-silence, hoping Miss Seeton was finding it all half as much fun. She was drifting off into a daydream when she heard, approaching in the distance, the rattle of wheels accompanied by a wooden, creaking sound.

The pony and trap came trotting down the road towards her, harness jingling, hooves clip-clopping. The hooves belonged to a sturdy little chestnut with a shaggy mane, whose reins were held by a man every bit as brown and shock-headed as his pony; equally shock-headed was the large grey dog which sat beside the man, who, as he drew near Anne, with a fine flourish of his whip pulled the trap to a halt, and leaned across to smile a gap-toothed, leathery smile as he chanted:

"Enn yole dahn — rags, bols, bones?" Anne blinked at the traditional cry, uttered in a strange yodel, obviously intended to carry. Was it likely that anyone in the middle of nowhere, as she was, would have a ready supply of scrap iron or empty bottles to sell? The weather-beaten man saw her surprise, and chuckled richly.

"Oh, pay no heed to me. I do nothing more than keep in practice for what people expect, that's all." His normal voice was a husky rumble, but perfectly articulate. "Today is a fine day for sharing laughter, is it not?"

"It certainly is." Anne returned his smile. "A lovely day all round, as far as I'm concerned, and I hope it's the same for you. Your trap looks pretty full — have you had much luck so far?"

"I don't complain." He flourished his whip once more, and the pony tossed its head. "Easy now, Bucephalus. Quiet you, Jasper," as the great lurcher at his side pricked up its ears. "Someone in the village back there has been minded to renovate a house, casting out the radiators for night storage heaters, and more besides. Not that I hold overmuch with electricity, mark you, but there's no accounting for taste — though it would never suit the likes of them to live as me and mine, to cook over an out-door fire and light the caravan with tallow dips. But there's the only real life, the freedom of the road." He glanced at her, and contrived to look wise. "Nothing and nowhere to tie you down, nobody telling you what to do — the sky for a roof in summer — the sun and the stars and the wind on the heath . . ."

"Life is very sweet," agreed Anne, with a straight face. After a startled moment, he laughed. Beneath the shaggy fringe his black eyes danced in his weathered face, and his white teeth flashed; even the dog Jasper twitched a knowing ear in sympathy with his master's mirth.

"You're a clever, well-read young lady, and if my woman was with me she'd tell you a good fortune, I know. But our camp's ten miles from here, and she busy cooking, and caring for the babes while we earn an honest penny, my brothers and me. Yet you're a long way from home too, aren't you?" The whip indicated the loneliness about them. "Lost, stolen, or strayed? Would the offer of a lift tempt you?"

"That's awfully kind — but it depends on where you were going. I wouldn't want to take you out of your way —"

"You talk like a fool," he broke in, and

flourished the whip with a crack. Bucephalus danced in his traces, and the dog Jasper uttered a sharp bark. "Steady, my friends. What was I saying a moment since about the freedom to go where I please? Step up now on the cart with me, and I'll carry you where you will — I'm in no rush to reach one place above another, so long as I'm home by nightfall and my cart filled with that which others don't want. Yet on a day like this, I'll put other people's wishes above other people's rubbish, and if you're wishful to be carried home . . ."

"My car's about a mile down that road," said Anne pointing, "in a lay-by. I left my aunt there admiring the scenery, while I went for a walk, and —"

"And you'll come back to her in style, in my cart. Not on Shanks's Pony, but pulled by the pony of Tawno Petulengro — if you will believe me," he added, showing his teeth in a grin. "Such a well-read young lady as you . . ."

And Anne's laughter mingled with his as she scrambled up beside the man who called himself Tawno Petulengro, and Bucephalus the chestnut pony trotted down the road towards the lay-by where Miss Seeton was sketching.

chapter
18

When Miss Seeton, perched on the trunk of a fallen tree, saw the totter's cart setting Anne down at the lay-by, she shut her sketchbook hurriedly and tucked it under her arm before crossing the field back to the car. By the time she reached the lay-by, Anne was alone.

She was standing by the closed boot of the car with a strange expression on her face. Miss Seeton said: "Have I kept you waiting, my dear? I'm so sorry, but I was enjoying the view — he sunlight on the beech leaves, so fresh and summery — and one cannot walk quickly across farmland, even when there is an adequate footpath."

"Waiting? Oh, no, I'm the one who's kept you waiting, and I hope you weren't too bored. But I was having rather a . . . an interesting little adventure, you see." Anne's gaze drifted down the road after the vanished pony and trap, then back to the boot of the car. She sighed, and shook her head. "Only now I can't help wondering . . ."

It wasn't like Anne to be indecisive. Miss Seeton's own thought processes were sometimes so incoherent that only she knew what she meant, but it always surprised her when anyone else displayed similar tendencies. She regarded Anne with an anxious eye. Going for a walk as the morning advanced — surely it couldn't be sunstroke? How would they make their way back to the hotel if dear Anne was unable to drive the car? "A pony and trap, I suppose," she murmured, and Anne's rueful chuckle made her jump.

"The pony's name is Bucephalus, and the driver called himself Tawno Petulengro, though I doubt if that's really his name. It's obvious that he's read George Borrow — you know, *The Romany Rye* — and worked up his patter into a pretty good line — he's certainly a persuasive salesman," as she gazed at the boot once more. "When I spotted it on the cart it seemed just the thing, but now . . ."

Miss Seeton quirked an eyebrow at her, and waited. Anne chuckled again. "I may as well show you — but you must promise not to laugh, Aunt Em. It seemed such a bargain at the time, and I was thinking of you anyway, which is why . . ."

She opened the boot, and Miss Seeton peered inside. Her eye was caught by something dark, patterned with flowers and gleaming. "Good gracious," she said, stretching out an exploratory hand. "That looks not unlike . . ."

"An umbrella stand, yes. Heaven knows why I bought it! Maybe thinking about you made me more receptive to the idea, when I realised how long I'd been gone and wondered if you minded, though you of all people don't need a papier-mâché umbrella stand. And nor do we! Bob put up a row of hooks for coats and macs, and neither of us has an umbrella, except the cheap collapsible sort. And this could hardly do duty as a coat stand, could it? But even if it's meant to be for umbrellas, I'll have to find something else I can use it for, or Bob will never let me forget it. I'm only thankful it isn't made out of an elephant's foot. He had such a gift of the gab, I think he could have talked me into buying something even that hideous."

"Good gracious," repeated Miss Seeton faintly. "You say it was a bargain, of course, so I suppose —"

"What's a bargain? Something you know you need before you find it, at a price you can afford when you do. Well, I won't say it was expensive, because it wasn't, but I really can't see that we need it. We'll have to tell Bob it's a . . . an unusual vase, for long-stemmed flowers, and I want to try my hand at arrangements or something. Unless," she said doubtfully, "you think it might come in useful for you . . ."

Miss Seeton regretted that she thought it would not, for all her umbrellas, as dear Anne knew, were clipped in a row in their rack on the wall, taking up as little room as possible in the hall of Sweetbriars. She really couldn't see that she had either the need, or the space, to put it, but if Anne thought Bob would be cross —

"Oh, no, he won't mind at all — I'm the one who's going to mind, and then only all the teasing. But, well, we're on holiday, aren't we? So why not a little extravagance, once in a while?" And she firmly closed the boot on her impulse buy, and changed the subject by asking to see what Miss Seeton had been sketching during her absence.

There were several quick studies intended, as Miss Seeton explained, for a larger, composite picture once she was home again; not that she really felt she could do justice to the beauties of the area, but she hoped it might at least serve as a reminder, once their little holiday was over. So much more personal, she always thought, than a camera . . .

Anne had reached the final sketch. "Oh," she said, and looked at Miss Seeton: who seemed unaware that it was in any way remarkable. But to Anne, who knew her so well, it was. Miss Seeton's artistic style was generally earnest, plebeian, and painstaking: personal (if she insisted), but the camera she despised could do as well, every time. Yet there were other times, with altogether another style: the style of the swift, almost instinctive line drawings, which had always, to Anne's knowledge, meant that they deserved more than ordinary attention.

"Oh," said Anne, and studied the sketch with care, while Miss Seeton watched a squirrel which, because the two of them stood so still, had scampered up the trunk of the beech and was running along a branch above her head. "Oh . . ."

There was the pony, pulling the trap, sturdy and shaggy and very like Bucephalus. But Anne couldn't be sure whether the driver bore any resemblance to Tawno Petulengro; there was no dog by his side, no whip in his hand, and his face was unclear, though every line of his body portrayed secrecy and haste. It was his companions who had startled her, however. Two men, or so it appeared, were beside him on the seat; but the third passenger was in the body of the trap, and had the distinct form of a woman: a woman scantily clad, indeed almost nude, for modesty's sake draped with folds of unspecified material in only a few strategic places . . .

Anne was a nurse, so nudity didn't embarrass her: Miss Seeton had attended life classes as an art student, and very little could embarrass her. But surely this sketch wasn't suggesting that she regarded Anne as a bare-faced liar, a brazen hussy or an adulteress — she'd only been married five minutes, for heaven's sake — even if the man might well not be Tawno Petulengro (or whatever his real name was) because, by the time Miss Seeton had come within sight of the road, he'd already disappeared, and it was therefore no surprise that she couldn't show his face. As for the other two in the picture, they looked even less like the Romany than the driver of the trap did. Besides — Anne peered more closely at the background to the sketch — those weren't, as she'd at first thought, pine trees in the distance, or strange-roofed houses, but soaring, ice-covered mountains. Of which there were remarkably few in the Belton Abbey neighbourhood, never mind what time of year it might be.

"Good gracious, how very strange," remarked Miss Seeton, looking over Anne's shoulder at her own sketch. "It does rather remind me — How foolish, at the height of summer . . ." Her voice fell, and Anne caught only a few words. "I do wonder why . . . him . . ."

"Him, who, Aunt Em?" Anne spoke calmly; she knew what importance the police, especially Delphick, placed in Miss Seeton's instinctive sketches, but she also knew that these same sketches were about the only things which embarrassed the little spinster. Art, she maintained — unless one had the good fortune to be a genius — should reflect only what one saw; and it seemed to disturb her every time she saw, and in her sketches showed that she saw, anything in a way nobody else seemed to do, looking right through any illusion to the reality behind. It was for these sketches that Scotland Yard paid her the retainer, but it was on the matter of these sketches that Miss Seeton, in her everyday dealings so painfully honest, preferred to ignore the truth.

"Oh, dear," said Miss Seeton, and murmured *foolish* a few times more. "In such hot weather, to be thinking — that is, of course, unless that is the reason for . . . the heat, you see. Perhaps we could call it wishful thinking, although I cannot suppose I would ever attire myself in such a fashion, no matter how high it rose — the temperature, that is. Not him, but hymn. From Greenland's icy mountains," sang Miss Seeton, in a cracked but only slightly flat quaver. "To India's coral strand — though an Indian summer is far hotter than an English one, which means that I must have been in rather a muddled state when I drew this, especially as I do not believe there are any rag-and-bone men in Greenland — or horses, either, and as for India, there are cows, of course, and they are sacred, which must remind one of the hymn, even if it makes little sense to have either a horse or a cow pulling a trap . . ."

And she seemed so worried by what she obviously thought of as an indication of mental fragility that Anne spent some time reassuring her of her undoubted sanity before coaxing her back into the car, and driving off in the direction of the nearest village likely to possess a teashop. Anne was a great believer in the restorative powers of tannin, and said so, very firmly, as they spotted a likely hanging sign and began to wonder where to park the car. Not doctor's orders, said Anne with a laugh, but nurse's —

"Oh," said Miss Seeton, "of course. Dear Mel," and gave a relieved sigh. "Poor thing, I wonder how she is?" And as Anne (who suddenly wondered if her adopted aunt really had suffered a summer brainstorm) gently asked her to explain, she told her of Mel Forby's letter, of the broken ankle, and of how she had tried to draw a get well card and it turned out so strangely at the first attempt — not unlike the picture she had just drawn, indeed . . .

And Anne, knowing Miss Seeton as she did, resolved that when she was speaking to Bob that night she would do well to mention the sketches Miss Seeton had most recently drawn.

It was late afternoon when they arrived back at the Belton Arms, pleasantly tired and planning an early supper followed by a restful evening in front of the television. Tonight's film, to which Anne and Miss Seeton had been looking forward all day, was *Queen Christina*.

Anne parked the little car, wondering whether to leave her day's purchases in it overnight or take them inside for further gloating over her bargains. Some of the larger items she'd acquired during the past few days had been left at the various shops for collection by Bob in a hired van once the holiday was finished: he'd grumbled about it, as she'd known he would, but cheerfully, as she'd also known. She wondered how cheerful he'd be when he saw the umbrella stand . . .

"But *I* like it," she assured Miss Seeton. "It rather grows on you, doesn't it? It's unusual — it has character," and she carried it happily with her as they went into the hotel.

It was almost an exact repeat of their first arrival. Once again, receptionist Beverley was flirting discreetly with a smiling young man: the smiling young Lord Edgar, who abandoned his lady as soon as they appeared, and hurried to greet them.

"Miss Seeton — and Mrs. Ranger, of course." A brief acknowledgement, a smile, then he turned back to Miss Seeton. "I've been hoping to catch you. It seems ages since we last spoke. Why haven't you been up to the Abbey again? I said you could come anytime, and I meant it. It's absolutely the least I could do on my family's behalf — the parents will be so wild not to meet you — do say you will. Come tomorrow. Let me send a car!"

Miss Seeton looked anxiously in Anne's direction. Would her feelings be hurt? The car was so small — hers and Bob's — his lordship no doubt had a Rolls-Royce, although he had said, had he not, that the Bremeridges were rather badly off — but surely, not compared to a young couple married for so short a time, and starting out with so few material possessions . . .

"My goodness, Mrs. Ranger." Lord Edgar had just noticed what Anne was carrying. "That's a rather jolly piece. Mind if I ask where you found it? Beverley tells me you've both been having fun around the local antique shops — I hope they didn't diddle you."

Miss Seeton smiled at him as Anne replied. So tactful, not to refer to them as junk shops — which was, after all, what one had to admit they were — but then they were noted for their tact. The aristocracy. Perfectly respectable, of course, but he made them sound far more the sort of place he himself might enter, or his family — the shops, although she was telling him about the totter and making him laugh, so at her ease, dear Anne . . .

"I've heard about them," said Lord Edgar, with a quick look at Beverley. "There's a gypsy camp about three miles to the south — the chap you met must come from there. Tough nuts, by all accounts."

Anne choked at a sudden vision of Miss Nuttel and Mrs. Blaine as gypsies, complete with tambourines and earrings. She hastened to make amends. "His muscular de-

235

velopment was rather splendid, certainly, but I suppose if you spend your time carting scrap iron around it's bound to have a toughening effect. He didn't talk like a thug, though — in fact, he didn't talk like a gypsy at all, in some ways. He sounded too much like one to be true, now I think about it — acting the part, you might say. He could well not have been born to it. Perhaps he saw himself as rather too old for rushing off to be a hippie, so being a gypsy was an acceptable compromise."

Eddie shook his head. "Dropping out may sound romantic, but I feel it's running away from your responsibilities . . ." Miss Seeton nodded, and looked pleased as he went on: "They seem to get themselves involved in rather too many punch-ups to be romantic, Mrs. Ranger. The local police haven't found it, but there are rumours that they've set up a still, and make the most fearsome firewater that makes them willing to tackle anyone, at any odds, if they're in the mood. I don't want to scare you, but I think you had a narrow escape."

Anne shrugged. "There's no point in my being scared now it's in the past, is there? I suppose I might have worried about it if I'd known at the time, but I didn't — and," with a quick look at Miss Seeton, "there are times when ignorance is definitely bliss . . ."

But it wasn't just Miss Seeton (whose almost permanent state of bliss was a matter for admiration — and anxiety — among her friends) whose ignorance must be maintained. Bob, thought Anne, might not care for the idea that his wife had been consorting with moonshine-maddened gypsies — except, of course, that her escort had been neither intoxicated nor, on reflection, a true Romany. But she supposed, looking back on her little adventure, that it had been rather silly to accept a lift from a stranger, no matter how romantic the idea of a pony and trap might be. Lord Edgar's words had woken uneasy echoes of Miss Seeton's uncomfortable sketch in Anne's mind. Maybe she'd been watching too many old films, and her wits had gone on holiday as well as herself . . .

Lord Edgar had turned his attentions back to Miss Seeton in a further attempt to persuade her to visit the Abbey and accept carte blanche to wander where she pleased. Today had been another "public" day, and he'd looked for her, and been disappointed: she must promise to come tomorrow, her niece as well, and bring her sketching equipment. He could assure her of the most marvellous views — the Palladian temple and bridge, the fountain in the middle of the lake, the yew walk, and the trellis garden — she'd love it, he knew. Wouldn't she say yes?

And, reminded again of dear Nigel by Lord Edgar's charm and enthusiasm, Miss Seeton in the end found herself agreeing that before many more days had passed, she would go to Belton Abbey.

chapter
19

When Bob rang Anne that evening, between (fortunately) dinner and *Queen Christina*, she barely had time to ask him how he was before he told her.

"Hopping mad, me and the Oracle both. There's been another Croesus, at least we think it must be — and it's not the Ilkley Moor painting that's gone — and there's another poor brighter with concussion and a cracked skull. Somebody broke into Bellshire County Museum and walked off with their stuffed polar bear — yes," as Anne couldn't help giggling, "it sounds funny, but this is serious, darling. Apart from anything else, it means they're heading your way instead of staying near London ready to raid Sothenham's and pinch the Ilkley Moor bait MissEss went to so much trouble to set up. I'm not sure now whether you're better off staying there, or coming back home, after all."

"The chances that they'd recognise us even if we did run into them — which I don't see why we should —" Anne began, then stopped. She knew as well as Bob that where Miss Seeton was concerned, you had to be prepared for anything. "Do you want us to come back? What does the Oracle say?"

"Nothing repeatable." Despite himself, Bob chuckled. "You'd swear he'd taken lessons from Superintendent Brinton at Ashford — the one they call Brimstone, remember?"

"We have," Anne reminded her spouse, "had the odd encounter — he came to our wedding, after all; and I lived in Plummergen for several years before I met you. PC Potter tells a good tale, when he gets going."

"Then you know what I mean. He's furious — the Oracle, that is. The poor devil with the cracked skull's in intensive care, and if he ups and dies on us as well I wouldn't like to answer for the consequences for Croesus when we finally nobble him — if," he added glumly, "we ever do. We've made no sense out of Aunt Em's sketches, of course. Why," and Anne could hear the frustration in his voice, "can't we ever understand what she tries to tell us in time to do something about it? She's got the answers, she must have. She always has before — and it's always the same. It never makes sense until it's almost too late . . ."

The newspapers next morning all carried stories on the Croesus case, asking questions about what the police were doing, and why they seemed to be having no success in combatting Crime In General. Raffles, it was pointed out, was still at large: it was deplorable that such dangerous men could stalk the countryside as far from capture as if they'd only just begun their campaigns of terror. Delphick cursed aloud, and muttered of irresponsible hacks distorting the truth to boost their circulation: Croesus, or his henchmen, might be ruthless, but Raffles (so far) was not.

Thrudd Banner, writing in *The Blare*, was the only journalist to give a remotely balanced view: but he could afford to be generous, because he had a scoop to announce to his readers. Somehow, he had found out about the loss of the Eykyn Emeralds, which he related in full, rejoicing in the almost farcical attempts of the police to capture the man who'd stolen them, and the clever trick he'd played.

"Makes us look fools," Delphick said, "and the trouble is, in this instance we are. Raffles is running rings round the police, and I can't deny it. As for Croesus . . ."

"Anne says MissEss has been drawing again, sir," offered Bob, as Delphick ran out of words. "Something to do with Mel Forby, she thought," and he described, as well as he could, the pony-and-trap sketch which had made Anne uneasy. "Mel's in on the Croesus business, after all, sir. I know she's by way of being a friend, but I can't help wondering — perhaps we ought to ask her if there's anything she's, well, not telling us, sir — because she's a journalist first and foremost, isn't she?"

Delphick shook his head. "Not Mel, Bob. She wouldn't behave like that — besides, resourceful though she is, I don't see how she can have found anything out that we don't know, not confined to the house with a broken ankle. Thrudd is another kettle of fish entirely, mind you," he added, in a thoughtful tone. "Even the Yard didn't know about the Eykyn Emeralds — but he apparently did. It's just possible that he's learned something about Croesus from one of his contacts which he might have mentioned to Mel, though I hope she'd consider herself enough of a friend to pass it on as she's done in the past, even if he didn't. We've worked together for some years now, on and off, and my faith in human nature would be really shattered if she meant to let us down just for the sake of a story."

"She might not mean to, sir. She might know something she doesn't know she knows, that even Thrudd didn't know was important when he told her, whatever it was. The way those two always try to outdo each other, he wouldn't have told her if there was any chance it was something important, sir, would he? You know how they niggle all the time about who has the scoop."

"It's an idea, I grant you, but somehow I don't see it. Thrudd has Raffles and Mel has Croesus — sharing the stories pretty fairly, I'd say."

"But it was Thrudd who first wrote about Croesus, sir," objected Bob at once. "And if he'd been there when you rang — well, it wouldn't do any harm to have just a friendly talk with both of them, would it? In the circumstances, I mean, sir. With us being, er, stumped . . ."

Delphick favoured his sergeant with a sideways look of restrained irritation. "Not while we have Miss Seeton on our side, we aren't," he pointed out, reaching for the cardboard portfolio which Bob had brought back from Belton Abbey two days ago. "Now that things seem to be hotting up a little, let's take another look at her offerings to see if they inspire any brainwaves . . ."

Delphick spread the three sketches out on his desk, and stared at them with as much concentration as he had already applied, unsuccessfully, several times before. The first showed a row of portraits, hanging on the walls of a panelled room which Bob had told him was very like the Belton gallery, the faces very like the Bremeridges.

"Anne says the chap who was showing us round turned out to be Lord Edgar Bremeridge," he reminded Delphick, as the chief superintendent pulled the picture across and held it at an angle. "I hadn't spotted it while he was doing his stuff, sir, but now I've seen this I really can't think why I didn't — the resemblance is obvious. They all look just like him, sir, or perhaps I should say he looks just like them, and the room looks just like the room — except that I didn't notice that cabinet in the corner," he added. "Not that I'm much of a one for furniture and stuff — I leave all that to Anne, I'm afraid. But I thought the cabinet was in the room the snuffboxes were taken from . . ."

"Yet Miss Seeton's shown it as under the protection of the eagle Bremeridge eyes, it appears. Generations of them: I wonder why."

"The snuffboxes were heirlooms, sir — great sentimental value and so on. That could be the reason."

"It could, yes. There's certainly a remarkably strong feeling that the Lord Edgar lookalikes are interested in the cabinet, to say the least . . ."

They passed on to the second drawing, without any idea of the indecision which had preceded its inclusion in Miss Seeton's portfolio. She had, after all, not drawn it for the benefit of anyone save herself — and it had gone wrong — but it was the police, which meant dear Mr. Delphick, who were paying for her little holiday, and for her services as an artist as well, and as she'd drawn it while on holiday, even though (so far as she could see) it was nothing to do with snuffboxes — or, indeed, with anything else . . .

"That's the Abbey in ruins, sir," prompted Bob, as Delphick sat and stared. "Goodness knows why, because it's not a ruin at all — Anne said it reminded her of a film set, and I'd agree with her. Like something out of Hollywood in what she calls the golden years — and MissEss as well," he added, with a grin. "They've been spending every night glued to the television, apparently, soaking up romantic atmosphere by the ton, though I'm pretty sure neither of them goes in for horror films. Why she's drawn that wolf and those birds — if that's what they are — goodness only knows."

"Vampire bats, perhaps," murmured Delphick, "though they may be birds — it's hard to tell. But with those teeth . . . No doubt about the harpy, however," and he pointed to the winged woman with the cruel face and grasping talons, hovering among the bats (or birds) near the snarling wolf which had been, in Miss Seeton's mind, the golden retriever from the lawn of the Belton Arms. "You said the face reminded you of the hotel receptionist? Odd."

He turned to the third drawing, a vivid mountain scene. Above the snow line, picking its lonely way with the help of a rope and an ice axe, was a figure of indeterminate gender, muffled against the cold in layers of bulky clothing. There was a deep ravine ahead of the figure, hidden from its view behind a massed bank of snow. "And, echoing your words, Bob — goodness only knows why she's drawn this," Delphick said. "In fact, none of these make sense, do they? With hindsight they will, of course — as ever — but at the moment . . ."

"These are three or four days old, sir," Bob reminded him. "She's had time to develop more of a feel for what's going on since I came away — I told you Anne says she's come up with that woman in the cart sketch, and how MissEss said it was a bit like the get well card she did for Mel Forby — which was before any of this really started, sir, wasn't it? She must know something, only she doesn't know what — and neither do we, but if we could take a proper look at everything she's drawn, together . . ."

Delphick nodded, and was about to say something, then frowned. "Anne might well be able to persuade her to let us have the drawings, but I can't say I'm too happy at the idea of entrusting them to the post. Registered mailbags are the first things a robber with any sense makes for — and I need you here, Bob, not rushing off to Belton now the protection racket looks like breaking." He sighed. "It must be three, four years since they put a man on the moon, and how many of the technological marvels we were promised have come about? One day, somebody's going to make a fortune inventing a machine that transmits documents over distances — I suppose some sort of cross between a photocopier and a telephone would do the trick — and I'd be the first to take advantage of such an invention. As it is . . ."

He stared at the collection of newspapers, all with their headlines of complaint. "Tell Anne, when you ring her tonight, that we'd appreciate the most detailed description she can manage for anything MissEss has drawn over the past few days. As for myself, I must dig out my little black book and have a word with Mel Forby . . ."

Anne and Miss Seeton, meanwhile, oblivious to the problems of Delphick and Bob, were once more enjoying a day out: but much closer to home, on this occasion. Lord Edgar had been so pressing in his invitation — Miss Seeton's conscience had begun to suggest that her modest refusals might be misconstrued as base ingratitude, not to say churlish — there were some tempting descriptions in the guidebook of the beautiful vistas about the Abbey grounds — Anne had hinted that she was a little tired of driving every day . . .

Fortunately for Miss Seeton's desire to remain unobtrusive, it was one of the Public days at Belton Abbey. Coachloads of trippers passed through the house, took photographs of the gardens, and (those whose feet were up to it) wandered further afield, admiring the Palladian bridge and the other sights they'd read about in the papers.

Those who observed an elderly lady in a neat tweed suit sitting with a sketchbook on her knee, diligently shading in the pillars of the bridge, decided that she must be one of themselves, and went to peer over her shoulder and make such giggling remarks as "Don't put me in it, will you?" or "Aren't you clever? I could never do that." They drifted away with warnings to her not to miss the bus, and left her in peace.

It certainly was a peaceful and delightful place. "Only think, Aunt Em," rapturised Anne. "Crinolines and powdered wigs and lovers' trysts — I bet if this bridge could talk, it would have a few stories to tell."

Miss Seeton gazed about her with pleasure, answering in an absent tone. "If only the skill of my pencil were equal to the view! It was most kind of his lordship to grant us the opportunity . . . such a very lovely day . . . take home such happy memories . . ."

"Do you want to go back now? You're not tired, are you? We haven't seen the Temple of Hiberna yet, and you said last night it would make a companion sketch to the bridge. But if the sun's too hot, or anything —"

"Dear me, no, indeed. I have never felt better in my life. There is no need at all for you to concern yourself about me — it is your holiday too, remember. But, as long as you do not find it tedious to accompany me —"

"Don't be silly, I'm having a marvellous time." Anne gave her a quick hug. "It's so restful here, apart from the odd occasion when you're besieged by people wanting to buy your pictures. I'm a great believer in doing nothing, from time to time, and so's Dad — he says half his patients could cure themselves immediately if they only stopped to *breathe*, once in a while."

"Inner harmony." Thinking of her yoga, Miss Seeton nodded. "*Trataka*, or do I mean *samadhi?* Your father is a most sensible man, my dear. It has certainly done wonders for my knees, over the years — breathing, I mean, although mostly I feel it must be due to the various postures — so relaxing."

Anne murmured her agreement, and sat back to enjoy the sunshine. Suddenly, she chuckled. "It looks as if we spoke too soon — about relaxing, I mean. Could we be due for yet another invasion?"

Miss Seeton followed her gaze across the parkland in the direction of the house. A solitary figure was making its way towards them, walking with an easy, proprietorial stride which she and Anne recognised simultaneously.

"Now we're going to have to sing for our supper, Aunt Em — that's Lord Edgar coming to check up on us. Better have your sketches ready to show him, and I'll make a point of saying how much we're enjoying ourselves, which is perfectly true, of course. This must be a gorgeous place to live . . ." Anne's eyes roved admiringly about the grounds, while Miss Seeton dropped her gaze absently to her sketch pad, and began to draw swift lines on a clean sheet as she remarked:

"Of course, romance is all very well, but one would miss the modern conveniences, particularly the plumbing, I fancy. My understanding of those days is that baths were somewhat infrequent, and as for washing clothes, silk and lace would take a very long time by hand — no central heating, you see, but one can certainly imagine, as you said earlier, all the gallant young men and beautiful girls who have passed over this bridge, and perhaps fought duels — the young gallants, I mean, all his lordship's ancestors . . ."

"Here he comes," murmured Anne, as Lord Edgar appeared at the far end of the bridge and waved to them.

And Miss Seeton looked up from her sketching block with a start. "Good gracious," she said.

chapter
20

"Good gracious," said Miss Seeton, "how very odd — but then I was only dreaming the other night, of course . . ."

She flipped the cover back on her sketchbook, set it to one side with a quick gesture, and smiled in greeting as his lordship drew near. "Good afternoon, Lord Edgar. Such a beautiful day, is it not?"

"Eddie," he corrected her, and turned to Anne. "Hello, Mrs. Ranger. I'm glad to see you finally persuaded your aunt to sample some of the other delights of Belton besides the house — have you been here long? How much have you managed to see? I notice" — with a bow towards Miss Seeton — "you have your sketchbook with you. May I look? I promise" — as she blinked at him, and made a nervous movement towards the closed cover, "I won't criticise. In fact, you're probably as good an artist as at least half the johnnies who painted the family phizogs — ghastly likenesses, some of them were, weren't they? That fashion for making people look a little green around the gills à la Reynolds . . ."

He had swooped, smiling, on Miss Seeton's sketchbook before she could utter a word of protest, and began to leaf through it to examine the sheaf of drawings, studies, and notes she had been making since Bob had departed for London. Most were landscapes, routine and painstaking and instantly recognisable. Eddie admired them, and produced names for them where applicable, so that, as he put it, when she had the labels printed she'd be sure of getting them right.

He wavered a little when he turned a page and came upon the pony-and-trap drawing which had startled Anne, but after a quick look at Miss Seeton spoke of it briefly as "an interesting concept," then turned tactfully to the next drawing as she blushed and laced her fingers together. Really, she had tried to explain that these were mere sketches — personal impressions — but one could hardly have refused, when it was, after all, by his lordship's kindness that she was enjoying these views on such a glorious afternoon, but one would so much have preferred to keep one's private thoughts, well, private — except, of course, when it was a matter of one's duty to share them with . . .

"The police," murmured Miss Seeton, as Lord Edgar found himself looking at her final sketch: the one she had dashed off just as he came over the bridge towards her, reminding her so much of his ancestors . . .

"The police? I'm not entirely sure," said Lord Edgar, with a frown, "when the Peelers were invented, but if you'll forgive my saying so, Miss Seeton, I'd have said Bow Street Runners were more historically accurate, in this particular case. Wouldn't you, Mrs. Ranger?"

He held the sketchbook across to Anne, who noticed the embarrassment in Miss Seeton's eyes but found it difficult to pretend his lordship wasn't there. She flashed an apologetic smile, and took the book. She studied the sketch.

It showed a couple in Regency costume, the lady with her hair in ringlets and her fingers, throat, and arms bedecked with jewels; her clothes were stylish and richly adorned, her face finely featured and bearing, Anne suddenly noticed, a marked resemblance to Beverley, the receptionist from the Belton Arms. Her escort, clad in silks and ruffles, carried a sword at his side and had a proprietorial air about him — and a face which bore a distinct likeness to Bremeridges of bygone ages, as anyone who had visited the portrait gallery would have agreed.

"Bow Street Runners — yes, I suppose so," said Anne, in a rather breathless tone, as she handed the sketchbook back not to Lord Edgar, but to Miss Seeton, who received it discreetly with a blush and a thankful sigh. "Mind you, this whole place is crammed with history, isn't it," she went on, as Miss Seeton set the sketchbook firmly to one side, laid her umbrella — not too pointedly, she hoped, for one did not wish to appear rude, but it was all so embarrassing — on top of it, and tried not to blush even more. "You can't help thinking of — oh, all sorts of things, like the Dissolution of the Monasteries, for instance, even if it was all hundreds of years earlier — we were saying so just before you arrived, weren't we, Aunt Em?"

"Indeed we were." Miss Seeton beamed upon Lord Edgar, happy now that an uncontroversial topic of conversation had been introduced. "Except that this is an abbey, of course, which means that it would not be . . . Unfortunately, I cannot feel that my poor efforts have done justice — such splendid scenery, wherever one looks — such a strong sense of history — and, while one tries one's best, it is not . . . But one can never stop *thinking*, Lord Edgar. Which is the basis, is it not, for the imagination? As I am always telling the children. Clearness of thought is essential, I believe, for accuracy of sight — and to see clearly is, surely, the essence of art. Communicating one's vision. Once I am home again, I plan to undertake a composite painting of the area — for which your comments, of course, will be most helpful. Perhaps a panorama, to give something of the atmosphere, though I am not sufficiently talented to do it justice, I very much fear. The labels — not that I would go so far as to have brass plates engraved as your ancestors did, but one does like to be accurate concerning where, and what, and, indeed, who, one has drawn, does one not?"

He blinked. "Yes, of course, but . . ." Then he rallied nobly. "But you haven't drawn everything of interest around here by a long chalk, Miss Seeton. There's the Temple of Hiberna, for instance. I'm sure you've heard all about the ghost of that poor maidservant — simply bags of atmosphere there, you know. You can't leave without visiting the temple. It isn't far — in fact, it's nearer the house than we are at present, round the other side. One of the showpieces of the place, especially the statue of Hiberna, or rather what's left of her. If you ask me," and he uttered a deprecating laugh, "the Venus de Milo does it better. Familiarity breeding contempt, I suppose. When you've had picnics since you were a kid with a goddess goggling down at you, it's hard to take her all that seriously. We call her Armless Arabella, I'm afraid."

Miss Seeton nodded, and smiled, and murmured understandingly. Eddie looked pleased. "I was afraid an expert like you would rather despise me for being a Philistine, Miss Seeton, and I'm so glad you don't — but honesty's the best policy, wouldn't you say? If I'd tried to pretend I adored the thing, you'd have been bound to catch me out. Besides, perhaps when you see it you won't like it, either. Let me escort you both round there now — and, talking of picnics, I'll have Faulkbourne bring you out some refreshment once I'm back at the house doing my duty by the next tour."

"That is most kind, Lord Edgar, but —"

"Eddie," he reminded her, with a laugh, as he picked up her umbrella and sketchbook and offered her his arm. "Don't thank us — indeed, I imagine Faulkbourne may very well thank you. He'll be spared having to take the next tour — he does hate it, poor man, and especially since . . . he's convinced Raffles came on an Open Day to case the joint, you see. He doesn't really approve of the lengths to which the parents have had to go to restore the fallen family fortunes . . ."

Half an hour later, Anne lazed on the grass beneath the Temple of Hiberna on its gently sloping mound — man-made, as Eddie had explained — watching Miss Seeton at work over her sketchbook. A summer breeze rippled the leaves in nearby trees, from whose branches the clamour of birdsong mingled with the chatter of tourists from below. Nobody, it seemed, on so hot a day had enough energy to climb the slope, even to see the legendary bloodstains (which Eddie insisted were the result of youthful orange squash). Miss Seeton's knees had been equal to the challenge, of course, but Miss Seeton, as Anne reminded herself, was unique.

"Isn't that Faulkbourne coming from the house?" asked Anne, as a distinguished figure threaded its way through the chattering throng with a tray in its hands. "Yes, I'm sure it is. Do you suppose," and she giggled, "that Lord Edgar's arranged for us to have smoked salmon sandwiches and champagne, like the gentry — or will it be sardines on toast and a flask of tea?"

Miss Seeton smiled at dear Anne's whimsy, and watched as Faulkbourne, dignity in every inch of his bearing, trod his stately measure towards them up the knoll. "His lordship is most kind," she murmured, "such a hot day . . . of course, one could not refuse his offer, though we may find it rather awkward explaining to the hotel, but . . ."

"Don't worry. I could eat a horse, I think, despite the heat. There won't be a crumb of either picnic left by the end of the afternoon — and we could always feed the hotel sandwiches to the ducks, or something, if we have to. Blow being extravagant, for once — we're on holiday!"

Miss Seeton couldn't decide whether to be shocked at the idea of wasting the Belton Arms offering on the birds, which at this time of year really didn't need to be fed — though it was, she admitted, delightful to do so — or whether it was a sensible idea, and so like dear Anne, but then a nurse had to possess a strongly practical side, whereas an artist . . .

She found herself doodling again as the steward drew near, and turned pink as she dropped her sketchbook on the grass and jumped — silently blessing her yoga-nimble knees — to her feet. "Mr. Faulkbourne," she fluttered, "this is such a very . . . so kind . . . his lordship . . ."

Neither she nor Anne, even standing, could see what the steward, so much taller than they, carried on the tray he held in his gloved hands. Having greeted them with a bow, he indicated to the ladies that they might care to partake of their modest refreshment in the temple, where it was far cooler. "And where the insects," he added, "may possibly be less of a problem," although from his tone it was clear that he felt the field would be open to all manner of onslaught from ant, mosquito, and wasp the instant the restraint of his distinguished presence was removed. "If you would care to follow me?"

It was a princely picnic he set before them: cucumber sandwiches, Madeira and rich fruitcake, scones with jam and cream, thin rolled slices of bread and butter, and tea in an elegant silver pot with paper-thin porcelain cups. "I trust that, should you feel this to be insufficient, you will tell me at once," said Faulkbourne, bowing again as Anne and Miss Seeton exclaimed with surprise and pleasure. "This is the very least we — I mean the Family, of course — could do for you, Miss Seeton, after all your help in the past. And your courtesy and cooperation in the future, perhaps," he added, with yet another bow. "Have you — excuse me — been drawing again, by any chance?"

For the second time that day, Miss

Seeton's sketchbook — it would, she reminded herself unhappily, be so churlish to refuse, when one had been so kindly welcomed — was subjected to interested scrutiny from a stranger who, one knew, meant no harm, but really . . .

"Most interesting," said the steward, having raised his eyebrows on seeing that last picture which she had drawn as he made his way across from the house. "Thank you for permitting me to see your work, Miss Seeton."

And, with a final bow, he walked away.

chapter
21

Anne was speaking on the telephone. At the other end of the line, far away in London, she held enthralled an audience of two: her husband, Bob, otherwise known as Detective Sergeant Ranger — and Chief Superintendent Delphick, whose office Bob shared at New Scotland Yard.

Nightclubs function, as the name makes clear, during the night: thus it had been not in a dawn raid, but in what Delphick was pleased to call a noon swoop that the protection racket had been wound up that day. Assorted heavies, roused from their (or, more frequently, others') beds, kicked their no-longer-booted heels in prison cells, and demanded to talk to their lawyers. Delphick, Bob, and the rest of the posse, pardonably pleased with the results of their labours, yielded the inevitable paperwork to the Yard's administrative team, and went off to celebrate their victory over pies and a few pints in a nearby pub.

On their return to the Yard, there was a message from Anne. Mrs. Ranger would be glad of a few words with Mr. Delphick at his earliest convenience, and she would be waiting at the hotel for his call. "Something about going to the pictures," added the switchboard, in a puzzled tone.

The Oracle frowned. "I know your wife shares with Miss Seeton a fondness for the cinema, Bob, but somehow I don't believe that's quite what she meant to say. Let's hope it doesn't mean someone's rumbled the Winter Wonderland business as a put-up job — or," frowning even more deeply, "that MissEss has got herself into any sort of trouble . . ."

Delphick allowed Bob to exchange a few fond words with his spouse before picking up the extension.

"Hello, Anne. I gather from Bob's end of the conversation that it's nothing too serious, thank goodness. We were imagining any number of things having gone wrong."

"It's just that you wanted to know if there were any more drawings," came Anne's voice in explanation, "and there are — two, of the kind you'd be interested in. I've got her sketchbook in front of me — she's in the television lounge," rather wistfully, "watching *Dangerous Moonlight.* I've never seen that . . . Still, you'd like a description. The first is one she dashed off when Lord

Edgar was walking over the bridge towards us," and she described, in as much detail as she could, the Regency couple, and mentioned Lord Edgar's words on the topic of Bow Street Runners. Delphick closed his eyes and tried to visualise what she was saying; but it was impossible for him to know how closely (or otherwise) his visualisation resembled what was on the sketching block in front of Anne, far away at the Belton Arms.

"The second is what she did this afternoon, when we were up on the temple knoll and the steward was bringing us our picnic tea, except that it was far grander than that." Anne stifled a giggle. "She was looking right at him as she drew it — and it looks just like him, it really does. He's walking along with an incredibly snooty look on his face, and carrying a tray — but the odd thing is that she hasn't drawn any tea things on it. I know that, at the time she started to draw, she couldn't see him clearly — he's pretty tall — but you'd expect her to show cups and saucers on the tray, wouldn't you? Instead of — well, what looks like heaps of little bricks, only they aren't regular enough in shape to be bricks. The corners are rounded off so that they're more oval than oblong, if you see what I mean, and there must be a couple of dozen of them."

There was a thoughtful pause. Delphick said at last: "Little bricks with rounded corners. A fair number of them, if that's what they are, which they probably aren't, on a tray carried by a butler . . . Anne, what were you talking about when Miss Seeton was drawing?"

"I've been trying to remember, in case it was important. Mostly, I think, it was about the history of the place — the Dissolution of the Monasteries and so on — and people fighting duels, and — oh, yes, and Miss Seeton said she'd been dreaming the night before, and how odd it was — I gathered that what she'd dreamed somehow resembled the sketch, so I suppose —" She stifled a yawn. "Sorry — it's been such a lovely lazy day, I'm half-asleep. Anyway, I suppose . . . it might just be that she's, well . . ."

"You suppose she might just be echoing her dream in the clear light of day?" Delphick looked at Bob, and shrugged. "It's a thought, of course, but somehow I feel there's more to it than that. You know how we've never decided whether she's psychic or not, in the generally understood sense of the word — but I'm convinced that, in her own, er, unique sense of the word she is. So, if she was dreaming about a heap of little bricks — no, that was later, wasn't it? The two of you were rapturising over history, as I recall. Anyone know anything about brick-making techniques in times historical? Would they have had rounded corners?"

"The only thing I know is that you can't make them without straw," volunteered Bob, as Anne confessed to her ignorance with a baffled silence. Delphick grinned.

"Somebody-or-other is famous for having found Rome brick, and left it marble, but I hardly think that applies in this particular case — and wasn't there a regiment of the Light Infantry known as the Brickdusts? Sir George Colveden would be the chap to ask about that, I imagine. Which is all very interesting, no doubt, but gets us no nearer understanding what MissEss is trying to tell us, does it?"

There was an expectant pause. "Sir," said Bob, "now the nightclub lot are in clink, we're not too busy . . ."

"Anne," said Delphick, "how full is the hotel? Would we be able to find rooms? Or, rather, one room, for me — Bob's all right with you, of course. I rather think we ought to come to Belton as soon as we can — expect us tomorrow unless you hear anything to the contrary . . ."

★ ★ ★

Anne crept back into the television lounge, and caught the last half hour of *Dangerous Moonlight*. Miss Seeton was so wrapped up in the story that she failed to notice her young friend's return; she had been transported back in time, and was watching it as she'd watched it first in a London cinema thirty years ago. She had agonised once more while the resistance workers waited for the Polish national anthem to be silenced, heralding the arrival of the Nazi jackboots; while the handsome young pianist met the American girl reporter in bombarded Warsaw, and they fell in love beneath the dangerous moonlight. When he escaped to England and fought in the Battle of Britain, she thrilled; when, injured, he failed to recognise his love, she desponded. His final playing of the piano — *The Warsaw Concerto*, so expressive — and the gradual return of his memory was almost too much to bear: she knew very well what was going to happen, and could hardly wait for it all to come true.

"Didn't I say I thought I'd seen that movie someplace before?" said a middle-aged American woman triumphantly to her husband, as the credits rolled up the screen. "It was when he joined the Air Force I remembered — but surely we call it *Suicide Squadron* back home? I guess now I've seen it again, I prefer the English title."

Her spouse uttered a vague grunt. His eyes were firmly closed, and could well have been closed throughout the film: he certainly gave no clear impression of sharing his wife's memories. She looked round at the other occupants of the residents' lounge. "Moonlight's a sight more romantic than airplanes," she said, and Miss Seeton, as she put her handkerchief away, nodded.

"It is indeed. There is a quality — shadows, you know — and so very much more effective in black and white. Imagine if it had been made in colour — the film, I mean. Not that there were no coloured films in those days, but of course they were more expensive, and, in this instance, infinitely preferable, I feel, to use black and white, which somehow does not give so much of a *grey* impression of moonlight as photographing in colour, I believe, would have done . . ."

As she finished speaking, her fingers began to dance on her lap in a way which Anne, still wishing she'd seen all of the film, recognised. Would there be another of her sketches to show Bob and the Oracle when they arrived tomorrow? She wondered whether she should let Aunt Em know that they were to have company, but, during the little chat on old movies and lighting techniques which Miss Seeton and her new friend seemed set to enjoy for a while, had time to think better of it. Once she knew Bob was coming back, Aunt Em would insist on relinquishing her tenancy of the four-poster bed: and what harm would it do to let her indulge her romantic daydreams just for one more night?

". . . Popular Culture," the American woman was saying, to Miss Seeton's evident interest. "They don't make them like that anymore, more's the pity. You can't have too much of the old romance in your life, that's what I say," and with a forceful elbow she dug her sleeping spouse in the ribs. He snorted, jumped, and opened his eyes. Anne stifled a giggle at his look of bewilderment, though she had every sympathy with his drowsy state. Perhaps it was all the fresh air today, but she found herself yawning in sympathy.

"Wake up, Howard. You can take me right along to the bar this minute and buy me a drink." She glanced enquiringly at Miss Seeton. "Would you — and your niece, of course," and she favoured Anne with a welcoming smile, "care to join us?

269

We couldn't help noticing the two of you around the hotel these last couple of days, and we've been wanting to make your acquaintance. Say you'll come — we won't take no for an answer, will we, Howard?"

Howard, his eyes now fully open, looked with interest on his wife's new friends, and promptly added his welcome to hers in tones every bit as insistent. Miss Seeton, who had at first seemed pleased by the invitation, after a quick glance in Anne's direction made attempts at refusal so very polite that neither Howard nor his wife appeared to hear them. They were touring England to see the sights and meet the people: what better way could they have of meeting people than in a good old English pub? Surely Miss Seeton and her niece could spare just half an hour for a little visit? Miss Seeton's niece, noticing a pause as they both drew breath simultaneously, jumped in with:

"Yes, do go, Aunt Em, and enjoy yourself — but if everyone will excuse me, I rather think I'll have an early night. I shan't feel so bad about leaving you to your own devices, though, now I know you've found some congenial company," and she favoured drowsy Howard and his wife with a grateful smile. "You'll be able to swap notes about more old films," she added, as Miss Seeton hesitated. "All the ones we've been watching since we've been here, for instance . . ."

The brightening of Miss Seeton's eye did not go unrecognised by Mrs. Howard, who exclaimed that she'd thought from the start they'd have things in common, and didn't it just go to show that Aunt Em here — if they'd excuse the liberty, she was Shirley Warren and this was her husband, Howard . . . that Miss Seeton, wasn't that nice and quaint and English, would have as much fun talking to them as they'd have talking to her? But she (Shirley) knew how young people were inclined to fuss over their elders, and Anne could rely on her not to keep her aunt up all night — only, if she had the slightest doubt, why didn't she change her mind and come along to the bar with them, if only for one quick drink . . .

In the end, Anne's sleepiness having apparently been accepted as genuine, Miss Seeton was gathered up in triumph by Shirley Warren and hustled merrily off to the bar with Howard, rubbing his eyes, in their wake. He winked at Anne as she parted from them at the foot of the stairs, and murmured that he wasn't so keen on the old movies either, but that sometimes, for the sake of peace and quiet, it was better doing it her way. Anne smiled politely, realising that his mix-diagnosis of her weariness as entirely tactical was her easiest escape route from what otherwise promised to be much tedious explanation.

Nobody followed Anne up the stairs: the night was still very young, and the bar of the Belton Arms was a welcoming place, with a cream-washed ceiling striped by age-darkened beams on which Bob, being so tall, had often risked bumping his head. Horse brasses fixed in rows to leather harness straps hung on the uneven walls, and Miss Seeton's eye had been caught on the first night by a series of prints which, she felt sure, were genuine. There were enough, but by no means too many, tables — and no piped music. Small surprise that it was a popular local, as well as a comfortable drinking place for hotel residents.

Anne yawned again as she made her way towards Room 25, and in so doing managed to drop her handbag, out of which she was just fetching her key, on the floor. Her exasperated "Bother!" coincided almost exactly with the thud of the falling bag and the clatter of the key ring. As she stooped to pick everything up, she froze.

From inside Room 25 she thought she heard a noise.

She listened, still frozen, for perhaps half a minute; heard nothing more; and decided it must have been imagination, compounded with tiredness. She finished picking up her belongings, and moved to fit her key in the keyhole.

It would not fit.

She checked the number on the door: perhaps, being so tired, she'd come to the wrong room . . .

She hadn't. All the doors in the Belton Arms were old-fashioned, solid wood, panelled — but with old-fashioned, solid brass numbers on them. Room 25. No mistake.

And, as she tried again to fit the heavy iron key in the old-fashioned lock, she heard a scuffling sound from within the room — and then silence.

chapter
22

Over a hundred miles away, in the Scotland Yard office, Bob Ranger yawned, stretched, and snapped shut his notebook with a sigh of relief. Delphick, who had also been ploughing the weary furrow of the nightclub protection paperwork, glanced across at his sergeant, and grinned.

"Broken the back of it at last, Bob?"

"Hope so, sir. If we're heading off to Belton first thing tomorrow, I don't want my notes hanging over me till we get back. My memory's not that brilliant."

Delphick nodded. "I know your position as my sidekick is justified by your many fine qualities and abilities, but it has to be admitted that one-hundred-percent accurate shorthand is not one of them. Excellent training for the memory, though."

"Yes, sir. Er — the voice of long experience, sir?"

Delphick looked pained. "Hardly as long as your tone would seem to suggest, Sergeant Ranger. The days when I was a humble detective like yourself are not, I trust, so far lost in the mists of antiquity that the skills of an archaeologist would be required to disinter them — and if this is a roundabout way of asking whether I'm now going, or have gone, gage, I shall ignore it. I wouldn't say there's much wrong with my memory — not when I recall very clearly that you owe me that last pint we didn't have earlier. Just in case you were hoping I'd forgotten."

"Certainly not, sir." Bob contrived to look simultaneously scandalised and hurt. He checked his watch against the office clock. "Time for a quick one, sir? And then off home ready for an early start?"

Delphick, too, was checking the time, and did not reply at once. "Bob, are you particularly tired? Desperate for your Bromley bed after the excitements of the day?"

In the act of stretching again, Bob stopped, and stifled a yawn. "No, sir. Could do with a spot of fresh air, mind you — and a change of scene," he added hopefully. After so many years working with the Oracle, there were times when he could almost read his thoughts. "How about you, sir?"

Delphick nodded. "A change of scene would suit me very well. And driving through the night, when the roads are far less crowded . . ."

"Pop home, pack, pick you up, and head west, sir," said Bob without hesitation. "It'd probably mean sharing some of the driving, though, especially towards the end, but —"

"But it would be worth the effort," supplied Delphick, a gleam in his eye. "Not, of course, that I believe for one moment there is any risk to Anne, or to Miss Seeton, in so quiet a place as Belton — but we both know from, er, long experience, that when MissEss is involved it does no harm to make sure . . ."

Anne was wide awake now. She rattled the handle of her bedroom door as she twisted her key in the lock, pushing and probing: but to no avail. She stopped, breathing hard, and listened furiously.

She thought she could make out further scufflings from within: deliberately mocking, muffled sounds which she could not identify. Yet the door was old, and solid wood: perhaps she was imagining things . . .

"You look as if you're having problems," said an unexpected voice, as one of the male guests came up the stairs. "Your key playing up, is it? I had just the same problem yesterday. They tell me there's a knack — would you like me to try if I can remember it?"

"That's very kind of you," said Anne, handing over her key with a smile, relieved that should there indeed turn out to be an intruder, there would now be two people to tackle him. This man was large enough to compensate for her own tiny frame, if it came to catching burglars . . .

But they weren't going to catch any burglars just yet. "Sorry, this one's beaten me," said the man, straightening from his third attempt at opening the door. "I'll slip down to Reception and ask young Beverley for the master key — she must be getting used to this by now. You wait there," and he was gone.

Anne waited. Whoever was in her room was trapped. Was she ready to make a grab at them as they tried (as would anyone with sense) to make their escape? Suppose Beverley or the Samaritan guest should be injured in the ensuing scuffle? Anne might be expecting a scuffle, but they almost certainly were not. They would simply be expecting to help her get into her room . . .

Her room. But it wasn't, was it? Not officially. Miss Seeton had been allocated Room 25, while Room 24, with its four-poster bed, had been given to Mr. and Mrs. Ranger — which was how matters still stood, in the hotel register . . .

Anne wondered what Bob, and the Oracle, would say she ought to do. Before she'd had time to work out an answer, back up the stairs came her new friend, with Beverley in tow and a look of *I told you so* on his face. The receptionist's look was one of deep apology. In her hand, she carried what was obviously a master key.

"I'm so sorry," she said, as she reached Anne and began to fit the master key, with an effort, into the lock. "It must be the hot weather — this keeps happening, I'm afraid. The door frames must warp, or something. All it's supposed to need is a sort of — ah!"

With a click, the door swung slowly open. Beverley said brightly: "Success! It's all yours, Mrs. Ranger — or rather, I thought this was your aunt's room?"

"She asked me to, er, fetch her sketchbook," said Anne absently, while she braced herself for mortal combat with whatever illicit form should now rush out upon them.

But nobody emerged from Room 25. Warily, she stepped inside; followed, for some reason, by the blond receptionist, though the helpful guest continued on his way after a few words of congratulation. "Oh," said Beverley, "I wondered where he'd gone," and pointed to Anne's bed.

Right in the middle of the counterpane,

his paws wrapped defiantly over his eyes, Orlando lay curled in a slumbering heap. At the sound of Beverley's voice, one ear twitched, and the tip of his tail flickered. "Orlando . . ." Beverley advanced on the bed with determination. "He's pretending," she told Anne, laughing. "He thinks he can get away with it — everyone spoils him."

Anne had done a fair amount of spoiling herself, but not to the extent of inviting the enormous marmalade cat to take up residence in her room. "How on earth did he get in?" she wanted to know, as Beverley began trying to wake him before carrying him away. The receptionist nodded towards the sash window, which was partly open.

"He'll have climbed up the tree and jumped across to one of the balconies, and then gone prowling along the windowsills looking for a way in. Just like Raffles the Ransomeer — our very own cat burglar," she said, laughing again. "It was one of his tricks when he was a kitten, though I'd have said he'd be too heavy for that now — but obviously I was wrong. Who's a clever boy, then?" As she stroked him, Orlando opened a wary eye, and began, very softly, to purr. "Who'd give an acrobat a run for his money, the cheeky old thing?" And Orlando, smugly, closed his eyes with pleasure at the obvious admiration in her tone.

Beverley turned to Anne. "I'm awfully sorry about this, Mrs. Ranger. I hope your aunt doesn't mind cats. He hasn't left hairs on the bedspread or anything, though, so . . ."

Anne said quickly, "No, she doesn't mind cats. In fact, Aunt Em is about the only person in her village who's not terrified of the policeman's little girl's tabby. Tibs has, well, moods — but my aunt stands no nonsense from her. She won't worry about Orlando."

"It was rather naughty of him, though." Beverley rose to her feet with her arms full of Orlando, who obviously expected his slave to carry him away. Anne, to show there were no hard feelings for her fright, tickled him gently under the chin and called him a trespasser. He opened one eye into a knowing black slit, and his throat vibrated with the strength of his purring.

"Better close the window, in case he tries it again," said Beverley. "Then he'll just jump back into the tree and come down again without bothering anyone. I hope."

Anne went to do as she advised, and stood for a moment studying the strong, thickly leaved branches of the ancient beech which grew so close to the hotel. As a conscientious householder, she wondered vaguely about root damage to the drains, and insurance policies; but decided that the Belton Arms had no doubt taken such factors into account. The tree was a graceful, living thing, and it would be a pity to take away its life simply for the convenience of —

"Don't forget your aunt's sketchbook," Beverley said, as Anne made to follow her from the room. "Isn't that what you came upstairs to fetch?"

"Oh yes, of course — thanks," said Anne. For a moment, she wondered if she'd taken caution too far in maintaining the fiction that this was Miss Seeton's room: then she reminded herself that she was the wife of a detective. Both her husband and his superior always said that where Miss Seeton was concerned, you could never be too careful . . .

"I'll . . . have to look for it," she temporised, knowing she was now committed to fetching the book, and to letting Beverley see her with it. The reception desk had too good a view of the stairs. "If you wouldn't mind lending me the pass key so I can practice, to explain to my aunt . . ."

"All right, but don't keep it too long, will you?" The key was handed over. "Is your aunt still in the bar with those nice Americans?"

To which Anne murmured that she believed she was; and, heading a few minutes later in that direction, she wondered how she was to explain her unexpected presence — and that of the sketchbook, as well.

In the end, it wasn't perhaps as awkward as it might have been. When having duly returned Beverley's passkey, she appeared in the doorway of the bar and stood scanning the crowd for Miss Seeton and her companions, Anne was almost immediately spotted, and beckoned across with welcoming smiles from all three at the table. The Warrens looked a little surprised, perhaps, on first seeing her, but concealed it well by the time she reached them; Miss Seeton looked delighted that she had changed her mind and decided to join them, though somewhat puzzled as to why she carried the sketchbook with her.

"Oh, yes," said Anne, as she took her seat. Howard had moved to the bar, buying her a drink; Shirley was hanging on every word. "Yes, well, I thought — as you said you were touring round, seeing the sights — neither my aunt nor I have a camera, but this might give you some idea of a few of the places we've seen while we've been travelling around on our own little tour. If you didn't mind, Aunt Em, that is."

By the time Miss Seeton had finished her modest explanation that these were only very rough drawings — she had not, she feared, captured even half as well as she would have wished the atmosphere of the Belton area — Howard Warren was back with drinks all round, and displaying a flattering interest in Miss Seeton's work. He would have removed the book from her hands to look through it himself, but Anne was firm in saying that her aunt must select just a few to show them. Somehow, it seemed important to her that the cartoon-type drawings she'd told the Oracle about should not be subjected to the scrutiny of strangers; Miss Seeton, she knew, would think so as well; perhaps the Warrens would consider it ungrateful, even rude, of their guests to be so secretive — but that, thought Anne, was too bad. These were, after all, not merely Miss Seeton's, but police secrets . . .

Anne really was tired. She stayed in the bar for about half an hour, but Miss Seeton caught her yawning more than once, and she began to fear that the Warrens would think her even more rude. She smiled, excused herself, and once again made for Room 25, and the promise of an early night.

The Warrens at last allowed Miss Seeton

to leave them, assuring her they'd enjoyed every minute of her company and if ever she came to the States she was to be sure to give them a call. Miss Seeton, who thought it unlikely that she would ever be able to afford a visit to America, accepted the invitation in the spirit she understood it to have been given, and in her turn went up to her room.

But not to her bed. She barely glanced at the plumped bolster and embroidered counterpane before she crossed to the window, where she stood looking out into the limpid, black-and-white summer night, illuminated by a silver moon riding above in majesty, drowning out the stars. There was not a cloud to be seen; in the distance, the song of a nightingale could be heard above the squeak of bats as they darted past the window, swooping for insects. Miss Seeton gave a sigh of pleasure as she drank in the view; and her hands began to dance once more . . .

The conversation tonight had been friendly — and stimulating. One would need to apply several of the most rigorous yoga techniques before one felt sufficiently calm to fall asleep — if, indeed, one wished to do so, even though the hour might be regarded as comparatively late. Mr. Warren had been so very kind — three glasses of sherry, so hospitable and the compliments he had paid on one's sketching skill . . . about which one could not help, well, wondering . . .

Maybe if Anne hadn't brought the sketchbook into the bar the idea would never have entered Miss Seeton's head. But she had: and, as she was leafing through the book, it had — the idea. Come into her head. Probably because she had so much enjoyed watching the film, which she rather thought had inspired it in the first place — the idea — although looking at the sketches had reminded her of just how inspirational the scenery was — and of how much she had enjoyed today's little excursion . . .

One lived, after all, in the country. It was not as if one was unaccustomed to walking. A matter of two miles, had dear Anne not remarked once? Which, now that one's knees were as fit as the remainder of one's person, was no distance at all. And Lord Edgar — had he not said on more than one occasion that one was welcome at any time? And one had no intention of disturbing him by going to the house. Nor, of course, did one wish to disturb Anne, who was so sleepy, and had made such sterling efforts to converse. But it was well known that one needed less as one grew older — sleep —

and really, on such a night it was a shame to spend any time at all in sleeping. The effects of moonlight . . .

Moonlight was not alone in having its effect on Miss Seeton; the effect of three glasses — generous glasses — of sherry should not be underestimated. She was hardly intoxicated — not even tiddly — but she was, perhaps, rather more exalted than she might otherwise have been. She would not normally have entertained the idea of going by herself for a two-mile walk in the middle of the night, bewitching with birdsong and moonlight though it might be . . .

Miss Seeton's dancing hands were quickly put to practical use. Sketchbook, pencils, eraser; torch — since one had become a country dweller there was always a flashlight in one's bag; the key to one's room, of course. One's umbrella, naturally. The sky might well be cloudless now, but in an hour or two the weather could alter quite dramatically — one had missed the forecast this evening while talking with the Warrens, but it was safe to assume that it was as changeable as ever. But, in summer, never cold. A warm summer shower might be rather pleasant — refreshing — and the play of light and dark among the falling drops . . .

Miss Seeton, smiling happily as she dreamed of the miracle which moonlight was to work upon her sketching skills, let herself out of her room and passed quietly down the carpeted stairs, through Reception, and out of the main door of the Belton Arms without anyone noticing her.

And set off for Belton Abbey, and the Palladian Temple of Hiberna.

chapter
23

Miss Seeton walked dreamily along the country lanes, drinking in the song of the nightingale and the scents of summer blossom. She rejoiced at the way moonlight mingled with shadow, at the faint gleam of stars in a soaring sky, and the turning of the world before her to pewter, pearl, and silver. She stopped, and looked about her, and breathed in with pure delight.

All at once, there arose in the distance a sudden, mechanical spluttering and choking as someone tried to start a car engine. Rather a discordant note, one could not help but feel, on such a night — the fresh, sweet summer air . . . the petrol fumes, the clouds of blue smoke, the noise — the glaring beams from the headlights as they swept across the horizon . . .

The car, mercifully, was gone, although so still was the night that the sounds of its engine continued to intrude for some minutes. Miss Seeton sighed. One recognised, during the hours of daylight, that what dear Sir Winston had called the infernal combus-

tion engine had its right and proper place —
but on a night like this it felt more like
wanton destruction . . .

As Miss Seeton turned in at last through
the gateway to Belton Abbey, her feet began
to make a crunching sound as they trod the
gravel of the long, curving drive. How very
loud, and carrying, and embarrassing! One
would infinitely prefer not to rouse the
household . . . Miss Seeton glanced at her
watch: no difficulty in making out the dial,
on such a night. Or, rather, morning — it
was well past midnight now. And, as
Scarlett O'Hara had said, tomorrow was another day. Or, rather today, which had been
tomorrow, and . . .

And Miss Seeton suddenly realised exactly what time it was, and where she was,
and what she was doing, or planning to do.
And wondered why on earth she had
thought of doing it. She didn't remember
the sherry: she supposed she must have had
a brainstorm of some sort. Her advancing
years . . . the yoga, one very much feared,
could only achieve so much — if only dear
Anne, with her nursing knowledge, had
been with her. She might have warned her
— but Anne had been so tired last night,
and it had seemed a kindness to let her
sleep, not to ask her to be one's companion

on what was, now one came to consider it fully, such a . . . an unusual excursion.

But it had been a beautiful night for a walk — so many sights to admire. And, having come so far, it seemed, well, rather a waste not to complete the last few hundred yards of the walk, to reach one's planned destination — just for one's own satisfaction — no need to draw or sketch, but one could at least study the temple and make mental notes for whatever one planned to draw or paint in the future . . .

Miss Seeton hesitated. She moved from the gravel to the grass verge, gazing up the drive towards the house and feeling, now that her sherried flush of enthusiasm had been well and truly exhausted, somewhat foolish. It would be a great pity, she acknowledged, not to see the Temple of Hiberna by moonlight: but it would be an even greater pity if wakeful eyes should peer from any of that multitude of watching windows in the Abbey, and notice her, and wonder . . .

Miss Seeton shook her head. Goodness only knew what had come over her, but she was (she was pleased, and relieved, to be able to say) now fully recovered. She would turn on her tracks and head back to the hotel this minute . . .

She stopped. Surely — as she was turning — a flash of light in the distance, through the trees . . .

She stood and stared. She saw nothing. She rubbed her eyes. One's blood pressure, perhaps — a seizure of some sort — the sooner one could consult dear Anne, the better. Miss Seeton shook her head, took a deep breath, and stepped out boldly — and carelessly.

"Drat," muttered Miss Seeton, her ankle turning under her as she moved from the gravel down to the grass. Trying to keep her balance, she dropped everything she carried: including her torch. Not, she reflected as she steadied herself, that one had any particular use for a torch, when the moonlight was so clear . . .

But someone definitely had. As she stumbled, she had twisted round so that she was once more facing that clump of trees through whose branches she thought she'd seen . . . and she had. Seen it. A torch —

Or, rather: "Several torches," murmured Miss Seeton, and felt decidedly more cheerful about things. It was plain that the night's charms had worked upon others than herself. No doubt Lord Edgar and some of his cronies were enjoying a moonlight picnic in the Temple of Hiberna — and they might, she thought, as she rubbed her ricked ankle, possibly have a bandage, or something similar. Now that she'd tried putting her weight on it, she realised that her ankle wasn't in such good shape as she had at first thought. A bandage — a cold compress, perhaps, mused Miss Seeton, with thoughts of iced champagne in her mind. If she could walk that far, of course.

She tried her weight again. She winced. Yes, she could walk — but with an effort. She bent down to collect her scattered belongings, and gratefully seized on her umbrella. How fortunate that one had always insisted on the crook handle, and the full-length shaft instead of one of the more modern collapsible models . . .

Limping slightly, leaning on her umbrella, Miss Seeton made her slow way across the grass in the direction of the moving torches in the trees near the Temple of Hiberna.

She wasn't halfway there before her knee, as well as her ankle, began to ache — the one opposite her ankle, the bad one — or, rather, the good one, except that it wasn't anymore, because with her weight being thrown upon it, despite the umbrella, it was no surprise that it was aching. People were meant to walk with their spines straight, reflected Miss Seeton: *Yoga and Younger Every Day* made a point of saying that one's posture should be relaxed but upright, if not positively stretched, as much of the time as possible . . .

Miss Seeton found a convenient tree stump, and stopped to rest for a while. Knee, ankle, and even (she sighed) hip were aching now — it had been foolish of her to forget that grass, no matter how smooth it may seem in daylight, isn't. Unless, of course, it happened to be a bowling green, or something of the sort — a quadrangle in one of the Oxford or Cambridge colleges, for instance, although at college, she knew, one was not permitted to walk on the grass, except in rags. Or should that be "during" rags? In Rag Week, anyway. Such festivities had been unknown at the London art school which she had attended, so many years ago. But perhaps that was what Lord Edgar and his friends — she could still see the torches moving about — were planning now, and not a picnic, after all. The young. Enjoying life so much, with such a sense of fun . . .

Miss Seeton's own sense of fun made her chuckle at the thought of the strange picture she would present, if any of Lord Edgar's friends chanced to notice her hobbling quietly towards them across the grass.

Might they, she wondered, think her the ghost of that unfortunate young woman who was supposed to have killed hers— No, of course not. That had been inside the temple, which she was not. Unlike his lordship and his friends, although they appeared to be leaving the temple now, from the way the torches were bobbing down the slope of the temple knoll. The picnic must be finished. And how considerate of him not to let his friends make too much noise throughout their celebrations. Even though the temple was a little way from the house, on such a night the noise was bound to carry . . .

Another — indeed, almost the only — noise came upon Miss Seeton's listening ear: a rattling of wheels, accompanied by a wooden, creaking sound and the jingling of harness. Lord Edgar and his friends, it seemed, had also heard it. There came a sudden muttering from the temple knoll — the torches moved faster — Miss Seeton hurried to catch them, and found herself tumbling again. Drat. This time, it seemed to take longer to retrieve one's belongings. Being in the shadow of the temple mound, of course; and a few clouds had appeared in the sky, from time to time drifting across the moon. The remarkable, uneven quality of the light — and how fortunate that one had brought one's umbrella. Which was, naturally, near to hand, though the sketchbook seemed to have vanished. And one could hardly abandon it. Quite apart from the notes and drawings it contained, should a strong breeze arise the sheets of paper would be torn out and scattered in all directions. One certainly had no wish to reward Lord Edgar's kindness by acting like a . . . a litter-lout . . .

The sound of harness and wheels drew nearer. Good gracious. On grass, not gravel — a pony and trap was approaching, and at speed. Surely that was rather reckless? Miss Seeton tried to imagine what Stan Bloomer, who tended her garden, would say if the hooves of a well-shod pony were to trample across her lawn. Maybe the grounds of an abbey were different. Not so smooth and even, certainly — which was why she'd tumbled for a second time — the moonlight was very deceptive — she still couldn't find her sketchbook, and the party from the temple were —

Good gracious. Another pony and trap. Moving away from the temple knoll. With . . . with . . .

"It can't be the ghost," said Miss Seeton firmly. "That poor girl killed herself inside the temple, not outside, and certainly not in a pony and trap . . ."

But it was strange. More than strange. Where had she seen this before? The pony and trap, the figures of men in the front and — good gracious. She hadn't supposed that his lordship and his friends would be quite so, well, uninhibited — young women nowadays were, or so she'd been given to understand, rather less willing to become the playthings of men than they had been in the past. Hellfire clubs and . . . and episodes of that nature. Miss Seeton hoped that this was merely another trick of the moonlight . . .

But there definitely appeared to be a naked girl, or one wearing very few, and flimsy, clothes, in the back of the trap. The trap being pulled by a pony about whose shoulders — was that the correct term? Miss Seeton thought not, but didn't know what else to call that part of the poor creature — a whip was being laid . . .

"Stop!" A man's voice, loud and sudden and insistent. There came a rattle and a rush as the second pony and trap sped past her in pursuit of the first, which hadn't got very far. Miss Seeton, who had been almost on her feet, stumbled again — then stood upright, forgetting her lost sketchbook. Good gracious. Surely this was taking a sense of fun rather too far? How could anyone find it amusing to pretend to be fighting with their friends?

And, oh dear, it sounded very, well, realistic. Oblivious now to the loss of her sketchbook, grasping her bag in one hand and her umbrella (for support) in the other, Miss Seeton hurried to intervene in what, it seemed, had degenerated into genuine fisticuffs . . .

The first pony and trap had moved hardly any distance before the second, driven by more skillful hands, drew close behind it. The first driver tried to pull the pony's head round in an attempt to block the second, and move away; the trap began to turn; but too slowly. From the second trap a fast-moving, four-legged, lean form came leaping, followed by four large and vigorous men, who proceeded to drag down to the ground the driver of the first trap, with his companions — all but the young woman. Who remained silent and still in the trap . . . frozen, no doubt, with fear.

Miss Seeton was shocked. This was carrying things too far. The swift and stream-lined shape revealed itself by growls and barks to be a dog, which rushed in furious circles about the fight — for the seven men were fighting now. Such colourful language, if a little, well, forceful for a lady's ears — if one could, indeed, so describe that rather immodest young person in the trap —

The trap which, while Lord Edgar and his friends were so busy with other matters, was continuing to move in the slow circle which it had already begun — moving, though that poor young woman was still rigid with shock — the dog's growling seemed to upset the pony, for the trap started to pick up speed . . .

Miss Seeton did not hesitate. She recognised that duty called her to stop the trap, if she could, and rescue that poor girl being carried away against her will. The pony was moving steadily, but not yet speedily — and almost in Miss Seeton's direction. With luck . . .

"Stop!" piped Miss Seeton, waving her umbrella almost as if she were hailing a taxi. The pony tossed its head and whinnied. In the moonlight one could see the whites of its rolling eyes. "Stop!" But Miss Seeton's genteel command was lost above the barks, and the sounds of battle from the seven men left behind. "Stop!"

Her ankle protested, but she ignored its protests. Into the very path of the runaway trap scuttled Miss Seeton, with her umbrella in her hand. She had remembered something she once read about a barking dog and a Japanese sunshade. She waited until the pony was almost upon her and then, with a flourish, opened the umbrella right under its nose. With a startled whicker, the pony showed its teeth, and stopped dead in its tracks.

"Thank goodness," said Miss Seeton breathlessly, taking a few faltering steps towards the poor creature's head and trying to furl her umbrella at the same time. Tucking it under her arm, she grabbed blindly at the strange confusion of leather straps and clinking metal which dangled from the pony's neck. Which part of the harness — bridle? reins? — did exactly what, Miss Seeton had no idea. Of course, one was aware that it was by such means the driver could control the animal, but the idea that anyone else should attempt to control it . . .

For one thing, it looked far larger, close to, than one had somehow expected. And Miss Seeton hadn't realised just how very menacing a pony's teeth could look, when it curled its lips and, well, one might almost say it snarled . . .

Miss Seeton, in her time, had controlled an entire class of schoolchildren, and had won several battles of wits with Amelia Potter's infamous tabby, Tibs. A solitary pony pulling a cart ought surely to be an easier proposition — one had always understood that one tugged on the reins, whichever these might be, and, well, instructed the pony to obey one's wishes.

Except that Miss Seeton had wished it to do nothing more than stop. Which it had. But now, evidently realising that the person who had stopped it had no real notion of what to do next, it was beginning to give the distinct impression that it didn't intend to remain stopped for long. It threw back its head once more and neighed. An answering bark came from the neighbourhood of the fighting men . . .

Miss Seeton recalled that one patted horses to soothe them. Tentatively, she patted the pony's neck. It was snatched away from her inexpert hand in irritation — and the reins with it. Miss Seeton heard, above the sounds of the still-fighting men, the sound of a stamped hoof, and the creaking jingle of harness. If it should start to run away again . . .

"I think, my dear," she panted, as she fumbled for the dangling leather once more, "that if you could possibly help me by, er, catching hold of . . . if you could prevent him from . . . I really am unable to hold . . ."

The poor girl made no response to this

disjointed plea, either by word or by deed. Rigid with shock, supposed Miss Seeton. Which was hardly surpri— "Stop!" The pony began to move off. Miss Seeton pulled frantically on every piece of leatherwork she could find: the pony ignored her. It was moving away — it was moving past — one could hardly seize it by the tail, poor creature, even for the sake of —

"Oh. But surely — Oh, I see. Good gracious — no wonder . . ." As the body of the trap lumbered past, and Miss Seeton panted alongside its creaking weight, she had looked desperately up to admonish the young woman and bid her play her part. Sometimes, when one was in a state of shock, a brisk slap about the face — not that one could easily reach her face, being so much higher, but . . .

But the deceptive moonlight was deceptive no more. Miss Seeton saw, as the trap rolled past, not a young woman — not exactly — a young woman, certainly, but not flesh and blood.

It was the statue of the goddess Hiberna.

chapter
24

No sooner had this shocking realisation
dawned on her than Miss Seeton realised
several other things, all at once.

The seven men were still fighting.

The pony was still moving.

The trap would soon be out of reach . . .

Miss Seeton threw one swift glance back
towards the surging, struggling, mass of
angry men, and knew she stood no chance
of interrupting the fight while everyone was
so preoccupied with hitting everyone else.
So preoccupied that they hadn't noticed
how the pony was pulling the trap away —
with the statue, which, no matter how high
the youthful spirits, she felt sure could not
have been, well, lawfully removed from the
temple. Because it had been there for over
three hundred years. It belonged there. And
now it wasn't there anymore . . .

Miss Seeton's sense of the rightness of
things made her forget all about her ricked
ankle and her aching knee. With a re-
proachful click of the tongue, she turned
away from the fight and began to trot after

the trap, slightly faster than the pony, saving her breath for the chase rather than waste it in what she knew would be useless exhortations to the animal to stop. She doubted whether it would. It sensed, she felt sure, that she had no proper idea of how to control it; like a child set unexpectedly free from the discipline of school, it was what one might call running riot. Or preparing to do so . . .

It was not easy for Miss Seeton to swing herself up into the back of the trap. She tossed her umbrella and handbag over the low side to leave her hands free, then made a grab as she continued to run — but failed to hold firm, and fell back. She braced herself for another attempt. She did not dare approach from the side: the wheels seemed as tall as she was, turning in their iron rims, creaking, heavy . . .

She made it. Gasping, she scrambled on hands and knees — she rather feared that her stockings must be laddered, but fortunately there had been no splinters as she fell on the wooden floor — past the statue and towards the front of the trap, where she knew the reins should be.

But where, to her dismay, they weren't. Of course. She must have pulled them off the . . . the driving seat when she first caught hold of the pony's head. No wonder it had been so, well, irritable — as irritable as, she recognised, the men she was rapidly leaving in her wake were. They seemed to have stopped fighting, and were calling after her.

"I can't stop," Miss Seeton called back to them, trying to make herself heard above the thump of hooves on grass and the rattling jingle of harness. "Oh, dear." And she found herself sitting down once more with a bump.

The men shouted again. Some of them began to run. "I can't," cried Miss Seeton, trying to make them understand. The shouts continued. The pony began to — trot, rather than walk? Gallop, rather than trot? It was moving faster than before, anyway. And she still couldn't stop it, no matter how much she was asked to do so.

The hubbub seemed to have aroused the house. In rooms all over the upper floors of Belton Abbey, lights came on. Miss Seeton found herself being carried willy-nilly towards the busy, watching windows: towards, past, and then beyond. Hurry as they might, the men behind her showed no signs of catching up with her; shout with amazement as they might, the people in the windows could not deter the pony from its onward flight.

Miss Seeton looked back nervously at the sight of Lord Edgar — then who was it, if not he and his friends, who had removed the statue from the temple? — trying to make sense of what was happening below, leaning — no, hanging — from the window, calling after her . . .

Miss Seeton gasped, and fell backwards. Useless to try to keep her balance; her dancing hands made abstract patterns in the air. The air which was moving past her faster than ever, as the pony, maddened now by the shouts of those who pursued it in the other trap, took the bit, literally, between its teeth. And bolted.

"Not much farther now, sir," said Bob Ranger cheerfully. He had slowed to read the name on a signpost, and would have played a high-spirited tootle on the horn had his superior not fixed him with a steely sideways look.

"Not much farther? We have made suspiciously excellent time, Detective Sergeant Ranger. I trust that there was no exceeding the speed limit during my innocent slumbers?"

Bob grinned. "All strictly legal, sir, but you said the roads would be clear at night — and they were. We'll have to camp out in the car until the landlord, or whoever wakes up first tomorrow, wakes up."

Delphick peered at the luminous numbers on his watch. "You mean today, Bob. Yesterday, you looked forward to seeing Anne tomorrow: and today *is* tomorrow, as it were. Great heavens, I'm starting to sound like MissEss. Put it down to proximity, although . . ." And he yawned. "No doubt, being half-asleep as I am, I am picking up psychic vibrations from her dreams . . ."

"Stop!" cried a tumult of voices to the rear; but the pony galloped on. Miss Seeton was bumped, and bruised, and helpless. One had never ridden in so much as a governess cart, suitable though such a conveyance might have b—

"Oh, no!" Now they were tearing down that long, curving drive in the direction of — surely not — but one remembered, only too well — the main road. Would the gravel, the uneven surface, drag against the wheels? Such did not appear to be the case. Miss Seeton shuddered. Suppose — if those pursuing her did not manage to catch up before the pony passed through the gates — a car were to come in the opposite direction? It must — she must — be stopped. The alternative was too awful to contemplate.

Miss Seeton groped for her umbrella, looking back as she did so. The second trap had taken a short cut across the grass, deceived by the moonlight into believing it to be a flat, smooth surface: it bounced and juddered and moved more slowly than she. They would never catch her up in time.

Miss Seeton, that keen cinema-goer, remembered the scene in *Stagecoach* where John Wayne is seen leaping from horse to horse to seize the dropped reins and restore control. Only, of course, it hadn't been John Wayne, but a stuntman. Miss Seeton shuddered again. The practice of yoga, while making one undeniably fit and agile, hardly prepared one for such daunting feats.

It did, on the other hand, impart a certain degree of mental agility. Better late, reflected Miss Seeton as the pony swept through the gates of Belton Abbey and turned up the main road, than never. The moon shone clear and bright, and she could see that the — traces? — the reins had somehow, as the pony skidded and turned, been caught — snagged — had been stopped in their slithering and sliding — had been held comparatively still, so that if one possessed a steady eye, a hand and wrist made skilful by many years spent wielding a paintbrush — and something like a stick, with a curved end to it — something like an umbrella . . .

"Talking of psychic manifestations, sir," said Bob, slowing the car to take a sharp bend, "perhaps we should keep an eye open for the tragic maidservant as we pass the Abbey turning — I know the temple mound's a bit far from the road, but, well, I've never seen a ghost. And if she's likely to come popping out in her draperies in front of the car . . ."

"There are other ghosts in these parts, older ghosts by far," said Delphick, drowsily. "The little dark people who fled west when the Romans came . . ."

"Boadicea," supplied Bob promptly. Delphick woke up at once. His sergeant was a dear chap, but . . .

"Boadicea, or Boudicca, was of the Iceni, a tribe of the east. She never came this far west — she began her revolt by burning Colchester and London. Camulodunum" — he yawned again — "and Londinium."

"Knives on her chariot wheels," said Bob, remembering history lessons at school.

"Also St. Albans," Delphick informed him, frowning at this perpetuation of what was generally accepted now as nothing but propaganda. "Otherwise Verula — what the hell!"

"Hey!" cried Bob, slamming on the brakes. "What — who — I don't believe in . . ."

But there, in front of his eyes — and, it seemed from the force of his exclamation, his superior's — the ghost of a warrior queen, in her battle chariot, came thundering down the road towards them, with another chariot appearing in hot pursuit around the bend. Another chariot that was gaining, as the first chariot slowed — that was drawing almost level — and then, as the driver apparently for the first time noticed the stalled car blocking the road, performing an erratic manoeuvre that was half overtaking, half evasion . . .

Or trying to perform. But failing. And ending up in the ditch . . .

Delphick and Bob, unclasping their safety belts as one and leaping from their seats to see what assistance they could render, were prepared for the bad language, and the groans, and the startled whinnies of the pony as it trampled in the mud, its traces broken. They were prepared for blood — and bruises — and broken limbs . . .

But they were most definitely not prepared to hear, from the driver's seat of the cart which had caused all the problems in the first place, a voice they both knew well.

"Why, good evening, Chief Superintendent Delphick," said Miss Seeton. "And dear Bob, too. How very fortunate that it should be you. I was thinking, you see, that it would be so useful if I could find a policeman . . ."

It was in Belchester police station, twelve miles away, that Delphick and Bob began to make sense of what had happened. They were not alone in their intense desire for enlightenment: Lord Edgar Bremeridge, his father's steward, and Miss Emily Seeton all knew part of the puzzle, but nobody could unravel the whole without the help of the others.

Lord Edgar, a quick-thinking, fast-moving, and extremely fit young man, had come pelting down the drive with one of the duke's shotguns in his hand, ready to repel intruders as necessary. He was followed at a surprisingly (for his age) close distance by Faulkbourne, brandishing one of the pikes from the armoury. The rest of the ducal household, following haphazardly in their wake with an assortment of weapons, were deflected from their immediate purpose by the sight of three staggering forms near the temple knoll.

The forms staggered all the more after the confrontation with the first footman, under-footman, upper housemaid (the under-housemaid being incapacitated by a wisdom tooth), and cook. These loyal domestics rapidly deduced that his lordship and Mr. Faulkbourne must, in their haste, have missed the trespassers; it was their clear duty to remedy the oversight; and they accordingly fell upon the hapless three, who were already battered and bruised from their encounter with the four large men in the pony and trap.

The rolling pin wielded by the cook had been the final inducement. The three men surrendered; and it was while they were being escorted in triumph back to the house that the party encountered Delphick, Lord Edgar, and assorted allies coming back up the drive with four more men under guard. (Jasper, trained for poaching, had headed silently home at his master's whistled command, there to await his return.) The four took one look at the three, and things seemed about to get out of hand; but Lord Edgar's quick wits again came into their own. His lordship understood at once that the malefactors could not be dealt with in Belton. The village police house had been designed for the odd poacher, tramp, or drunk: there was nothing so formal as one cell, let alone seven. Belchester it must be: but the transporting of so ill-assorted a group would cause problems, unless the chief superintendent agreed to co-opt Lord Edgar and Faulkbourne as what might be called emergency volunteers. With the loan of the ducal Land Rover . . .

"Not quite how I expected our journey from Town to end," remarked Delphick, as he sat with his auxiliaries drinking a welcome cup of coffee. "An altogether stimulating finish, thanks to you, Miss Seeton."

"Chief Superintendent, I assure you —"

He ignored her pinkened cheeks and fluttering hands. "I repeat, stimulating — and rewarding, undoubtedly. For, with your help, Miss Seeton, and that of his lordship, and Faulkbourne, of course, not to mention those unable to be present for, er, various reasons — we can be confident that we have collared a vital cohort of the Croesus Gang . . ."

chapter
25

"Good gracious," said Miss Seeton faintly. Delphick smiled, regarding her with amused affection. Goodness knows how she always managed to come up trumps — but she did . . .

"The Croesus Gang?" repeated Lord Edgar Bremeridge, with a frown. "I had one of the local coppers — crime prevention or some such — call on me the other day, nattering about the Croesus Gang, and security at the Abbey. But he certainly never gave me to understand that the risk of being robbed by Croesus was particularly great. If I'd known . . ." He broke off to sigh, and shake a rueful head. "Oh, well . . ."

"At the time, I don't suppose he realised the risk *was* particularly great." Delphick thought it better not to let his lordship suspect that the crime prevention officer's visit had been more in the nature of an attempt to advise on the Raffles robbery, about which the police had then known, officially, nothing. He glanced towards Faulkbourne, who appeared slightly uncomfortable at

Lord Edgar's words, and gave him a reassuring smile as he continued:

"If your lordship had only seen fit to report the loss of the Belton snuffbox collection, we might not have been taken so much by surprise when the news was broken later by the tabloid press. As it was, however, the papers had a field day — and every detail of the Bremeridge history was broadcast to the general public. Most members of which, of course, read it with no more than ordinary interest, maybe decided to visit the Abbey on a day trip, nothing more — but Croesus, as I shall continue for the present to call him, was a rather more avid reader than most. He read about the Temple of Hiberna — and decided at once that the statue must be his. Accordingly, he —"

"Why?" broke in Lord Edgar, echoed by Faulkbourne, whose expression was unreadable. "What on earth possessed the man to pinch Armless Arabella? He must be mad."

"Very probably. The consensus of expert opinion" — here Delphick shot a quick look at Miss Seeton, and smiled — "is that he's not only mad, but that his madness takes the form of an excessive interest in all things cold: what we might call cryomania, perhaps, or hypolepsy. No doubt the trick cyclists have a proper term for his condition, which is not only chronic, but severe. It is also irrational, in that the intrinsic value of the items he desires is of no importance. They may be priceless — or without price. All that matters is that they catch his fancy —"

"And he fancied the statue of Hiberna?" Lord Edgar broke in once more. "But why, Chief Superintendent?"

"Because he read the newspapers with rather more care than any of us. We supposed — not unsurprisingly, I feel — that the temple was in honour of the goddess of Ireland, or Hibernia. A understandable misreading for Hiberna — or," he spoke with slow emphasis, "the goddess of Winter . . ."

"Good gracious," said Miss Seeton again, as the others sat back on their chairs in amazement. It was so obvious, once it had been pointed out, but . . .

"But," said Lord Edgar, "they didn't get away with her, did they? Whoever *they* were. Surely the chap isn't so mad that he employs two separate groups of people to acquire the loot on his behalf? If he does, he must have money to burn, as well as being barmy."

"If the little we have managed to learn of him so far is correct," Delphick said slowly, "then he does, indeed, have an ample financial basis to support his mania — but you will understand that it is legally impossible for me to supply details, Lord Edgar. Suffice it to say that there is a suggestion, no more, that the man who has been responsible for a great many art thefts over recent months is a multimillionaire with an international reputation for being a recluse. He lives in a part of the world noted for its low temperatures and almost permanent snowfields, and is in the process of building himself a massive underground palace which he intends to furnish in accordance with his, er, particular requirements —"

"Chrysander Bullian!" exclaimed Lord Edgar. "Nutty as a fruitcake, by all accounts — the American Armenian nobody ever sees. It must be him. He's forever waiting for World War III, from what I've heard: it's not so much a palace he's building in Alaska as a nuclear shelter, Mr. Delphick. He's mad, all right. But can he really be mad enough to pay double the going rate, whatever that might be, for two lots of people to pinch Arabella?"

"He," said Delphick, "whoever he might be — and I name no names, Lord Edgar — has only employed one, er, gang of thieves throughout his entire European operation.

There was a degree of madness in his method, to that extent: but it was madder still to make it plain that money was no object. The three men he employed grew greedy. They also began to regard themselves as invincible — with the almost inevitable result that they grew careless. Not so careless that they didn't realise a lorry or truck would make too much noise so close to the house, but careless enough that instead of hiring the pony and trap from the gypsies, they elected to, er, cut corners and steal it. A course of action to which the gypsies, not unnaturally, took exception."

"The other four men, of course." Lord Edgar nodded. The expression on Faulkbourne's face was still unreadable. Miss Seeton looked shocked, and mildly disapproving. Delphick continued:

"Don't ask me how, but they managed to track the pony's progress from their camp to the Abbey grounds, and realised, once they arrived, that they had the advantage of the Croesus Gang in physical size and fitness as well as in number. In righteous wrath also, of course — which, I gather, added some, er, zest to their chastisement of those they assumed to be the entire band of pony thieves — until it came to their attention that the pony was being, er, removed by yet another player in the drama . . ."

Miss Seeton said, "Oh, dear," and blushed. She looked both embarrassed and agitated. Delphick chuckled.

"Cheer up, Miss Seeton. Believe me, you need have no fear of being charged under any Road Traffic Act with driving an unlicenced vehicle on Her Majesty's highway without due care and attention and without lights . . . We're all much too grateful to you. There's a good chance we'll retrieve most of the gang's latest acquisitions — they hadn't got round to shipping them out just yet — and, even if we can't bring a prosecution directly against their employer, because he's in another country and a hearsay link is insufficient — we can definitely fire a warning shot across his bows, with a little cooperation from our American colleagues. Another success notched up to your credit, Miss Seeton, and I congratulate you . . ."

As she blushed again, and looked slightly bemused, Delphick noticed the expression on Faulkbourne's face, which displayed mingled admiration and disappointment. He had at last observed the renowned MissEss in action — but it hadn't been the action he'd expected. Lord Edgar's face, however, wore an expression of great relief.

"What the parents would have said if they'd come home to find Arabella gone, I tremble to think," he told Miss Seeton with his most charming smile. "I wish I could find more to offer than the freedom of the Abbey grounds — you already have that, haven't you? Faulkbourne, we must put our heads together and think of something."

"Very good, your lordship." The steward's head inclined at a very slight angle. It might have been in acquiescence: it might have been to hide a yawn.

"It's very late," Delphick said at once. "Or, rather, it's very early. Either way, I feel that the rest of this discussion should be postponed to a more hospitable hour," and in his turn he yawned. "No doubt we will see you later, Lord Edgar . . ."

When everyone had surfaced from their slumbers and had something to eat, Delphick assembled his little band for what he was pleased to call the Great Exhibition.

"Of your pictures. Some of them, anyway," he told Miss Seeton: who clutched the sketchbook she'd feared lost until the cook found it, and murmured that of course, Chief Superintendent, one knew one's obligation to the police, but —

"But Anne tells me you've come up with a

319

couple of small masterpieces since we've been gone," he said firmly. "Which I should very much like to compare with those you did before — if you wouldn't mind?"

Miss Seeton, remembering the retainer, murmured that she didn't mind. Not really. But she so much hoped he wasn't expecting too much, because one recognised all too clearly that one's talent was, well, very *ordinary* . . .

Delphick took as much notice of her protestations as he ever did, and was soon sitting with all her drawings, including those brought back from London, spread on a low table in front of him. Anne prepared to give a running commentary as necessary, and Bob looked merely bewildered. He'd never got the hang of Aunt Em's scribbles — the Oracle seemed to make sense of 'em, and Anne didn't do too badly, but he'd rather detect crime in the normal manner, any day. Nobody could call Miss Seeton normal . . .

He peered over Delphick's shoulder at the pony-and-trap sketch of the near-nude woman with Greenland's icy mountains in the background, and grinned. She'd been spot on, same as always. Once you knew what she was — not exactly talking about, but Drawing, with a capital D — you could make sense of it. Only, making sense of it meant you had to do everything, well, back-wards. Lucky the Oracle was pretty agile, mentally, though it didn't take a genius to make the connection between the snow and ice and Croesus — the muffled, lonely figure heading for the hidden ravine — there was symbolism there, even Bob could see that . . .

But what did the other sketches sym-bolise? Not much to do with Croesus, surely. True enough, MissEss had nobbled his gang — as they'd hoped she would, even if it hadn't been in the way they'd all ex-pected — yet the unexpected was what you always seemed to get, with MissEss. They ought to be used to it by now. These other drawings, though, didn't seem to have any connection at all with the mad millionaire recluse from Alaska. Why had MissEss drawn the Abbey as a partial ruin, the recep-tionist at the Belton Arms as a harpy? Did she feel that nothing was ever as it seemed to the outward eye? Why had she shown Beverley for a second time in Regency cos-tume, escorted by one of the Bremeridges? And the portrait gallery — more Bremeridges — and what on earth was the significance of the pile of little bricks which the steward Faulkbourne was shown car-rying on a tray? Faulkbourne. Bob suddenly sat up straight. It had been the steward who first requested Miss Seeton's presence at Belton because of —

"Raffles," remarked Delphick, completing his sergeant's unspoken thought as he studied the drawings one by one once more. "I can't believe there's no hint — the coincidence — I refuse to believe she hasn't . . ."

Miss Seeton was pink as she said, twisting her fingers: "I assure you, I know very little of this Raffles person, Mr. Delphick, always excepting what dear Martha tells me she has read in the popular press. I understand that he has, well, considerable athletic ability, and a sense of humour — but apart from that . . ."

He regarded her dancing fingers with a whimsical smile. "Very little, Miss Seeton? I think perhaps you know more than you realise. Over the past few days, you must have heard people talking — you must have gained an impression, of sorts. Would you care to rough it out for me on paper? I'd be most interested to see it. Suppose I were to let you have your sketching block, for just so long as you need to produce your impression of Raffles — your impression which," and he looked again at her dancing fingers, "I feel sure is going to be of great interest to us all . . ."

Having settled her by the window, Delphick then appeared to ignore Miss Seeton utterly as he ran through the Raffles case for the benefit of his enthralled audience. He stole covert glances at her from time to time, however and seemed pleased with what he could see. At first, Miss Seeton had sat and looked, as she so often did when faced with similar requests, rather uncertain; she kept trying to still her restless fingers, without much success; she closed her eyes, shook her head as if to clear her thoughts, then suddenly reached for her pencil, sighed, and with swooping strokes sent it back and forth across the paper, filling it with the picture which would be, Delphick hoped, the final clue in the Raffles mystery.

"We know," he said, as he waited for Miss Seeton to make her first marks on the blank sheet before her, "that Raffles must be a superbly fit individual: agile, athletic, and with an excellent head for heights. Incidentally" — with a nod in Anne's direction — "we've no particular reason to assume Raffles is male: none of the robberies we know of has needed particular physical strength, though some of the methods employed suggested that the thief would be unusually tall for a woman, if only slightly above average for a man." Lord Edgar shifted on his chair, his long legs stretched in front of him. Had he, wondered Bob, inherited his height from his father's side of the family — or his mother's?

Delphick's gaze drifted past Lord Edgar towards the window where Miss Seeton sat with her eyes closed in thought. He coughed. "However, I believe I'll refer to Raffles as 'he' in deference to Hornung's original. Whether or not he plays cricket, of course, is one of the many things we don't know about him. What we *do* know, apart from the physical aspects, is that he possesses, as Miss Seeton has pointed out, a sense of humour — and a remarkable sense of the value of what he steals to hold to ransom."

Miss Seeton, oblivious now to the mention of her name, was engrossed in her drawing, driving her pencil across the paper as if inspired. The chief superintendent had a gleam in his eye as he went on:

"I don't just mean monetary value, although we have to suppose that Raffles knows a fair amount about antiques and objets d'art — but he also knows the sentimental value the victims of his crimes have in certain instances attached to what he has taken. He is a good psychologist, in short, if a psychologist with a sense of humour is not a contradiction in terms." Anne, remembering some of the people she'd met during her nursing career, hid a smile. Delphick winked at her before continuing:

"He understands his victims — because, it seems to me, he knows them, and knows them well. But not, I suspect, as an outsider, calculating profit and loss and risk — Raffles knows them as one who moves in their world — not necessarily of it, but certainly in it." Lord Edgar shifted again, long legs nervous; Faulkbourne, steward to his father — to the Duke of Belton — cleared his throat with what seemed to Bob unnecessary force.

There came a sudden harsh squeak from over by the window as Miss Seeton pushed back her chair and rose to her feet. The eyes of everyone except the chief superintendent turned towards her as she hesitated, the finished drawing in her hand. Delphick raised his voice above the stirring in the little room, to remark quite calmly:

"And, because he is in that world, he needs money, more than most of us, in order to maintain his position. Raffles has turned to a life of crime rather than lose face among those he regards as his equals — his *peers . . .*

"Isn't that so, *your lordship?*"

And, reaching for Miss Seeton's sketch, Delphick fixed Lord Edgar Bremeridge with a sharp, accusing stare.

chapter
26

"Master Eddie!" A man of normal height would have covered the distance in five, perhaps six paces: but it took Faulkbourne only three swift strides before he was standing close by the chair of Lord Edgar Bremeridge. He dropped a warning hand on the young man's startled shoulder. "Don't you say a word, lad, not one word! Do you understand?"

Delphick, himself taller than average, judged that even he would have needed four steps to move from the steward's chair to that on which the son of his master sat. The chief superintendent had wondered whether his words might surprise anyone into acting out of character: yet he had hardly supposed it would be Faulkbourne who was so obviously shaken from his habitual professional composure. Indeed, the man seemed more than shaken: he was positively alarmed. Beneath his grip, Lord Edgar winced, and writhed again.

Delphick regarded the little tableau with quite as much interest as everyone else in the interview room. Everyone, that is, apart from Miss Seeton. A gentlewoman does not permit herself to indulge in vulgar curiosity. Besides, now that she had completed the sketch for which dear Mr. Delphick had asked, she wished him to have it as soon as possible. It was, she reminded herself, for her sketching abilities that the police paid her such a generous retainer fee . . .

Ignoring everyone else, Miss Seeton trotted across the room and, with a shy smile, offered her drawing to the chief superintendent. "I fear this may come as something of a disappointment to you, Mr. Delphick, because one should never permit one's fancy to run away with . . . the foolish reference to *numbers* and *tickets* is obvious, of course, but in such a serious matter it seems very wrong to . . . not that I would ever stoop, of course," she hastened to add, "to the picking of anyone's pocket, execrable though the pun might be. Only I would not wish, you see, people to think that I undertook my duties in any — any *frivolous* fashion . . ."

"Dr. Johnson," murmured Delphick, returning her smile as he accepted her sketch. "Or, wait — wasn't it really one of the seventeenth-century critics who was so scathing about the pun? A chap called John

Dennis, in conversation with Purcell, if my memory serves me correctly — but please don't let it worry you, Miss Seeton, whoever he was. Nobody could ever accuse you, even for an instant, of being in the least bit friv— Ah, yes. Yes, indeed." And he gazed long and hard at the drawing he now added to the collection on the table before him.

Bob, sitting next to him, leaned across to look; retiring, baffled, almost at once. Yet Delphick appeared delighted with the results of Miss Seeton's most recent labours: goodness only knew why, mused Detective Sergeant Ranger. He leaned across again, and stared harder: it made little more sense to him, for all the Oracle's evident gloating, than it had done before.

Miss Seeton had sketched in a high wall, as of a great house, with windows far above the ground, and storm clouds gathering overhead — clouds from which oblong drops were falling. But not drops of rain — not with numbers written on them like so many . . . *raffle tickets,* thought Bob, with sudden realisation. Where Dr. Johnson came into it all, he had no idea, even if MissEss and the Oracle both seemed to know what they were talking about — and perhaps now the rest of it made a bit of sense, after all. It didn't take any great brain to work out that she was probably referring to Raffles the Ransomeer in her sketch; so the figure on the ledge of one of the windows — no, leaning out of the window, on second thoughts — must be her interpretation of what was known of the Raffles method of thieving.

Bob nodded, pleased with himself, and squinted across at the sketch yet again to see if he could beat the Oracle at his own game. Pretty dangerous, the method MissEss had shown: even more risky than usual. That rope hanging from the roof above the window looked as if it could hardly carry a child, let alone the full-sized adult — taller than average? — who appeared to have climbed down it. But what was the significance of the little brick-shaped objects piled in that neat pyramid on the sill of the neighbouring window? MissEss obviously thought they were important, from the way they were so clearly illuminated in the flash of lightning which was directed at one corner of the . . . yes, the Abbey, Bob decided. He glanced anxiously in Miss Seeton's direction. Did everything she'd drawn go to suggest that, while the rest of his family were enjoying their adventures in the wintry Andes, Lord Edgar ought to prepare for the destruction of his home by fire?

Delphick broke in gleefully upon his sergeant's musings. "Miss Seeton, you have done us proud, as ever — as I knew you would. This," and he tapped the sketch with his finger, "is just the ticket, I assure you. Especially when taken into account with your other drawings." His smile was all the reassurance she needed that he meant what he said, and that she hadn't been wasting his time. Pink with pleasure, Miss Seeton retired modestly into the background as the Oracle continued:

"That neat little structure on the next-door shelf looks to me as if it is made either of very small bricks, exactly like those on the tray carried by Faulkbourne in this other picture. Very small bricks, or — or very small boxes, perhaps." He paused. "Snuff-boxes, at a guess . . ."

Someone in the room caught their breath. Delphick could not tell who it had been: nor would he waste time trying to find out. Because now, with Miss Seeton's help, he *knew*. "Raffles the Ransomeer," he said, softly but with every syllable weighted. "He stole the Belton collection — as we all know . . . *Or did he?*"

There was a general murmuring. The Oracle's smile, as he surveyed the room, was one of triumph. "According to the latest evidence," he announced, indicating Miss Seeton's new sketch, "he didn't. Because he had no need to — because to steal something means breaking and entering the property . . . which Raffles never did." And, above the general murmur of growing astonishment, he concluded firmly: "Why go to all that effort, when — you live there already?"

He turned towards Lord Edgar, still sitting beneath the warning clasp of Faulkbourne's hand. "The general appearance was of an outside robbery, but we'll find proof enough, now that we know, that it wasn't. Miss Seeton's drawing shows the rope as a flimsy thing, incapable of bearing an adult on so dangerous a mission, so high above the ground. And for *flimsy* read *transparent* — except that we weren't supposed to see through the trick, and without the help of Miss Seeton we might not have done . . . I'm sure that Raffles went through the motions, and left the right traces for any investigation which might follow — investigation which he did his best to thwart, one way or another." He had not taken his eyes from Lord Edgar's face; now he let his gaze drift upwards to observe the steward's anguished expression. "One way or another," said Delphick again, "it was some time before anyone knew about the loss, or should I say supposed loss, of the snuffboxes. Supposed loss," he repeated, still staring at Faulkbourne as the steward's hand clenched, white-knuckled, on Lord Edgar's shoulder, and his pale lips parted in an attempt to utter — a further warning? A denial? Delphick did not give him the chance to speak.

"Why," he demanded, "were you so keen for Miss Seeton, a far less official investigator than any police detective, to enquire into the disappearance of the snuffboxes?" And now it was Lord Edgar's turn to react. Faulkbourne pushed down as the young man tried to rise from his seat, and Lord Edgar subsided, with a nervous cough. "Was it," went on Delphick smoothly, "because an official investigation would have been rather more likely to act upon whatever was discovered — to act in what you, with your long loyalty to the Bremeridge family, feared would bring discredit on those you had served so faithfully and so well? Obeying orders to the best of your ability . . ."

"Mr. Delphick," the steward managed to gasp, before once again his protests were lost beneath the chief superintendent's persistence. The Oracle was speaking now in his most oracular tones, making the conclusions he had deduced from Miss Seeton's drawings the very matter of truth.

"The missing snuffboxes," announced Delphick with absolute firmness, "are . . . copies. Which was what you feared an official investigation would bring to light — whereas Miss Seeton, if she achieved the safe return of what you believed to be the stolen property, would be rather more willing to accept whatever version she was told . . ."

"Copies!" Lord Edgar Bremeridge cried, as Faulkbourne uttered a hollow groan and closed his eyes. "*Copies* — but surely — not *you*, Faulkbourne!" He twisted on his chair to gaze up at the steward's pale face. "If this is true," Lord Edgar rallied, and spoke with severity, "it will just about kill my father — my parents, when they come home — we all trusted you, Faulkbourne . . ."

"And rightly," Delphick informed the young man, while to everyone's surprise Faulkbourne, instead of seeming crushed by his lordship's accusation, drew himself up proudly to his full height once more, his eyes sparking defiance. "A good and faithful servant," quoted the chief superintendent, with every evidence of approval. "The duke trusted you to such an extent that he allowed you to organise the making of the copies, and the disposal of the originals, didn't he? Apart from yourself and His Grace, nobody else was allowed to know in just how poor a financial position the Bremeridges are, were they?"

"His Grace, who did me the great honour to take me fully into his confidence, thought it best that the Family should remain free from worry for as long a time as possible," said the steward, through pale lips. "Had he known, however . . ." And his eyes flickered down towards Lord Edgar, then away as soon as he realised his error. Delphick, however, had been waiting for such a revelation. At once, he pounced.

"You suspected Lord Edgar of being Raffles," he said, no hint of doubt in his voice. Everyone in the little room was holding their breath — everyone except Lord Edgar, who wore a bemused expression as he looked in turn from his father's trusted steward to the chief superintendent, and back again. "As, of course," concluded Delphick, "he is"; and, while the others waited for Eddie to deny the accusation, Faulkbourne put his other hand on the young man's shoulder, and gently shook him before he had time to say a word.

"His lordship," the steward informed the accuser of his young charge in tones that barely trembled, "is not prepared to say anything at all until he has consulted" — his voice broke momentarily, but he cleared his throat and continued — "the family solicitor . . ."

Anne and Miss Seeton had completed their packing, and sat now with Bob and Delphick in a secluded corner of the Belton Arms coffee lounge, enjoying a light meal together before heading homeward in their separate vehicles. Anne was to drive her own little car, taking Miss Seeton (despite the latter's protests that she had no wish to be any bother and could easily catch a train) back to Plummergen before returning to Bromley; Bob, still on duty, would whisk Delphick down the motorway straight to Scotland Yard for the writing up of yet another official report.

A report which all four of them were in the process of pondering as they finished their snack.

"All for the love of a lady," murmured Delphick, having first looked over his shoulder in case Beverley, the unwitting instigator of Lord Edgar's downfall, should be within earshot. It seemed unlikely, since the hotel proprietor had advised his guests of her absence (caused by the proverbial, and providential, sick headache) before their feet had barely crossed his threshold; still, nobody reaches the rank of chief superintendent without learning that it is always better to make more than doubly sure. The only living creature in sight, however, was Orlando, curled once more on his favourite chair, his paws over his ears.

"No woman's worth losing your freedom for," said Bob, "let alone your reputation. Catch me turning crook!"

Anne, fond wife of his bosom, sighed gustily and tried to look disillusioned, but with little success. Her dainty form simply could not suggest the harpy-like greed and seductive skills of the absent Beverley: she was, after all, a trained nurse, not an adventuress. She smiled across at Miss Seeton.

"Now you know why your pictures seemed so sinister, Aunt Em. She pulled the wool over everyone else's eyes pretty well, though I admit there were times when I wondered . . ."

"Hindsight," scoffed Bob, as Miss Seeton shook her head.

"He reminded me so much of dear Nigel," she said. "Such an eye for an attractive girl, although perhaps rather more makeup, especially nail varnish, than I would think any of the Colvedens would approve. But he is, of course, a great deal *steadier* in character, is he not? Farming makes so many physical demands — and the discipline, as well. One cannot be too self-indulgent in such a career, if one wishes to be as successful as he is sure to be — Nigel, I mean. Than Lord Edgar. Steadier. And for all his invitations to address him by the diminutive, somehow I never felt . . ."

"He was trying too hard to be friendly," supplied Delphick, as she hesitated. She nodded, and sighed.

"So much charm, yet so superficial, I fear. Not likely to be a reliable character in later life unless he becomes rather more, well, thoughtful . . ."

"There'll be plenty of time for thought in prison," Delphick pointed out. "With the advantages that young man had, he ought to have known better. Birth, background, breeding, education — I always said Raffles was a crook with class. And when the privileged classes go to the bad, they do it so much more thoroughly than the rest of us. Cocking a snook at authority — pulling the wool over the eyes of the plebs — among whom we must number ourselves, Bob. The thick-headed, flat-footed bobbies who only exist to have their helmets pinched on Boat Race Night, and who are unable to pronounce the aristocratic surnames correctly when they come to read out their statements in court . . . But his arrogant young lordship was wrong about us — and especially wrong about you, Miss Seeton. He didn't realise you were a force, if I may say so, to be reckoned with. He tried to be too clever. It is fortunate that he wasn't as clever as he supposed . . ."

"His poor parents," said Miss Seeton, shaking her head in slow motion. "What a sad shock this will be for them on their return from South America." And, for just one moment, she looked almost guilty at what she had helped to achieve. She rallied quickly, however, knowing that in her own quiet way she had once again served the cause of justice — or so dear Mr. Delphick had been kind enough to say, though one was doing no more than one's duty, of course . . .

Bob said, "Clever, the way he made the point he didn't much like the adventurous life." He grinned at Anne. "No more mountain climbing for him once he was old enough to say no, and so on — but it was only last year he stopped, and he's a fit sort of bloke. Still easy as pie for him to shin down ropes and crawl through sewers — he'd had enough practice with his parents since he was a kid, hadn't he?"

"He protested too much," Delphick said, and Anne nodded vehemently. "I did wonder," she murmured again, as Delphick continued, above Bob's disbelieving snort:

"His parents, prompted either by their own instincts or by a few heavy hints from their younger son, left him alone at the Abbey while they went adventuring on this particular occasion — alone, and ostensibly in charge. But the attractions of Beverley were altogether too much for him — he came to need more money than his personal allowance for wining and dining her, and whatever else is done during the courtships of today's blue-blooded youth. He turned to the Raffling, and very profitably, for a while. As several police forces will testify," he added, with a wry smile.

"But then he grew greedy, and lazy, as successful crooks often do — only look at the Croesus Gang — and came up with a less energetic method of making money: steal his father's prized collection of snuffboxes, then pay out the ransom to himself, the one who'd been left in full financial charge of the family estate . . . or so he thought. It would have been an awkward moment for him when Faulkbourne looked like putting a discreet spanner in the works . . ."

"He is bound to feel the shame most acutely, poor man," lamented Miss Seeton, feeling guilty again. "How he must dread having to give Their Graces the news of their son's arrest, when they finally come home."

"Like a storm waiting to break," Delphick agreed, thinking of her sketches, and their hint that Belton Abbey was to undergo the indignity of inundation: not only over-whelmed by disgrace, but by the media as well. He made a mental note that he should inform Mel Forby and Thrudd Banner of this surprise outcome to their involvement in the Croesus and Raffles cases; and hoped for Faulkbourne's sake — it would be the steward who must bear the initial brunt of the onslaught — that the reporting hordes would be sympathetic in their questions. He knew he could trust Thrudd and Mel, of course, but some of their colleagues . . .

In his turn, Delphick sighed, shook his head, and then glanced round at his com-panions. He pushed back his chair, and rose to his feet. "Time to be on our way," he said.

Closely pursued by Miss Nuttel, Mrs. Blaine burst into Plummergen's post office and prepared to make her announcement before Eric could beat her to it. She paused just inside the threshold, blocking Miss Nuttel's path, and took a deep breath as she surveyed the animated little crowd clustered near the revolving book stand.

But the irruption of The Nuts into their midst did not intrigue Mr. Stillman's customers as much as usual: indeed, they hardly seemed to notice the new arrivals at all. They were too busy listening to the lamentations of Emmy Putts as she heard the grim tidings her mother had brought from Brettenden.

"Taken by totters, that's what it was," repeated Emmy's mother, as if she could still barely believe it even after the third or fourth telling. "Thought it was scrap metal put out for collection, so they did, and only just in time to stop it being melted down . . ."

"Poor Mr. Marsh," moaned Emmy, while everyone commiserated with her at the same time as seeing the funny side of it. There could be no doubt of the topic under discussion. Mrs. Blaine, her blackcurrant eyes a-gleam, all thoughts of Miss Seeton's return to the village driven from her mind by this new sensation, threw one triumphant look in the direction of Miss Nuttel before enquiring:

"Surely you can't be saying that the so-called sculpture from outside the biscuit factory has been found — in a junkyard! Too humiliating for that man Marsh, if it's true!"

"Oh, it's true, right enough," came a chorus of affirmation, at the centre of which Mrs. Putts might be observed, brooding. She felt somehow cheated. When she'd gone to the trouble of having her photo took — and then it hadn't been no more Croesus stealing it than he'd pinched that garden gnome the Murreystone crowd took from The Nuts. Which had been at least deliberate, thought Mrs. Putts, aggrieved; not just a daft mistake . . . But she'd managed to be first with the news of what had really happened to *Food Chain*, bumping into that young copper Foxon in his fancy clothes laughing his head off with some of his mates, and one of 'em being a bit sweet on Emmy's cousin Kimberley and easy enough to pump — not that it was set to be any great secret, so far's Mrs. Putts could see . . .

"So much for Marsh, then," gloated Mrs. Blaine, as Miss Nuttel thought furiously at her side, a frown on her forehead. Not Art, after all. Not worth stealing. Not worth quarreling with Bunny about! Better apologise . . .

But not here. Abruptly, with a toss of her

head, Erica Nuttel turned on her heel and strode from the post office. Mrs. Blaine, after one startled squeak, went panting after her. "Eric! Do wait, Eric — where are you going? What's the matter? We haven't done the shopping yet!"

Miss Nuttel paused. She waited for Mrs. Blaine to catch up with her. She took a deep breath. "Sorry," she said, at long last. "Very sorry, Bunny." Bunny's eyes widened in surprise. "About Humphrey Marsh," Miss Nuttel enlarged, and Bunny's eyes narrowed into anguished slits.

"Please, Eric," she begged, "don't keep saying that name — too upsetting for me, you know it is."

"Know?" Erica Nuttel blinked. "No. I don't. Why?"

"Oh, Eric!" Mrs. Blaine allowed vexation to flare in her little black eyes. "You, of all people — after such a long time, I would have expected *you* to understand . . ."

Without apparently knowing she did so, Mrs. Blaine raised one plump hand — her left — and brushed away imaginary tears from her eyes. Miss Nuttel's own eyes, puzzled, widened in their turn as revelation suddenly dawned. For, on the third finger of that plump left hand — a finger itself so plump that no amount of soaping would free it — was the gold wedding ring which had, so many years ago, been placed there by Norah Blaine's husband . . .

"Humphrey," breathed Miss Nuttel, in horrified accents. A shudder shook her bony frame as she closed her eyes, and Mrs. Blaine uttered a groan of anguished reminiscence. She permitted herself a bleated "Yes" of acknowledgement, and for some moments the air was frantic with silent communion.

"Sorry, old girl," said Miss Nuttel at long last. "For everything," she added, expansively. "Over and done with now, though. Best forget about it." And her eyes met those of Mrs. Blaine, which brightened with relief.

And with the realisation that there still remained their own little titbit to impart to Plummergen: that Miss Seeton, accompanied by Anne Ranger-who-had-been-Knight, was again in residence at Sweetbriars.

For, taking all things into account, it was as well to be beforehand with the news. Because nobody ever knew just what Miss Seeton was likely to get up to next . . .

Hamilton Crane is the pseudonym of Sarah J(ill) Mason, who was born in England (Bishop's Stortford), went to university in Scotland (St. Andrews), and lived for a year in New Zealand (Rotorua) before returning to settle only twelve miles from where she started. She now lives about twenty miles outside London with a tame welding engineer husband and two (reasonably) tame Schipperke dogs. Under her real name, she is currently working on a new mystery series starring Detective Superintendent Trewley and Detective Sergeant Stone of the Allingham police force.

We hope you have enjoyed this Large Print book. Other Thorndike Press or Chivers Press Large Print books are available at your library or directly from the publishers.

For more information about current and upcoming titles, please call or write, without obligation, to:

Thorndike Press
P.O. Box 159
Thorndike, Maine 04986 USA
Tel. (800) 257-5157

OR

Chivers Press Limited
Windsor Bridge Road
Bath BA2 3AX
England
Tel. (0225) 335336

All our Large Print titles are designed for easy reading, and all our books are made to last.